THE GOLDEN CATCH

CATCH

A THRILLER

ROGER WESTON

This book is a work of fiction. The characters, names, incidents, dialogue, and plot are the products of the author's imagination or are used fictitiously. Any resemblance to actual persons or events is purely coincidental.

CHAPTER ONE

November 16ᵗʰ, 1995

Frank Murdoch figured he had at least a fifty percent chance of surviving the hour. Navigating his ice-covered crab boat away from the epicenter gave him some relief. Having his ten-year old son with him did not. Frank stood wide-legged in the wheelhouse of the *Hector* and clung to the helm. He took a deep, strained breath of the frosty morning air. Fierce winds dragged streaks of foam across the wave tops. Morning had arrived with a sub-marine earthquake, epicenter the Aleutian Trench, apex of the Pacific's rim of fire. Fortunately, no tsunami had followed, at least not yet. Frank knew that an aftershock could trigger one at any moment, hurling forth a seismic wave, taller than the sea cliffs of Kiska Island that stood on the horizon.

It was no coincidence that Frank and his late wife had built their ranch house on the other side of the island. The Pacific side of the Aleutians had seen colossal tsunamis in the past. The hundred-foot wave that took out Scotch Cap lighthouse years ago came to his mind. The rim of fire was the most active seismic location in the world.

If that wasn't bad enough, Frank knew that the already pounding sea, light snow, and blustery winds were about to deteriorate into a williwaw, a violent storm with cyclone-force winds. He was eager to get his boat around the island and into the protected harbor of his home. For a minute, he questioned the wisdom of living on one of the most remote islands in the world, but that thought evaporated quickly. With a past like his, he figured he had no choice. If not for Kiska, he would've been dead long ago. Not a good alternative for a single father.

But the kid's actions had complicated Frank's day. Luke had snuck away from home to look for his dog. He'd taken off on his horse and rode across the island. Frank had gone ashore and found the kid at their sheep station, a glorified shack where his ranch hands bunked down sometimes. He glanced over at his son, who stood looking out the window at the storm. Spray splattered the windshield and froze. The *Hector* bashed into a thundering wave and thousands of tons of salt water cascaded across the frozen, white decks. Vast dark cloud cover drifted above like a tide of liquid lead, pouring into a bulging dark horizon.

Up ahead, a 4,000-foot volcano hid in the storm clouds, but the coast was visible, and lifting his binoculars, Frank scanned the rough terrain for a while.

As they passed Musashi Inlet, Frank noticed something.

"Hey, Luke, did you say Brian and Clay were planning to run the sheep up the Volcano Tundra Trail?"

"Yeah, they said we might get a tsunami."

Frank focused the binoculars. "That quake was powerful, eight-point-two'er for sure. Cracked the trail in half."

"What?"

"Hold on. . . Wait till the boat rises again. . . Look. . . The entire cliff has cracked open. I've never seen anything like that."

"You mean the quake broke the cliff? Can I have a look?"

"Just a minute. That's gotta be several yards wide." Frank panned the binoculars along the base of the mountain. "What the …?"

"What?" Luke reached up for the binoculars. "Let me see."

"Wait a second. It looks like there's a new crater near the base of the volcano." The boat shuddered as she dug her nose into the dark face of a twelve-foot wave. Frank handed the binoculars to Luke and hung onto the wheel.

"Get ready to look when we crest on the next wave," Frank said. "All right, here we go….Wait a second. Okay, now. You see the crack? It runs all the way from the breakwater to the top of the cliff. You see it?"

"No."

Frank pointed. "It's right there, above the shoreline where those black cliffs rise real jagged."

"I see it."

"That's bad news. From the looks of it, the crack goes right across the trail. Clay and Brian might drive the sheep that way, and if they do...."

Frank called up Vassily Prilimoff on the radio. Vassily was an old friend of Frank's who lived on Attu and worked at the tide station there.

"It's ugly," Vassily said. "Aftershocks are a major danger right now. We've already had two."

"I need to go ashore to check out some damage."

Vassily grumbled. "If there's another earthquake, you could be looking at multiple tsunami waves, possibly six or eight in a row."

"I doubt we'll have a second quake of that magnitude all in one day."

"Every quake is unique. It could be ten times smaller and still produce a big set of waves."

After he hung up, Frank turned to Luke and said, "I'm going ashore."

Frank maneuvered the *Hector* into Musashi Inlet, a fjord rimmed with basalt cliffs and black-sand beaches. Billows broke against the black hull, and spray cascaded across the deck. Even here on the island's protected coast, wind whined a sinister high-shrill in the rigging. Ice was thickening on the boat's deck and superstructure. Chilling white frost crusted over the ice while ominous dark clouds crowded in the sky. The rumble of the engines shifted.

"How come you're slowing down?" Luke said.

"There's a shipwreck up there. The wheelhouse and stack are just under the surface."

"Another Japanese shipwreck?"

"Yeah, but this one's different."

"What happened?"

"I scuba dived on her once. She's called the *Musashi*. Name's right on the hull. That's how I named this cove. What's different is she's not listed in any of the history books I've read about World War Two. The Japanese say she was never here."

"How can they if she is?"

"I don't know. I had a friend look into it for me once. He came up with nothing." Frank glanced at the color depth sounder and eased the wheel to starboard. "Right now she's a ghost ship."

"You mean she has ghosts?"

"No, she's just invisible to the world. Nobody knows about her. It appears she was abandoned. Her hulls are empty. There's no sign of life, no cargo, nothing. She can sink us if we're not careful."

"Like the ones in Kiska Harbor?"

"Anything hidden just below the surface is dangerous. We don't want to wreck on her."

Luke moved to the windshield and began searching in earnest. "I can't see it."

"That's why she's so deadly. You can't see her till you're up close. Just keep looking."

As the *Hector* rumbled into Musashi Inlet, Frank tried to think less about the ship's murky history and more on keeping a safe distance. He moved several controls and watched his color depth sounder as the *Hector* rolled past the sunken *Musashi*. The monitor painted a vivid color picture of the bottom beneath. The sunken ship rested alow in the surging waters off the port beam. Frank glanced at the sonar display and fathometer.

The old, ice-covered crab boat plowed onward through the frigid, sub-arctic elements and swirling gray mist. Surf crashed against the base of black cliffs and stone monstrosities, causing a continuous froth of churning white water along the rugged shore.

Well clear of the sunken Japanese cargo ship, Frank slowed the *Hector* to a crawl. He closed his eyes and took a deep breath. He opened them and glanced out the window. For a moment, his eyes fixed on a colossal mass of fallen cliff. Thousands and thousands of tons of solid rock. It looked like the product of a mammoth volcanic cataclysm. The titanic slab of rock rested where the high cliffs leveled out onto a sprawling shelf of lava just above the water. The rock had always been there, but it was so imperious he couldn't help glancing at it.

He pulled his eyes away and quickly looked up toward the sky. He remembered the picnic he and his late wife Melody had enjoyed at this cove when he dove on the *Musashi Maru*. Even brief thoughts of Melody brought feelings of love and respect and sadness. Her memory emphasized how quickly life could come to a crashing halt. He knew that she would be frightened to see her young son in such a dangerous situation. Frank didn't like it either, but he had to deal with circumstances. He couldn't ignore a hazard that could cost his ranch hands their lives. He had to go ashore to check out the chasm.

Weather conditions were holding for the moment, but Frank knew that was short-lived. He looked over at Luke. "You stay here and monitor the radio for changes in the weather. I'll be back in twenty or thirty minutes. You know what to do if she drags anchor."

After he dropped the anchor, Frank craned the skiff over the side into the choppy gray waters. Moments later, he climbed down the ladder and jumped in the skiff. Glancing up, he saw Luke standing by the ladder. When Frank turned towards the shore, he felt a jolt shake the skiff. He whirled around and saw Luke standing in the shore boat with his arms crossed.

"I'm coming with you. I want to see it, too."

Frank's gut felt raw at the thought of bringing his son with him, but if the *Hector* dragged anchor, she could wreck on the lava shelf. Either way, it wasn't safe. At least this way, they would be together.

Frozen rain came like pellets from a gray nowhere. Frank and Luke fought the elements, running the skiff through the wind and spray, over bucking black swells, toward the stark, black shoreline and finally putting ashore, riding a wave up on the beach like a surfer.

They climbed all the way up the ravine. As they summited on the high ridge, wind bowled Luke over. After making sure the kid was alright, Frank helped him up over the crest and into the blow. They hiked a hundred yards to the northeast, where they found the volcanic fracture. The new fissure ran up over the edge of the ridge and continued on in a dramatic, zigzag procession.

"Alright, come on," Frank said. "I need to see if it crosses the Volcano Trail."

The two made their way along the crevasse until it crossed the trail. It was worse than he had expected. The trail was now separated by a six-foot wide abyss.

Frigid, numbing cold air was snaking inside Frank's sweater. He wanted to get the kid back to the *Hector* and get the boat safely away from the coast. Still, his ranch hands were headed this way and didn't know of this new danger. If they got too close and the edge gave away, they'd be dead. Frank didn't want to be responsible for anymore death in his life. He'd seen enough of that.

"We've got to create a barricade so Brian and Clay can see the crevasse. Let's move those boulders in front of the trail." Working up a sweat for twenty minutes, they grabbed every big rock they could find. They worked tirelessly to create a makeshift diversion. They branched out for a hundred yards on each side of the trail seeking the largest boulders they could carry.

On one run, Luke yelled for Frank: "Dad, look over there!" Luke was pointing inland.

At the edge of the tundra, where the solid, flat lava field began, a large crater had opened up. Frank glanced seaward and saw his boat rocking precariously in Musashi Inlet. "Come on," he said, turning back to Luke. "Let's take a look."

They jogged through the freezing squall, up the gently rising meadow, to where the lava began. Arriving at the crater, Frank stopped Luke from standing too near the edge.

"Over there," Luke said, gesturing toward the other side of the crater.

Carefully, Frank inspected the black pit: fifteen-feet deep and thirty-feet across, round with vertical walls. On the other side, the collapsed ceiling was extra thick and now formed a jagged ramp down into the crater. Steam rose from cracks in the broken lava slabs below. Opposite, a cave disappeared into the volcanic earth. Despite the wind and rain, Frank could smell traces of sulfur and saw tendrils of steam curling out of the cave and vanishing in the gusts.

He turned to Luke, but the boy was now standing on the other side of the crater and pointing down. "There, look!"

Frank walked over and joined him. Now he saw what Luke was excited about. Down in the pit, next to a slab of lava, lay a gold sword. Looking at the partially collapsed, four-foot wide slab of lava that had been part of the ceiling and now formed the ramp, Frank said, "You wait up here. I'll take a look."

"I want to come."

Frank took a deep breath. "Stay here."

Luke peered down the ramp.

Frank put his hand on Luke's shoulder. "You do what I tell you."

As Frank moved closer to the cave's mouth, the smell of sulfur got stronger. He grabbed the gold sword. He started to unsheathe the find, but stopped.

Looking the mouth of the cave over for stability, Frank stepped a few feet into the eight-foot high cave. Instantly the groaning gale was quieted by the shelter of the cave. He looked up at Luke shaking in the brutal wind above. He cupped his hand around his mouth and yelled for Luke to come down.

Luke ran down the ramp and straight for his dad.

"Let me see that," Luke said, snatching the sword out of Frank's hands.

Frank took it back. When he flipped the sword over, they were both mesmerized by the gold and silver bands ringing the handle, by the scabbard with its gold "S" designs, its gold leaves, and the little gold balls around all the edges.

Turning back toward the ramp, Frank said, "Time to go."

"Maybe there's more," Luke said. "I want to see."

"We'll come back later," Frank said, but he didn't move. He was listening to the howling wind and wondered if Luke was right…

Frank put his hand on Luke's back, gently pushing him several yards into the cave. The warm, steamy air met them inside, stinking of sulfur.

CHAPTER TWO

They walked up a slightly-rising round black tunnel, about nine feet high and wide. Water dripped from the ceiling, and running water covered the cave floor. Their feet slapped in the shallow streamlet, causing splash sounds that echoed around them. Frank kneeled to touch the water, finding it as hot as bath water. "Stay close behind me," he said. As long as there were no more aftershocks, they should be fine. As for the *Hector*, he hoped she was okay.

At first, the light from the entrance was enough, but after they'd gone just fifteen yards underground, Frank got out his flashlight. A little further and they entered a large cavern.

Frank swung the flashlight around. The illumination cut through the rising steam and froze. "Look, right there, see that. It looks like a lava formation, but it's a crate covered with a canvas tarp and lava dust."

Luke moved closer, but Frank grabbed his shoulder.

"Don't touch it! If that crate is old war remnants, it might still be booby trapped. Don't touch anything." Frank's voice echoed through the chamber.

The faint sound of wind howling at the cave's mouth penetrated the cavern.

Frank took a step and kicked something. He shined his light to see what it was.

Luke backed up, his head bumping Frank's elbow. "Bones," he whispered. "They're all over."

Frank slowly swung the light beam through the steam. The bones of at least six skeletons sprawled across the cave floor along with strips of tattered old Japanese uniforms. Scattered among them were dozens of gold treasures: a solid gold vase, a golden dragon head, a cup, a pitcher, another sword, a Buddha.

Frank aimed the light down the tunnel and spotted more crates.

Luke kneeled down by a rusted rifle and examined it. The rifle lay beside a frying pan and a fire pit, circled by stones. "What is this place?" His voice was barely a whisper.

"It looks like one of the old Japanese supply tunnels," Frank said. "Go stand over by the entrance until I tell you it's alright to come closer. Don't kick anything." Luke obeyed. Frank carefully stepped over the skeleton and walked to the crate. He started to pull the canvas tarp back, but the material crumbled. He lifted the lid an inch and shined the light inside, checking for booby traps. Volcanic dust floated densely through the flashlight's beam. He pushed the lid back. Shining the light inside, he held his breath. Glitter filled his vision.

"Come here." He heard Luke's footsteps echoing. Then he felt him breathing next to him.

As Luke reached out and grasped a cup, it clanged on another piece of gold; a chime pierced the stillness. Luke held the piece in the light for closer inspection.

Water trickled against the far wall. Shivers of uneasiness ran up Frank's neck. This was no ordinary Japanese supply tunnel.

As Luke slowly turned the cup, Frank held the flashlight still, but its beam shook. The intricacy of detail was incredible: landscapes of animals and foliage etched into the cup; cylindrical foot; rose-bud knob on the lid.

Frank reached out. "Let's hold onto that." He accepted the cup, then reached into the crate and removed the companion saucer stand. "We'll bring them with us."

Pushing the set in his coat pockets, he found it wasn't enough. He stuffed both their pockets and filled a gold burial urn with artifacts. Leading the way down the cave shaft with Luke close on his heels, he came to the next crate. It was full of gold too.

"Where did all this come from?" Luke said.

"I'm not sure."

Then it occurred to Frank. *The Musashi Maru.*

The connection should have been obvious. How long had he been trying to solve the mystery of the *Musashi*? How many times had he wondered about the empty cargo hold he'd scuba dived in? So these skeletons were the missing crew. The treasure came from Japan. Perhaps the *Musashi* was sinking and the crew managed to evacuate the cargo in time. War plunder? On Kiska?

As they made their way down into the tunnel, Frank could still hear the blow faintly moaning through the crater at the cave entrance forty yards back. For a moment, after finding the gold, he'd nearly forgotten about his boat. But even if there was an aftershock, that didn't mean a tsunami was imminent. He needed to get out of this cave, but he could take one more minute.

He had to at least get a better idea of what they'd stumbled upon.

Progressing deeper into the shaft, they came upon another skeleton. It's crooked finger bones lay beneath a gold bracelet.

Luke stepped back, pointing. "It looks like he died screaming."

Frank squinted his eyes.

They walked farther into the shaft.

"Cracks in the floor," Luke said.

When Frank got a look around the corner--he stiffened.

The shaft widened into a steamy cavern. Four large crates backed up against the wall on the right. Broken sides spilled their contents, forming a three-foot high mound of pagodas, dishes, pots, crowns, swords, vessels, animals, dragons, Buddhas, eggs, tigers, tiger claws--all of it gold. More skeletons lay at the base of the treasure and sprawled on the stack as though the men died while crawling over the mound. A wide area reached around the mound on the left. Water flowed down the steep continuation tunnel on the far side.

"It's all treasure," Luke said. "Japanese."

Frank held the light on a gold suit of armor at the far side of the chamber, standing erect.

With Luke following, Frank walked to the far side of the chamber where the tube exited the back side, upturning and angling too steeply to stack any more crates.

Frank flashed the beam around the cavern. The light stopped on the cave's wall.

"What's that?" Luke said, pointing his finger.

Frank stared at the cave wall. A huge petroglyph shown crimson against the inky black: A strange ship etched into the lava, a chiseled sculpture that could have been chipped out by a prehistoric hunter, if not for the vessel's more recent cast in history. The old ship was propelled by oars and armed with cannons. Spikes studded her humped back, and a square sail rose high above the bowsprit that reached out like the head on a turtle.

Luke reached up and touched the carving, which loomed high above him and stretched long to his left and right.

A vibration shook dust particles from the roof. A rumbling quavered through the cavern. A stalactite broke free of the roof and hit the floor next to Frank. Jumping back, he grabbed Luke and held him tightly for a moment before letting go of him. The volcanic nature of the underworld manifested itself in Frank's mind. He was strangely reminded that he was an unforgiven sinner, and he envisioned a river of blood boiling below him in the black volcanic depths . . .

Frank felt Luke edging up close to him. "Let's get out of here," Frank said.

CHAPTER THREE

After grabbing two survival suits from the storage locker, Frank ran up the stairs to the wheelhouse of the *Hector*. He sat in the captain's swivel chair and tossed the suits on the chair next to him. Sparking the crab boat to belching life he eased her ahead, resisting the urge to go faster. He brought the *Hector* around, powering forth over watery ramps and then plunging down perilously close to the submerged *Musashi*.

Luke came in the wheelhouse.

"There's a survival suit if you need one," Frank said, pointing to the two orange suits thrown on the seat next to him. "Do you remember how to use one?"

"Yeah, Dad," Luke answered.

"Good." Frank looked out at the storm. As the *Hector* broke over a wave and crashed into the next, glittering rivers poured over the bow, and spray froze on the windshield. "That was quite a find we made today, wasn't it?"

"I can hardly wait to show Brian and Clay."

"Son, we can't let anyone know about what we found."

"Why not? It's ours, isn't it?"

"Well, I don't know. I need some time to figure that out, okay?"

As they rumbled directly over the *Musashi*'s central deck, Frank glanced at the CRT monitor, which showed orange clouds of fish conglomerating over the wreckage. The hazard slept off the starboard beam, where the sunken ship's superstructure and elliptical funnel rose dangerously near the surface. Glancing out the side window, he saw the menacing carcass looming beneath wave troughs. Luke joined him at the console, and Frank pointed out the sunken ship. He would be glad to get out of this cove and into deeper water. He shut thoughts of gold out of his mind and focused on getting his kid to a safer place.

After building up speed, Frank moved levers on the control consul; the *Hector* accelerated through the surge of Musashi Inlet. As they approached the mouth of the inlet, they passed towering lava cliffs on either side. Waves swelled where they heaped up over the underwater shelf. The *Hector* dipped and doused onward. As she broke over a wave and crashed into the next, glittering rivers poured over the bow, and spray froze on the windshield.

Frank guided her out into the open water where the sea was lifting and tossing his boat. White foam from breaking waves blew in streaks.

He glanced at his watch and then over at Luke, who was peering through binoculars. If there was any trouble, Luke would tell him.

Frank began to relax. Soon they would be in deep water. Gazing out at the ocean and storm play, he remembered the strange carving on the cavern wall. Something about it was familiar. But how could an eerie carving of a spike-roofed boat be familiar? What was it?

"*Now I remember*." Frank snapped his head around toward Luke. "Mr. Lee told me a story one night on his processor boat. It was about the spike-roofed ships of a famous Korean admiral. Something about ships resembling turtles. I think that cave carving is a Korean battle ship. From the 16th century, I believe."

"I thought it was Japanese."

"The *Musashi Maru* was. Those old rifles and bayonettes were Japanese. I'm not so sure about the old ship in the cave carving. I'll have to do some research when we get home. Why don't you go get us some hot chocolate and we can talk about it more then."

"Okay, Dad." Luke ran to the door and took the steps down to the galley.

As ocean sounds descended upon the wheelhouse, Frank looked at the anemometer. The wind peg was jumping wildly. His watch indicated four hours since they left the range station. Probably would take them another hour to round the island.

A few minutes later, Frank noticed the seaward current strengthening. He grabbed the binoculars and looked at the shoreline, which was still only a couple hundred yards away. Visibility was shrouded, and he only saw a blur. The current was now a rip tide-- worse than any he'd encountered on the west side of the island where they were notorious. In this area that meant… His eyes opened wide.

"Oh no!"

The *Hector* upthrust on a monstrous swell. Frank's knees buckled as millions of tons of water swept beneath them. At the crest the *Hector* caught air. The hull moaned out in ghostly distress. Frank heard pots and pans crashing in the galley.

"Luke!" he yelled, "hold on!"

"Dad!"

The boat dropped down the backside of the titanic surge like a runaway elevator. Frank's stomach sank as he braced himself for impact. The boat crashed and rumbled. Frank slid across the wheelhouse and slammed against the bulkhead. A bedlam of water imploded upon the *Hector*, swallowing her in the throat of the ocean.

The submerged *Hector* heeled violently to starboard. White water churned furious. Frank expected the windows to implode under a flood of liquid, but his boat broke the surface. He rolled over and saw

daylight behind a curtain of cascading seawater. To port, to starboard--
the *Hector* heeled.

He struggled to stand up, but lost his balance and landed on his
side and rolled.

Thunder roared as a tsunami burst upon the rugged coast.

The *Hector* rocked deeply, but Frank pulled himself up by the
handrail. The boat was now turning in a huge whirlpool. The storm
was still blowing, but for a moment, as the *Hector* swung around, Frank
saw the entire coast engulfed in an unbridled torrent of white water
wrath.

"Luke!"

CHAPTER FOUR

From inside the log ranch house, Ingrid stared out the window at Opelia
Harbor. Looking out the rain-spattered panes, through the gray fog
toward the beach, she wondered why Frank and Luke weren't back yet.

Taking three logs from the alcove next to the giant river-rock
fireplace she added them to the flames. Standing in the warmth for a
minute, then walking into the kitchen's big pantry, she picked up her
list of long-anticipated supplies:

200 pounds of flour
75 pounds of sugar
100 pounds of rice
150 pounds of beans, soups . . .

The list was seven pages long, all pre-ordered from a shipping
supply company in Seattle, Washington, whose minimum order was 40
cases. They put out an inch-thick catalog that she knew by heart. As
Luke's nanny, ordering food was one of her chores.

Twice a year Frank made the 1400-mile trip to Dutch Harbor to pick up the supplies ACME shipped from Seattle. He planned to leave in five days. Even though she longed for a taste of civilization after six months on Kiska Island, she would stay home and help Luke with his lessons and chores around the ranch. Sitting down at the kitchen table she added a few items to the list, but couldn't concentrate. Luke should never have gone out during a storm.

Why didn't they call? One last look for the boat and then she'd try Frank on the radio again. The fire crackled, and she felt a wave of heat as she walked into the living room. From the window she saw the *Hector* docking. Luke was tying up. Ingrid sighed with relief.

Back in the kitchen, she added logs to the wood stove. Luke charged in, almost running her over. His cheeks were red from the cold, but round as a plum from his smile.

"I went on the boat with my dad! We almost sank!"

Ingrid stared at him, unsure how to respond. She was afraid that if she did respond, she might start crying or even yell at him.

Frank walked in. "Are you alright?"

She nodded. "I was worried."

Frank looked at Luke.

"I'm sorry," Luke said. "I won't do it again." His shoulders sagged, and he looked down at the floor for a moment.

"It's okay." Ingrid forced a smile.

"Did you hear from Brian and Clay?" Frank took off his dripping rain coat and hung it on the back of a chair.

"Karen came by an hour ago," Ingrid said. "Brian radioed her from a bunker. He
said a tsunami hit the east shore."

"Glad they made it."

Luke smiled. "The wave went right under us."

Ingrid looked at Frank.

"Gave us a fair jolt, but we were in deep enough water and the tsunami hadn't risen much yet."

Ingrid gasped.

"The boat jumped," Luke said.

"Jumped?" she repeated. "You shouldn't have left by yourself. You didn't even ask. Do you have any idea how worried I was?"

"Sorry." His shoulders sagged and his chin touched his chest.

"Boat got pretty roughed up," Frank said. "I've got a lot more work than I planned on to get ready for the trip to Dutch." Frank looked over at Ingrid and gave her a smile. "Luke can help me."

***

For three days Frank worked with Luke preparing the *Hector* for the voyage to Dutch Harbor. They attacked all the disarray in the galley, Frank's office, and then the rest of the boat. Clay Krukov, Frank's Aleut ranch hand, attended to the engines and electronics, fine-tuning, adjusting, cleaning. By the fourth day, they were stowing the boat with provisions, and Frank was moving dunnage into his stateroom. During this time, Frank thought about the problems he would face if their treasure discovery was revealed to the world.

As a reclusive former crab fisherman and sheep farmer, he was invisible to the world, and that's how he wanted it to stay. Trying to secure a claim on a high-profile archaeological discovery while remaining anonymous would be near impossible. Since Kiska Island was a national historic monument, Frank, as owner, had a copy of the state laws and regulations regarding cultural resources. Included in that package were the state laws applicable to archaeological finds. Going over these, he reasonably assured himself that since the treasure was found on his private property, his claim was superior to that of the state government. Still undetermined was whether his claim was superior to that of the federal government or a foreign government. The treasure had probably been on the island for less than sixty years, unlike typical artifacts which may have spent hundreds of years or more buried underground. And the treasure was far removed from its cultural heritage.

From the *Hector*'s wheelhouse, Frank anonymously called an attorney in New York by radio-telephone on the single sideband.

"So you want to pay me to talk about a 'hypothetical' ship," the lawyer said. "As I understand, you're dealing with treasure trove, finders, and lost possessions. In a matter like this, I need all the information available to formulate an opinion you can rely on."

"I just need an opinion of where I would stand," Frank said, "whether or not my claim is defensible."

The lawyer gave a long sigh. "There would no doubt be a contested court proceeding. I'd need to know more about the events surrounding the disappearance of the ship. Why and when was the cargo moved ashore? Who owned the ship? Under what circumstances did the cargo disappear? Were efforts made to find the treasure or was it abandoned? Is the original owner still alive? Where was the discovery made? I need hard information--the more, the better."

"The owner of the cargo might have been Japanese or Korean. Let's say the ship had a vague and mysterious background."

"I'm not in the business of making assumptions. However . . . false documents could strengthen your position or complicate matters. If there was anything clandestine about that shipment, finding information might prove extremely difficult, if not impossible. Shady details might work in your favor, or they might snap back on you later like a trap.

"If you want to proceed, you'll certainly have to be a lot more candid with me. Naturally, I'll need my retainer and a signed fee agreement before I do anything."

"You've already been helpful. I'll call you if I have any more questions."

Frank went to his cabin, sat at his desk, and took off his boots. Thinking about all that had just occurred, memories of his dark past, his wife, and her tragic death entered his mind. Shame filled him, and he ached with agony. How did his life end up this way? He was just trying to raise his kid right, keep him from the horrors he experienced. Frank's own parents had tried to protect him, but as a missionaries' son in Guatamala who'd befriended the local rebels, the CIA took an interest in him. At first it was simple information gathering, but then the stakes got higher.

Frank tried not to remember. He went ashore and walked over to the barn. In the tack room, he removed the false bottom from his walnut seaman's chest. He flipped through several passports and credit cards with alternate identities accompanying his photograph with altered appearances. Finding the passport for John Blake, he looked at it closely. Flashbacks splashed across his mind like a tragic documentary. A dark cape of regret shaded certain images. He snapped the passport shut and put it down. He carefully picked through a collection of hair tints and dyes, trays of theatrical cosmetics and make-up brushes, toupees, wigs, fake mustaches, spectacles, color-tinted contact lenses. Everything was in order, and he set a few items aside.

Not prepared to tell a total stranger where the treasure was and other details he might later regret, he realized he must go to Korea and Japan to research the facts himself.

Going to Japan didn't bother him. South Korea, on the other hand, did. His three previous trips there were conducted under various umbrellas for very high fees. What occurred on his last visit was the capstone of a stained life, but this visit would be different than the others. He would go under the cover of an American tourist. There was danger in going back, but Frank had once been the best in managing danger. If he could get the information he needed, he might be able to accomplish the impossible. He would stake everything on seizing it.

There was one person Frank trusted who might be able to help him. After getting his cabin in order, Frank returned to the wheelhouse and called him by radio-telephone.

"What's all that static, Frank? Where are you calling me from this time? Argentina, or is it Brazil?" Mr. Lee laughed heartily.

"I'm in Alaska. I don't travel as much as I used to."

"When will you come to Seoul? You would like my country very much."

"Actually, I'm traveling to Korea soon. Should be there in about a week."

"This is good. You must come to my house."

That night Ingrid made pizza for everyone. Frank told her that he'd decided to extend his trip and go to Korea for a week. He wanted to visit an old friend.

CHAPTER FIVE
November 25th

The plane touched down at Kimpo airport in Seoul, South Korea. The flight was full, and Frank felt cramped up. Weariness clung to him after six days of nearly sleepless travel, having spent hours replaying his horrible past in his mind.

The airport was packed with thousands of people. They were lined up and shuffling everywhere, people filing this way and that. He felt a chill crawl up his spine as he watched the customs agent look over his false papers, so he thought about Melody on their wedding day. They stood in front of the young pastor who read their vows in the back office of the church. Melody wore a yellow dress, Frank an olive suit. Their short time together was a happy time. Her smile floated in his mind, her lost warmth now returning to him, but the sadness too. The customs agents let him through.

Outside he caught a cab. "Lotte Hotel. Downtown," he told the driver.

Seoul was home to eleven million people. Over the next hour, the cab barely moved. The standstill traffic was ten lanes deep. Frank decided he could cover more ground riding a horse on his ranch.

The cab driver rasped at him in Korean. They'd arrived at the hotel. Snow was starting to fall. A bellboy offered to take his luggage, but Frank decided to carry his own burden.

The lobby was luxurious and filled with rhythmic waves of a foreign tongue. Frank checked in, found his room, and went to bed before opening his duffle bag.

Morning came after five hours of uneasy sleep. He showered in the modern, western-style bathroom. Before leaving his room, he spent fifteen minutes at the window, where he gazed down through the still-falling snow, watching the shadows of the alleyway below. The darkness of his past returned to him.

The hotel lobby was as busy as the night before. The time was past nine. Being in Korea again, a heightened alertness came back to him. As he strolled through the lobby, he observed his surroundings. A glow of expectation that he would soon secure a claim to the treasure helped him to mask his tension. On the way out, he picked up a city map at the front desk.

The sky was a dense, dark-gray layer of clouds. Snow blew down in thick flurries. Most melted on the ground, though white patches accumulated in places. The Han'gul alphabet filled vertical signs overhanging the streets. Cars crowded the asphalt and lined up endlessly at traffic lights amidst the cement and steel skyscrapers.

Frank noticed the details of parked vehicles, faces, cabs and drivers. Women were slim with short, bobbed hair. Men in business attire were hardly distinguishable from one another. All walked in moving crowds. Occasionally, he would spot a person who broke the pattern.

Two blocks from the hotel, he spotted a sign that said "Coffee" in English. He went in and inhaled the sweet odor. He found a seat by the window and sat down, his wooden chair scraping the floor beneath him. Sipping the hot liquid, he looked over his notes.

There were several sources of English information in Seoul. While researching for this trip, he'd picked a hotel that was centrally located by these sources. Noticing a pay phone in the back corner, he went over and jotted down the number.

Back outside, walking to the USIS (United States Information Services), a fetid odor rose along the sidewalk. He held his breath and walked quickly past a sewer grate. The USIS kept only a few books on Korea.

Back out on the street, he followed a long stairway into the dimly-lit subway system. People shuffled through wide cement corridors and bumped him from all sides. The smell of Kimchi and exhaust fumes wafted in the warm, subterraneous air. Frank found another payphone and wrote down the number. He called Mr. Lee and set up a time to meet.

He made his way through the crowd and purchased a ticket. He fended his way down another flight of stairs and waited. The train arrived shortly. Bulging at the seams, it spewed a flood of people as the doors rolled open. No sooner had the crowd poured out when the next mass entered, Frank, the only westerner among them.

Garlic breath followed the crowd, invading the subway car with its musty scent. Nearly every Korean began his day with the fermented garlic-laden dish, Kimchi. It brought back memories. Not good ones. Frank's last mission in Korea haunted him the most. It was the one that caused him the greatest shame. It made him realize how far he had fallen. His only consolation was that his parents never knew. Melody, on the other hand … he'd promised her it was over. But he was unable to protect her, to prevent the unthinkable. He tried to shut the thought out of his mind.

He looked at his fellow passengers. A few wore surgical masks to protect them from pollution and viruses. He remembered being surprised about this years ago. The doors closed automatically, and the train sped into the darkness of the tunnel.

The train entered the next station and he got off. Walking in the flow of a river of people, a crooked old lady elbowed her way past him. The mass of foot slapping sounded like a herd of cattle moving through. Filling the wide corridor, over a thousand heads bobbed in front of him and as many behind. Frank moved with the crowd.

Climbing cement stairs up to the street he could see gray-white sky. Below the sky, brilliantly painted ancient buildings appeared through the falling snow. Turquoise, red, orange, and green contrasted with the white dusting of snow that covered the ground. He took several deep breaths of the brisk, cold air. Unlike the skyscraper-filled area he had just come from, this area was graced with traditional historical structures, remnants of an ancient kingdom. Pulling out his wallet, he looked at a picture of Luke and smiled. He flipped to a picture of his wife, gazed at it for a while, studying her features carefully. He pocketed the wallet and caught a taxi.

The British Council Library was on the first floor of a pale five story building next to the historical Toksugung Royal Palace. He walked down the ally along the palace's perimeter wall with its roof of traditional tiles. The library was small, but Frank found what he was looking for in a matter of minutes, a book on Korean national treasures.

The colorful images on the pages grabbed his attention immediately, and he found himself examining the photographs carefully. He stared at the pages, comparing the relics in the pictures to the ones he'd seen among the Kiska treasures. Many were different from the Kiska treasures, but others were similar. And while there were similarities, a striking difference was that only some of the relics in the book were gold. On Kiska they were all gold.

He learned a fascinating piece of archaeological news: A tomb discovered in 1972 by a construction crew was the tomb of King Muryong (462-523 A.D.), the twenty-fifth king of the Paekche dynasty and his queen. The crypt sat untouched for centuries in Kyongju, Korea. Over two-thousand objects were excavated including elaborate gold works, gold ornaments for crowns, painted lacquer wares, bronze mirrors with designs, copper bowls, pottery, wooden pillows, irons and hornblende tomb guardian animals. Many of the artifacts attested to the refined sense of beauty and highly developed sense of handicraft of the Paekche people.

As he flipped pages, he came across references to other archaeological digs in the 1970s and thereafter where artifacts were discovered. All of the artifacts were on display in national museums. He found no mention of any missing treasure. The treasures in the book were dated 300-700 A.D. and originated with Shilla and Paekche dynasties. He made notes and photocopies of general background information he felt might be useful to an attorney building a case.

He found his fascination growing, and time passed quickly as he devoured information on Korean culture and relics. But questions remained unanswered. Convinced the Kiska treasure originated in Korea, he wondered how it ended up on an Alaskan island? What was the *Musashi Maru* doing in those waters with a cargo like that? And what about the turtle ship carving on the cave wall?

With pages of notes in hand, he caught a taxi to the Royal Asiatic Society. The bookstore resided on the fifth floor of an old office building. The room was no bigger than a large bedroom, but English books about Korean culture lined the shelves. A Korean woman was talking with another westerner when Frank walked in. He left a half hour later with a dozen reference books.

After checking out of his hotel, he left by the side entrance. He walked several blocks, cutting down alleys and doubling back once. At crosswalks he waited till the last possible moment to cross. Pausing under an awning for a few minutes he watched the street behind him. At the subway station, he dialed the payphone and waited. A man answered, spoke in rapid Korean.

Frank said, "Colonel Kim, this is John Blake."

There was dead silence on the receiver. . . . Finally, a deep hesitant voice said, "John Blake?"

"I'm sure you remember me."

Another pause. "I didn't expect to hear from you again—ever."

"I need some information and knew you could help."

"Yes, I—I understand. This is not a good time for me."

"It could get worse."

"Wha— You don't understand. Right now it is impossible. I'm sorry."

"I need your help, Colonel. I know you won't let me down."

"What is this about?"

"You help me now in a simple matter, and you'll never have to think about me again."

"How can I be sure?"

"Obviously I forgave your part in what happened, or you'd have ended up like the others."

A long silence. "Okay, okay. Maybe I can help you."

Frank said, "I need to find out if there's any record of Japanese taking shipments of gold out of Korea during the occupation period."

"Yes, these things are difficult with the bureaucracy. I'll need money."

"You'll get what you need."

"It's not so simple. These things can take time. Maybe it's impossible. The Japanese occupation was a long time ago."

"I wouldn't have called unless I thought you could help."

"Very few people can access such sensitive information. The documents you're looking for are stored in a classified section of the government archives."

"The war's over," Frank said.

"Over? You know better than that."

Wrinkles formed on Frank's forehead. He didn't respond.

"I will contact you tomorrow afternoon."

"I'll call you," Frank said.

"I won't be near a secure phone," the Colonel said. "I'll have to call you. It's the only way."

Frank gave him the number of the pay phone he'd noted earlier in the subway. "Call me at exactly three." He paused. "One more thing, Colonel: you won't discuss this with anyone. I'm paying you to be discreet. I'll be gone within a week, and as long as you forget you ever saw me, you won't see me again."

Frank hung up the telephone. He didn't like trusting Colonel Kim. He scanned the horde of people shuffling through the station. None wore uniforms. That was good, but the real threats would blend in. After a slow, deep breath, he strolled toward the subway exit.

It was dangerous now, but the colonel wouldn't sell Frank out without incriminating himself. The past would stay buried. Frank smiled at a legless beggar, then stopped and gave him a hundred dollars.

The taxi ride swept him through a familiar cityscape. Modern high-rise apartment buildings carpeted Seoul. Smaller apartment buildings, called villas, squeezed between them. Occasionally Frank saw tree-covered green hills. He got out in Yoksam-dong, where he checked into a small, non-descript hotel under a new identity. After a short nap, he returned to the streets and caught another cab.

Togok-dong, one of Seoul's nicer residential areas, was mixed with big and small apartment buildings as well as single-family homes behind high walls. The taxi driver found Mr. Lee's brick apartment building on a narrow, one-lane street. The building was five stories high, modern, and no more than a few years old.

Frank located the right apartment and knocked. The door opened and a small, friendly-looking Korean woman stood smiling. She bowed slightly, spoke in Korean, and invited Frank in with a wave of her hand. Pointing at his shoes, she spoke again in Korean, and Frank removed them before proceeding.

The apartment was a large modern townhouse with hardwood floors and wood-paneled walls. Numerous bookcases with glass covers graced the walls in the living room. Antique chairs held stacks of books and magazines. The kitchen in the far-right, back corner opened up to the living and dining area. The left wall backdropped for a huge oak desk with leather-bound books stacked atop in numerous piles.

Mr. Lee was a retired fisherman and sea captain. While the Japanese bought ninety percent of the annual Alaska king crab harvest, Americans also had joint-venture contracts with the Koreans and Russians. Frank had contacts in all three countries from his time spent as a crab fisherman and for other reasons. Years ago, an inexperienced crane operator dropped a full brailor of crab on Lee, breaking his back. Frank hadn't seen him since, but kept in touch and knew he retired to Seoul.

Using a cane, Mr. Lee limped out of the kitchen area, hunched over somewhat with a crooked back. He was smiling, his face as jolly as ever, maybe more than Frank remembered. His hair was graying now. The captain greeted Frank and introduced his wife who didn't speak English. The wife bowed and returned to the kitchen.

"You ought to be fishing this time of year," Mr. Lee said.

"I'm a rancher now."

"Of course, you are, a rancher on Kiska. Amazing." The captain smiled curiously at Frank and steered him into a wooden antique chair.

"This is your first time to Korea, isn't it?"

Frank's gaze strayed to a book shelf. "Yes," he said, mechanically.

"What do you think?"

Well, now, there was a question he could answer. Frank elaborated glowingly on his impressions about Korea. Korea was great. And then the captain guided the conversation back to Alaska.

"You were never timid going after the crab," he said. "I remember your stories about the savage seas and screaming wind-tunnel passages of Adak; as I recall you even hunted opelia crab on the edge of the polar ice cap. You're probably lucky you got out while you're still alive."

"Luckier than you know," Frank said.

They talked on about old times, Alaska, fishing. Mrs. Lee returned with rice water. They drank and the captain made recommendations of places Frank should see. Frank found his eyes wandering about the bookcases gracing the walls and the volumes stacked in piles on the desk. "Looks like you've been hard at work."

"Yes, yes. In work I find one of life's great joys. So, on the telephone you didn't say why you were coming to Korea."

"Just visiting, always wanted to see this part of the world. You once told me a story about a Korean turtle ship. I've been intrigued ever since. It was a long time ago, and I forgot the details. I just remember the turtle ship. Do you recall what I'm talking about?"

Mr. Lee smiled. "The turtle ship is famous in Korea." He nodded and looked toward a bookshelf, then back at Frank. "In 1592, Japanese Shogun Hideyoshi launched his campaign to conquer China. Korea's Yi court wouldn't participate. In retribution Hideyoshi attacked Korea with 150,000 soldiers. By land, Hideyoshi's army easily overwhelmed Korea in less than a month; they raped and pillaged Korea to such a degree that even today many Koreans resent the Japanese."

Frank squeezed his cup and listened intently.

"However, their sea campaign was another matter," Mr. Lee explained. "Korea's Admiral Yi Sun-shin gave our navy a surprise advantage with his invention of the world's first armor-plated warships, called turtle ships due to their humped appearance. The turtle ships were propelled by oars and heavily armed with cannon. They were compact, highly maneuverable vessels. Their decks and gunwales were plated with spike-studded sheets of heavy iron. This made them impossible to board and practically invulnerable to enemy projectiles. Although the Japanese greatly outnumbered the Koreans, Admiral Yi's turtle ships sent the Japanese into a panic, and during eight battles they sank over two-hundred and fifty Japanese ships. Over a six month period, the Japanese lost over five-hundred ships in encounters with Admiral Yi. Yi forced them to withdraw before the Japanese set foot on Chinese soil."

Mr. Lee paused. Remaining in his chair, he touched the floor with his cane and pushed to straighten his posture. "In 1597, Hideyoshi launched another attack on Korea. However Admiral Yi had lost his post due to court intrigues. The Japanese slaughtered his successor, leaving only a dozen vessels in the Korean fleet. Admiral Yi was quickly reinstated."

The captain's eyes crinkled at the corners and he smiled. "And with only this handful of ships at his disposal, Admiral Yi again vanquished the Japanese fleet. He sank or captured most of their ships and routed the rest. During the final battle of the war, Yi was struck by a stray bullet and killed; however, both he and the turtle ships live on in Korean legend. Hold on a minute."

Mr. Lee directed Frank to a bookcase with glass covers. Frank removed the book indicated and returned to his chair. Mr. Lee flipped through the pages, then passed the book to Frank.

The turtle-ship drawing on the open page looked like the petroglyph Frank saw on the cave wall. He studied the picture in amazement. Mr. Lee leaned over and pointed.

"The mouth of the turtle-head bowsprit carried smoke generators that emitted sulfur fumes and hid the ship from view. This caused confusion among their enemies. Sometimes the turtle's mouth was used as a gunfire hole."

"The turtle breathes a hail of bullets," Frank said. "Impressive."

"There was another gunfire hole beneath the turtle tail astern and several on each side. During engagements, the spikes on the roof were covered with a straw mat to hide them. Then the turtle ship dashed into the enemy at seven knots. Not recognizing the spikes, the enemy sailors boarded. They stumbled and fell down over the protruding spikes."

Both men looked at the picture with affection, as if it were a photo of a newborn baby.

Mr. Lee said, "Finally, surrounded and attacked by enemy ships, warriors aboard turtle ships would fire a volley from the bow, the stern, the starboard, and the larboard--which prevented the enemy from approaching to attack. The turtle ship had fourteen mounted guns and were manned by a hundred and thirty men. They destroyed the enemy at will."

"How big were they?" Frank asked.

"There was variation, but figure a hundred and thirteen feet long, thirty-four feet in breadth."

"You're quite an expert on these turtle ships."

"As I said, they're famous in Korea. Anyway, most of my time is now devoted to history."

"Really," Frank said. "What do you know about the Japanese occupation of Korea before World War Two."

Mr. Lee nodded and frowned at the same time. The lines on his forehead became deep creases. He called Mrs. Lee, and she poured more rice water. The captain contemplated intensely as he took several sips. "At first, Russia was competing for Korea. After Japan defeated China in the Sino-Japanese War, a series of pro-Japanese and pro-Russian governments followed each other at Korean court. The consequence was the Russo-Japanese War of 1904, and the Japanese prevailed. In the aftermath Japan occupied the peninsula, making Korea their colony. Japan's resident-general became the ultimate authority in Korea. The economy was shaped to exploit Korea's resources and maximize returns for Japan."

Frank sipped his rice water slowly.

"In the beginning, Japan ruled Korea in a fashion that would have pleased Machiavelli, ruthlessly suppressing all opposition; although, Machiavelli would have parted with their policies that dragged out the suffering of the people indefinitely. After Korean nationalists published a "declaration of independence" in 1919, demonstrations began, and Japanese police attacked patriots relentlessly, leaving thousands of unarmed civilians dead." Squeezing his walking cane tightly, Mr. Lee shifted it in his hands.

"As World War Two grew near in the 1930s, a campaign of cultural genocide was launched to erase Korean culture and replace it with Japanese. Masters of Korean arts were killed; Korean history was banned from schools; the Japanese language, manners, and customs were forced upon the people; thousands of Korean men were shipped abroad--slave labor for the war effort--or forced to fight to the death for their Japanese oppressors; Korean women were . . ." Anger entered the captain's voice. "They were rounded up. Japanese government policy. The women were kidnapped and forced to be sex slaves for Japan's occupation troops." He shook his head vigorously. "*Comfort women,* they were called." His eyes were watering and he looked away.

"Bastards," Frank said, surprised by the captain's emotion.

Mr. Lee shifted in his seat and straightened his back a little. A grimace crossed his face. "The atrocities were terrible. When Japan lost the war, Korea finally regained independence. But the damage can never be undone." He stabbed the floor with his cane. "*Never!*"

Silence descended upon the room. When the hush was broken by the tinging sounds of dishes from the kitchen, Mr. Lee rose and caned his way to the kitchen. He was gone for several minutes. When he returned he sat down, smiled, and said, "So that's part of our history."

"Did the Japanese steal from Korea?"

"The Japanese tradition of stealing from Korea goes back hundreds of years." Mr. Lee's voice was more relaxed now. "During the Invasion of 1592--that's the one involving the turtle ships--the Japanese stole a huge amount of treasure. Besides the glory of the turtle ships, the campaign was a disaster for Korea. Artists and intellectuals were taken to Japan as prisoners. Korea's temples and palaces were burnt to the ground. In Korea, history tends to repeat itself. What's this all about, Frank?"

"There's a rumor about a lost shipment of Korean treasure. I'm trying to find out if there's any truth to the story."

"So, you've become a treasure hunter, too?"

"Something like that." Frank shrugged and looked vaguely over toward a bookshelf.

"There's plenty out there to find. We historians owe a great debt to treasure hunters. They find us relics to study and learn from. There's plenty of treasure in the Seoul National Museum. You should go."

"I will. I'll be here a few days. Then I'll go to Japan. See what information I can find in Tokyo."

"This shipment you speak of. You mean an ocean-going ship?"

Frank nodded as he sipped his rice water.

"What ever happened with that sunken ship you called me about a few years back? What was that called? The a . . . a . . ."

"*Musashi Maru.*"

"That's it, sure. That was mysterious. We never could find any record of the *Musashi Maru* sinking in the Aleutians. Japanese archives said she sank off Puson."

"Nine months after the Battle of Kiska," Frank added.

"Sure. I think it was an error. I think it was just another supply ship for Kiska air base. If not, the shipmaster was a mad man. No, just a mistake in the records. Don't you think so, Frank?" The captain watched Frank carefully.

"Well . . . you never know."

Mr. Lee grinned at Frank. "I think you would want to keep something like this quiet."

"Of course." Frank took a deep breath.

"How will you do research in Japan?"

"I suppose I'll visit libraries and museums, that sort of thing."

"You don't need to go to Japan. Like my father, I dabble in politics. Although not to the degree that he did--"

"You once told me about your father," Frank said.

"I'm sure I did. My own involvement in politics is more complicated, but I have contacts in political circles including some in Japan. I will have one of my associates in Tokyo look into this for you."

"You mean the fellow who looked into the *Musashi Maru*."

"I think this is too important. I have someone else in mind. He has more access."

"It's nice of you to offer, but--"

"I will contact him today. You will waste your time in the museums of Tokyo, and besides, you don't speak Japanese, do you?"

"There's really no need for you to get involved."

"This is fascinating, this lost shipment you speak of. I'm glad to help. My friend Koichi Kazuka can access government archives in Tokyo. He will find out what information can be dug up on this shipment. He will do this for me. You could spend months in the museums and learn nothing."

Frank turned his cup in the saucer. "Perhaps your friend will be resourceful."

"I'm thinking of someone else to refer you to as well. I think she can help you. She's an archaeologist, an American archaeologist, who lives here in Korea. You can trust her. She's like family to us. She's very knowledgeable about Korean artifacts, Korean treasure, those kinds of things. An amazing woman, Frank. Several years ago, I captivated her interest with some Aleut relics, and she developed a fascinating theory on the Aleutian Islands. Be sure and ask her about it."

Walking along the street, Frank thought about what Mr. Lee told him. He found himself amazed that such a slice of history ended up on his ranch. Later that evening, he called Mr. Lee from a public phone.

"Good news," Mr. Lee said. "I spoke with my associate in Tokyo. He can access the government archives there. I'll let you know what we find out. Also, I talked to Abby Sinclair in Kyongju. She's anxious to meet you."

Back in his hotel room, Frank looked at the stack of books he now owned on Korean history and culture. Since coming here years ago, he tried to forget Korea. Slowly, he opened a book and started skimming. Having already narrowed the origin of the treasure down to the *Musashi Maru* and the World War Two era, he was able to go to the appropriate sections and time periods. He spent the rest of the evening skimming books. At seven, he took a break and ordered room service for dinner. When it arrived, he found he couldn't eat.

He studied for a couple more hours. His reading expanded in scope. Over the centuries, Korea was overrun, pillaged and plundered continually by one dynasty after another; and with each new dynasty came new kings, more treasure, and more tombs laden with gold. Some of the dynasties, such as Paekche and Shilla lasted for long periods, producing many kings and many tombs; others didn't last at all, but left Korea with more tombs teaming with priceless relics.

Years passed, old dynasties were wiped out; old tombs were forgotten amidst constant war and upheaval on the peninsula. Archaeologists were still finding these tombs, excavating them, and producing treasure every year for bulging Korean museums. Treasure-filled tombs were turning up around Korea like mushrooms in the woods after a fresh rain. The tombs were producing ancient gold treasures. Many of these treasures appeared hauntingly similar to the Kiska treasures.

Sometime around midnight, Frank took up Dante's *Divine Comedy*, a graphic descent into hell, one of several books he purchased on his layover in Anchorage. As he read, his thoughts flashed back to the treasure cave. Sleep came hard that eve, and during snatches of laborious slumber, he convulsed in grisly nightmares

CHAPTER SIX
November 27ᵗʰ

The building lay on the outskirts of Seoul. Large enough to contain a football field on each of seven floors above ground and five below, the Seoul government stacks were a mind boggling maze of files, boxes, and walkways--a warehouse for government archives. Despite the building's immensity, the archived files were organized.

Colonel Kim arrived first thing in the morning. The guard, spotting the colonel's rank, stiffened. Colonel Kim introduced himself and explained that he wanted free and complete access. Reluctantly, the guard told the colonel he could not allow him access to the building without written orders. The colonel lay eight-hundred thousand South Korean Won in the guard's hand. The guard, finding this more credible than a written order, pocketed the cash and told the colonel to take his time.

For the next six hours the colonel scanned computers and files. Finally, deep within the stacks, after exhaustive searching, he found what he was looking for in a gray file cabinet.

As he withdrew the file, a hidden trigger was released that sent an electric current through a wire. Behind the wall, a super sensitive tape recorder began recording. Overhead, a camera hidden in the light fixture lit up, rolling its tape, watching with a quarter-inch lens. An electric current ran through the RG11 coaxial cable through the wall and up the side of the building to a transmitter on the roof. Across town, a computer alarm sounded.

***

The computer alarm sounded at the DowKai security center. DowKai was a multinational conglomerate founded and chaired by a man named Mok Don. Soo-man, Mok Don's security chief, was a muscle-bound body builder. When the alarm went off, Soo-man was thinking about the girl he was with last night. He hadn't been able to think of anything else all day.

Soo-man looked at the computer monitor as if it were suddenly working in Arabic. Initiative Three? That was a function he'd long since written off as one of Mok Don's eccentricities. Was it a computer error? A possibility, but not one he had the option of exploring at the moment. In case of this eventuality, his instructions were clear: Follow procedure, don't waste a second.

Soo-man made a call.

The telephone pole was on a busy corner, four blocks north of the Seoul Government Stacks. Behind the lid to the terminal box, were over five hundred terminal pairs; each linked a phone with the telephone company's main office.

Years ago, Mok Don obtained the coded number of the cables in the terminal box that linked the Seoul Stacks phone. He secretly leased the backup cables to the stack's sixth floor from a telephone company executive. His technical specialist hooked up a tiny device called an infinity transmitter.

When Soo-man placed the call, the backups were silently connected with a tiny microphone camouflaged in plaster and broadcasting from the wall behind the file cabinet inside the stacks. With the transmission completed, two listening devices and a video camera simultaneously monitored every sight and sound within twenty feet of the rigged file cabinet. While the tape recorder was a backup that retained hard copy audio surveillance, the video and hidden microphone both transmitted to the security center at DowKai.

Soo-man listened intently into the phone receiver for any dialogue. There was none. His eyes scanned the emergency alarm warning on the computer screen:

Immediately insert tape into VCR. Push Record. Turn on Channel 47.

Soo-man followed the instructions. With the VCR recording, he watched in fascination as an image emerged on the screen of the TV: A man, a colonel, stood in a hall between two rows of file cabinets.

The colonel paged eagerly through a manila file folder. He stopped, showing marked interest in a particular sheet. Removing the sheet, he scanned it.

"What's this . . . ?" the colonel said aloud, his eyes widening.

Soo-man pushed the button on the phone indicating another line out, then he dialed a number.

"This is Soo-man. Initiative three is active. Move! A colonel is in the Seoul Stacks right now. Follow procedure, the clock is ticking."

Soo-man pushed the button for the other line. Again he listened through the microphone behind the filing cabinet. Nothing. He looked back at the TV screen. The file drawer hung open. The colonel was now on the phone at the end of the hall.

Soo-man had a tap on that phone and heard every word.

The colonel spoke into the phone in English: "John, this is Colonel Kim . . ."

As the colonel elaborated, Soo-man crinkled his broad forehead and listened carefully. He understood only snatches of the rapid-fire English, but there were phrases that were unmistakable. He couldn't believe it.

After the colonel finished an oration of English, he hung up the phone and walked back to the file drawer. Several sheets of paper went into his pocket. The file he returned to its place in the drawer. He continued shuffling through the files.

The tape recorder and camera remained up and hot.

CHAPTER SEVEN

Dressed in army fatigues and a camouflage cap, looking like one of the thousands of American soldiers stationed in Seoul, Frank waited under an awning in front of a small French bakery, eating a pastry.

The sidewalk in front of the bakery was extra wide. A child darted out of the way as a quiet Hyundai drove onto the sidewalk and parked by the other cars already parked there. The busy street ran between high-rise office buildings and cars lined up at a traffic light half-a-block down.

For what Frank had in mind, he'd already approached two likely people, and both times he was turned down. Time was short now.

The bakery was two blocks down from the subway entrance. He casually scanned the area, looking for parked vans with lots of antennas, people sitting in parked cars, loiterers, anybody who might be staking out the entrance to the subway. The colonel could have traced the pay phone number by now.

Frank could think of no credible reason why the colonel would do something so foolish. He would have to be crazy or suicidal to turn Frank in for past crimes or set him up. By an action like that, the colonel would not only risk his life, but also implicate himself in the same crimes. Still, Frank wasn't going to link the assassin John Blake to a time and place without reasonable caution. As he'd expected, nothing caught his eye.

Elderly women walked by, businessmen, children. Many of them looked at him, which under the circumstances made him only slightly nervous since he was getting used to attracting attention. Westerners were scarce in Seoul. A young man with platform shoes, crisp white tie, and short spiked hair stared as he walked past. Frank smiled. The boy grinned back.

"An-yang-haseo. You speak English?" Frank said.

The boy stopped. "Sure."

Frank tossed the last of his pastry in the trash. "Maybe you could help me out and make some easy money," he said. "My friend is supposed to call me in a few minutes at a pay phone at the bottom of the subway stairs over there, but I'm meeting my wife. I'm already late, and she'll leave if I don't hurry."

The kid started looking around uncomfortably. He looked at his watch. "I don't know."

"It's easy." Frank reached into his pocket, and handed the kid twenty dollars. "The pay phone is over there at the bottom of the subway stairs. My friend will be calling in a few minutes." Frank handed him a piece of paper. "Just give him this number and tell him to call me. When you're done, come back here and the baker will give you another twenty dollars."

The kid adjusted the shoulder strap on his backpack and looked at the handwritten number on the paper. "That's all?"

"He should call right on time, but you might have to wait five or ten minutes. I really appreciate your help. If I didn't show up, my wife would never forgive me."

The kid raised his eyebrows at Frank, shrugged his shoulders. He stuffed the paper in his pocket. "I just give him the number, okay?"

"You've got to hurry." Frank glanced at his watch. "He'll be calling soon."

The boy's shoes thumped as he walked away.

Frank bought a dozen pastries and left the twenty dollars with the baker, who was happy to do a small favor.

Taking the long way around, Frank strolled to the coffee shop he'd visited earlier, which was around the corner and two blocks again from the subway entrance. He was more relaxed now and wondering what Colonel Kim would have for him. Inside, he bought a cup and sat at the table by the payphone.

CHAPTER EIGHT

The DowKai Building, located in northern Seoul, was far from the buzz of downtown. The twenty-story building was a bleak, dull-yellow hue. Guard posts, electric gates, and high fences topped with three strands of barbed wire--the structure appeared to be a foreign embassy or government building.

The twentieth-floor office was large and decorated in an opulent fashion that contrasted with the stark appearance of the building's exterior. From baseboard to baseboard, the black marble floors shined from their daily waxing. The full-wall window shaded with its one-way tint. Behind the gleaming desk, a long, matching, red-oak credenza backed up against the wall.

Sitting behind his big red-oak desk was Mok Don, a Korean man with gray hair and obsidian eyes. He headed the DowKai Group, a *chaebol,* a multinational conglomerate comprised of dozens of varied businesses.

In his left hand he held a manila file folder. While he quickly flipped pages, taking each in a glance, the red light on his phone flashed and a voice came over the phone speaker: "Soo-man is here, Mister Don."

Mok Don slapped down the folder, hissing and scrunching his nose with resentment. Pressing his elbows against his desktop, he pinned his eyes shut and touched his temples with his index fingers, moving the tips in slow circular motions against the painful building pressure. He felt liquid passion course through his veins like vials of wrath.

He continued flipping pages, but snapped the pages a little more sharply. "Send him in."

Moments later Soo-man walked through the door wearing his blue DowKai jumpsuit. Looking up, Mok Don took notice of him with particular acuity today. He'd been on the payroll ten years before Mok Don brought him on full-time as security chief. During those years, Soo-man was wrestling champion of the entire Seoul police force. After years of shooting a fortune in Deca-Durabolin steroids to enhance his intense weight lifting regimen—he bulged as a monstrous abnormality. He carried two pounds for every one of Mok Don's. He had a broad forehead and his eyes portrayed confidence. Carrying a VHS tape, he walked up to Mok Don's desk and bowed his head deferentially. His massive chest muscles flinched reflexively.

Mok Don smiled coolly, giving no hint of his anger. He had just found out that Soo-man had taken advantage of his daughter and he hadn't decided what to do about it yet. "What are you doing here?"

Soo-man looked up, and Mok Don thought he saw a hint of a smirk on his face, but wasn't sure. "Initiative Three," Soo-man said. "The computer alarm for Initiative Three was activated--"

Mok Don stood up straight. Perhaps he would deal with Soo-man's betrayal later. He stared at Soo-man like the man had just come back from the dead. Years ago Mok Don had made a one-in-a-million long shot at tracking down a lost shipment of plundered treasure that would make his collection the premier collection in the world of Korean gold artifacts. In 1980, he bought access for a researcher to the Seoul government stacks. The man found reference to a lost cargo shipment that left Korea during the Japanese occupation. Further research and first-hand accounts verified that the ship disappeared en-route.

Mok Don hoped that if the shipment turned up, the finder would check its origin through government archives. Or, if anyone was to search for the shipment, he'd wait and watch while they did the work. And if they hit pay dirt, they'd better have protection. He had the file rigged to set off electronic surveillance. He knew success using this approach was a long shot, but his instinct told him to try. After all, his chances of success were as good as any treasure hunter. He called the operation, Initiative Three. For sixteen years nothing had happened.

"What's going on?" Mok Don demanded.

"A colonel by the name of Kim was paging through our file. All the equipment worked. I have the video right here."

"What happened?"

Sweat was beading on Soo-man's broad forehead. He lifted his head, but looked past Mok Don. "He made two calls," Soo-man said softly.

"I assume you traced them." Mok Don walked over to the full-wall, tinted window. He stood with his back to Soo-man, facing the city view.

"We used phone company records. The first call was to a public phone at a subway stop in Central Seoul. Someone answered and said the colonel should call another number. We traced the second call to a coffee shop nearby." Soo-man's voice faded off to a mumble.

Mok Don looked angrily over the shoulder of his silk suit. "Speak up when you talk to me. Why would the call be relayed like that?" He turned away again.

"The colonel's dealing with an American named John Blake. We checked all the nearby hotels. Nobody had him registered, so we greased the gears and got the information we needed on American guests. There were nine. We did background checks on all of them. One of them was a fisherman. I found him the most interesting since the colonel is researching old ships and cargoes."

"Yes, what did you find?" Mok Don turned around, smoothing his tie.

"Name is Frank Murdoch. American. He was staying at the Lotte Hotel, but he's checked out."

"Find him!"

"We got a hold of the hotel security videos and saw him checking out. I've got thirty men with his photograph checking every hotel in Seoul. I've alerted our contacts in law enforcement, and they've posted an alert for his passport at the airport. I expect we'll find him within two hours."

"Excellent. What's on the video?"

"The colonel mentioned the Japanese occupation, royal tombs, also something about a shipment—"

Mok Don's hand shot out. "Let me see that."

Soo-man handed him the VHS tape with two hands. In Korea, it was a sign of respect to pass things with two hands. This ancient royal tradition was originally required by law to ensure another person wasn't carrying a weapon. It was meant to safeguard kings. It was a tradition Mok Don took seriously.

He accepted the tape and walked across the office to a large black television resting on a round, red-oak table. The table was a rare antique from the Choson period. The TV was a Samsung with a built-in VCR. He turned on the unit and pushed the tape in. The video was low resolution to compensate for the poor lighting, but clear. A Korean man--a Korean colonel--was dialing on the bugged phone. The man waited while the line was ringing. . . .

He spoke in English: "John, this is Colonel Kim. I found something. During the occupation, there's reference to Japan's governor-general obtaining information on certain royal tombs. The information was given by an unnamed Korean, a former government official. That would explain why this was kept secret; the trader would have been disgraced. The records of this event were shuffled away and lost in a bureaucratic catacomb for five decades. There are export papers here--Quarantine and Agriculture Declarations in duplicate, a Cargo Manifest, Load Line Certificate, Register, Private Parcels List, Bill of Lading, letters, and other forms. The contents were shipped out, bound for Tokyo. . . . My thoughts exactly. I'll be here a while longer, then call later." He hung up the phone, walked back to the file cabinets, and began shuffling through more papers. "Yeah, Blake," he mumbled. "I'll get you your files. Then I don't want to hear from you again in this life."

"There's no more calls," Soo-man said. "After that he just searched for information."

Mok Don eyed Soo-man and laughed at the bizarre twist of events. He was suddenly remembering his daughter's tears, her humiliating story about Soo-man's strength. Mok Don wondered if she'd left the house today. How unfortunate that he suddenly needed Soo-man more than ever. What were the colonel's exact words?

Mok Don rewound the tape. He listened to the phone conversation again, then a third time. "What else do you know about the American?"

"Files an individual tax return listing a P.O. Box in Seattle. No known address or phone number. No known relatives. Couldn't find anything on him except that he owns a crab boat. We traced his flight itinerary back to Dutch Harbor, Alaska. It appears he's traveling alone."

Mok Don sighed and breathed more easily. He smiled. "A Bering Sea fisherman . . . . Good, Soo-man. How long has he been a fisherman?"

"Seven years, according to the IRS."

"They're very helpful."

"I haven't found out the name of his boat yet. I'm working on it."

"The Bering Sea. . . ." Mok Don walked over and stood facing Soo-man. "The *Pinisha* is in the Gulf of Alaska, isn't it?"

"Just left Anchorage. I contacted them. They put a man in Dutch Harbor."

"Who?"

"The *Pinisha*'s first mate, Won-song. He's walking the docks, asking questions."

"Good work. Dutch Harbor's a small fishing village. If Murdoch owns a boat, someone there will know where we can find it."

Mok Don couldn't believe what he was hearing. A crab fisherman. His black eyes bored in on Soo-man. "Find out the name of his boat, the location--do whatever you have to."

Soo man nodded.

"If he's really a crab fisherman," Mok Don said, "why would he have used an alias when he called the Colonel? That doesn't add up."

"We haven't figured that out yet."

"When you find him, don't let him out of your sight. If he talks to anybody, find out who they are. I want to be sure this Frank Murdoch and John Blake are the same person. Follow him around the world if you have to. Find out who he is, what he's doing? If he's found Korean gold, I want every detail. Don't mess this up."

"I'll have a complete file on him soon. If he has a family, I think they'll make excellent leverage. I'll begin preparations to take them."

Mok Don tapped his forehead with his pointer finger. "Wait until I give you the go-ahead. And keep me informed." He thought about Soo-man and his daughter and a vile impulse tainted the joy he felt from the good news about the treasure. "Don't screw this up, Soo-man. You know what we do with incompetent salary men." Mok Don pointed at the door.

Soo-man bowed and left the office.

Mok Don sat down and leaned back in his chair. He looked around his large office. Resting on one end of the credenza was a black mother-of-pearl inlaid lacquer box. The lacquer box, a ninth century antique crafted during the Koryo Dynasty, was one of Korea's finest in quality.

The office's long wall, off-white and opposite the view window, was decorated with three rare appointments:

Farthest from the desk stood a three-shelf book chest of matching red oak: the doors, shelves, side, and top panels were paulownia; the museum quality piece was a nineteenth century antique from the Choson period.

Nearer the desk hung a landscape painting by the famous Korean artist Kim Myong-guk. Art scholars said that a painter of Myong-guk's talent only comes along once in a hundred years.

Closest to the desk, a four-shelf open étagère: the skeletal structure was crafted from a pear tree, the shelves from paulownia. During the Choson period, art objects were displayed on this tall exhibition piece. Currently, Mok Don used it to display four of his finest gold artifacts: The bottom shelf boasted a solid gold Buddha from the Unified Shilla Dynasty; the second shelf displayed a fifth century gold cup on an openwork stem from the Old Shilla Dynasty; on the third shelf rested a sixth century gold vessel from the Paekche Dynasty; and the top shelf flaunted Mok Don's finest piece: the solid gold Sarira Reliquary.

Mok Don leaned forward for a closer look at his most cherished treasure. A lotus stem stretched from each bottom corner of the casket, and Lokopala, Four Guardian Kings, sat atop of each stem. The only one of its kind, the Sarira Reliquary was in excellent condition--and during his earlier years, Mok Don personally plundered the treasure from a Shilla burial mound.

A great patron of the arts, he took pride in the fact that everything in his office belonged in a museum. Though his taste for

Korean antiques and art masterpieces was insatiable, he especially coveted gold artifacts from the Three Kingdoms Period. While he purchased various pieces abroad in Japan and China from time to time, he knew of collections in Japan that were superior to his, collections that were plundered during the Japanese occupation.

Any commonplace citizen could buy a collection, but for a collection to boast supreme glory, the collector's acquisition must follow the age-old tradition of plunder and pillage. For centuries conquerors like Genghis Khan plundered the Korean peninsula; in this tradition Mok Don wanted to amass his own collection of historic artifacts. Was he any less of a man than the conquerors of the past? Of course not. Perhaps his day of opportunity had finally arrived.

CHAPTER NINE

Frank Murdoch awoke at four a.m. and studied Korean history and archaeology for an hour. For two hours he devoured *Dark Night Of The Soul*, by St. John of the Cross, another of the volumes he acquired in Anchorage.

Putting his book aside, he pondered his reading and the destiny of his soul. He looked at Melody's photo for a long time. His thoughts drifted back . . .

Led by the wailing cries of their colicky baby, Frank, exhausted from sleep deprivation, walked into the dim kitchen. In a small pool of illumination around the little oven light, Melody held her baby in her arms, calming him in the middle of the night, singing lullabies. Her voice was soothing and comforting. Frank sat at the kitchen table and lay his face on his arms. He wondered how he got so lucky to spend the rest of his life with such a precious wife.

Frank checked the time, looked out his hotel window at the awakening city, into the clouds. In life, he was worth a fortune, and yet his money was now useless. Melody was forever out of reach. So many regrets. He could never forgive himself for his choices.

He remembered the tsunami, a cold testament of his mortality. Yet the treasure was his opportunity to make up for his past.

He wondered what Luke was doing. The boy was forbidden to go across the island until his father returned. Would the boy be able to resist that kind of temptation?

Kiska Island posed an extensive set of dangers. And there was always the possibility of a problem luring Luke away from headquarters. That dog, Taiga, for example, was a wanderer. Even in storms the animal preferred to stay outside and was prone to disappear. If Luke wandered too far off looking for Taiga and got caught in another storm, he could freeze to death quickly.

If he went fishing and misjudged the ice on Icy Creek, he could fall through. Hiking along dozens of different mountain ridges, a snow cornice could collapse and bury him in an avalanche. He could be thrown by his horse. And then there were the caves and tunnels. The list went on and on. Luke had common sense, but he had curiosity, too.

Everything was probably all right on Kiska. Frank would go back as soon as he wrapped up his business here.

He locked his room and took the elevator downstairs. Koreans moved about the busy lobby. Frank strolled into the restaurant and ordered the breakfast buffet. Afterwards, he found a pay phone at a subway station nearby and called Mr. Lee.

"Frank, my friend has researched your questions. I'll try to explain his findings in a historical perspective. Let me say first that many Korean royal tombs have been robbed at the time of excavation. There are numerous stories of Japanese occupation forces stealing gold artifacts during the 1930s and 1940s. For that matter, numerous stolen Korean artifacts are scattered around foreign museums in several countries.

"Recently a small scandal flared up in Japan when a man named Umezu Hayashima repatriated 3,031 artifacts to the Korea National Museum. The artifacts--his share of an inheritance from his father--

were collected in the 1920s and 1930s. During that time, his father bought stolen artifacts from every grave marauder he came across."

"Umezu must have felt guilty," Frank said.

"Scared too. At first he donated the artifacts anonymously, fearing his deed would be hindered when reported by the Japanese press. Later he took credit. He said he wanted to atone and asked forgiveness for the Japanese annexation of Korea."

Frank was silent in thought. Finally he said, "How old were the artifacts?"

"Very. They came from the Paekche, Koryo, Shilla, and Choson Dynasties."

Frank said, "The old collector probably thought his son would appreciate his inheritance, but he inherited a legacy of guilt. The son probably looked at those relics and saw only the countless victims of the occupation." Frank paused. "It seems every decision and action can knock over dominoes that topple through generations."

"Yes, yes, that's right . . . So true. And there are other stories. As the war escalated in the early 1940s, sapping their resources, the Japanese sought to compensate by stepping up the plundering of Korea and other occupied territories. Though their atrocities against Koreans were already staggering, they grew even more ferocious.

"While some Kyongju royal mound tombs were missed by the Japanese--and later found intact by Koreans--many were not. In the 1930s, excavations were carried out by Japanese colonial authorities at numerous royal mound tombs around Korea. When treasure was found, the excavations turned to looting."

Frank made notes on a pad so he would remember details later on.

"In addition to systematic excavations and looting," Mr. Lee went on, "there were chance discoveries. For instance, many Korean Kings were buried in remote locations to guard against grave robbing.

"Once, while the Japanese were constructing a work camp, they discovered hidden Shilla and Paekche burial chambers laden with ancient gold treasure. They ransacked the tombs like scavenger dogs."

"That's a shame," Frank said.

"You mean a crime. Those tombs constituted a significant piece of Korean wealth, culture, and heritage. After plundering them, the Imperial Army destroyed the catacombs, caved them in, and sealed them off with bulldozers. No traces remained. There was nothing for the Korean people to find. No books mention these particular tombs. The incident was lost in a maze of bureaucratic archived paperwork. In the Tokyo archives, there are no direct accounts of the thefts, just bits and pieces, offhanded references, dropped crumbs that mark a trail, but enough to put the puzzle together."

"I appreciate all your help. Please pass on my thanks to your friend Koichi Kazuka in Japan. Unfortunately he pieced together a sad puzzle."

"Sad--" The captain hesitated. "Yes. The Imperialists didn't just rob tombs, they raped a nation, inflicting every humiliation in an attempt to strip Korea of her national identity, erase our culture, and fuel the war at our expense." Mr. Lee paused. "I try to stay objective about all this, but it's not always easy."

"Your country's been wounded by foreigners."

"Yes," he said bitterly. He took a long deep breath and added, "While researching this issue, my associate uncovered evidence of a lost shipment--a mother shipment. For ten years the governor-general kept a guarded compound where thousands of these stolen gold artifacts were hoarded. He was keeping the best for himself. When Tokyo got wind of this--the hoard was worth an estimated fifty million dollars-- they sent a detail to Seoul and demanded the entire stockpile be shipped to Japan."

"Fifty million . . ." Frank trailed off. "And that was decades ago."

"A staggering fortune. In a desperate effort to raise funds for the war effort in the Pacific, the Imperialists had the audacity to try to sell Stalin the entire shipment--a piece of the pie Russia lost out on twenty-five years earlier during the Ruso-Japanese war. The shipment was held briefly in Tokyo, then redirected to sail for Russia.

"Gold Buddhas, pagodas, dragons, animal statues of the Oriental Zodiac, eggs, tigers, tiger claws--these are just samplings of the fortune in historic golden artifacts. And it almost worked. But Stalin changed his mind. I don't know why. And what became of those treasures after he turned them away? They disappeared; the crumb trail ended; officially, they never existed at all. As I said, we pieced this story together with crumbs."

After he hung up, Frank felt better about his decision to return to Korea to deal with the discovery. The relics were too valuable and could put his friends in danger. He could only pray that his secret remained secret...at least until he could take steps to safeguard the catch. He trusted Mr. Lee thoroughly. The colonel was a necessary risk.

CHAPTER TEN
Kyongju

Frank checked into the Kyongju Chosun Hotel, which sat on a lake surrounded by tree-covered mountains. He read for a while in his room and skimmed a book by a survivor of the communist prisons, a man who preached to thieves, murderers, and sinners, men who were as flawed as Frank. The man said that our lives are defined by our actions. Frank was eager to get on with his mission, so he took the city bus into town, where he had seaweed soup at a little restaurant. Afterwards he took a walk around.

Kyongju was a relaxing town with a traditional feel. Clay tiles topped traditional houses. The area, a virtual outdoor museum, was one of the great archaeological wonders of the world. Capital city of North Kyongsangbuk-do Province, Kyongju was known to Asia's ancients as Kumsong, home to powerful shaman kings.

Frank found an open-air market and browsed a few shops. He was in a match-box sized convenience store when he saw something that disturbed him. He glanced out the window and saw that a Korean man in casual clothes was watching him from across the street. The man looked away when Frank noticed him, then turned and started walking. He'd seen that face before. Was he being followed? . . . Or was he just imagining it?

Trying to appear casual, Frank left the store and went to meet Abby Sinclair at the Shilla Tombs in Tumuli Park. He took time getting there and saw no more hint of any surveillance. The Shilla tombs were an amazing and ghostly sight. Due to their size and unusual appearance, Frank was captivated by them several blocks before arriving at the park. Right in the middle of town, surrounded by neighborhoods of traditional Korean architecture, a range of huge mounds rose prominently. The mounds were rounded, grass-covered heaps as smooth as greens on a golf course, but brown and frosty for winter.

Frank found his way to the entrance while walking beside a high wall topped with clay tiles that surrounded the whole park. Abby was waiting for him in the bitter cold, a gorgeous young woman. Her dark brown hair was twisted in a bun, secured by a pencil. She had melting brown eyes and wore jeans and a dark jacket over a gray, V-neck lambs wool sweater. Frank noticed her shapely figure.

He introduced himself and they shook hands. Abby smiled, smoothing back a stray piece of her hair.

Frank said, "How do you know Mr. Lee?"

Abby smiled again. "He's an old friend of my father's. I'm very close to the Lees. Mr. Lee told me you're interested in learning more about Korea's ancient history."

"He said you're the person to see."

Abby's face brightened and she gracefully motioned to the park entrance. They started walking. "Mr. Lee said he knew you from crab fishing."

"I used to own crab boats, and I often sold him our catch. Now, I'm a sheep farmer."

Frank escorted her through the gate. Once inside, they were facing a mountainscape of dramatic mound tombs. "This is quite a place. I feel dwarfed standing next to these mounds. Must be nice to work out here."

"Yes, but I've been free of my last excavation for a few months now. I've been making inquiries about a new project for the spring."

"Then my timing was fortunate. Mr. Lee told me you're an expert on Korean treasure."

"I have a strong interest in artifacts of the Three Kingdoms Period. This is a good place to get a feel for where Korean treasure comes from. Many of Korea's finest artifacts were excavated from tombs like these, especially gold artifacts."

Frank nodded. "They're really something." He gazed across the mounded domes of varying sizes. "How old are these tombs?"

"Well, there are twenty tombs here in the park. They were originally heaped into place as early as the first century. Many have been excavated in recent years. Wonderful treasures have been unearthed here. Later, if you'd like, I'll show you some of the them at the National Museum."

"That'd be great. It's nice of you to show me around."

"It's fun to talk to someone who appreciates ancient artifacts," Abby said. Her eyes sparkled.

Frank glanced over at a particularly huge mound they were passing. "I've never seen anything like this place."

"From an archaeological point of view, this is hallowed ground you're walking on. Almost every year archaeologists here uncover another treasure trove of precious relics. Kyongju is truly an amazing place. Even a casual stroll around the hills is very exciting. The mountains you see surrounding the city are full of cultural and historical sites, the whole area. You could get lost, wander aimlessly, and have an extraordinary cultural tour. The whole valley is spotted with burial tombs from the 1st to 8th centuries, Buddhist temples, multi-tiered pagodas, granite sculptures, fortress ruins, palace grounds and other remnants of the Three Kingdoms Era. You could wander around here for weeks without running out of fresh new archaeological,

historic, and cultural sites to visit, even miles up into the mountains."
She tilted her head slightly.

"I'm confused about the Three Kingdoms," Frank said. "Why three?"

"During the first century B.C., many tribal states were united through wars into three kingdoms called Shilla, Paekche, and Koguryo, which ruled different areas of the Korean Peninsula. Shilla ultimately became the most powerful of the three kingdoms, and they flourished through the eighth century."

"You're quite an expert."

"I'm fascinated with ancient cultures and the people who lived in them, how they lived day to day, that sort of thing. It fascinates me that civilizations rose and fell, that people lived and died before I ever existed. That probably sounds a little strange."

"No, I can see where you'd get hooked."

"Really?"

"It's amazing stuff."

Abby smiled. They walked a ways further. She pointed to what appeared to be a cement entrance leading into the depths of one of the mound tombs. "This is Ch'onmach'ong, the Heavenly Horse Tomb. We can go inside."

The cement corridor led to a cavern in the belly of the mound. The crypt was dim inside, with some display lighting. In the center of the chamber's floor, crushed rock surrounded an excavation site. The archaeologists had uncovered a golden crown and girdle and other artifacts; selected imitations lay in the dirt, on display beneath security glass.

Abby leaned over and pointed. "See how ancient Korean artisans crafted the girdle with square links and hinded rings to each. And look at the end ornaments: a whetstone, fish, knife, tweezers, medicine basket, carved beads of jade and glass."

After examining the gold crown and necklace, they moved to a display highlighting a painting of a white flying horse on a birchbark saddle mud-guard. Frank admired the wavy horse that seemed to be dancing on fire.

"Over ten-thousand artifacts were taken from this tomb alone," Abby said. "The artifacts you see in this tomb room are reproductions. The real ones would be worth millions of dollars."

Frank walked to a display of a gold crown similar to one he'd seen on Kiska. He couldn't get over how much the real one would be worth. His focus on material wealth made him uncomfortable. His soul would one day be weighed in the balance. He couldn't let it be found wanting. Yet he saw the irony. Material wealth could feed the hungry and clothe the naked.

Abby said, "The artifacts found in these tombs are very important to the Korean people. They've worked hard to reestablish their cultural roots since the Japanese tried to erase it during the occupation period."

Frank turned and looked at her soft features in the dim light. He said, "It's a shame to think of grave robbers breaking into tombs like this . . . plundering all the treasures for themselves and private collectors."

Abby nodded. "I'm also a believer in artifacts belonging to everyone, not just one person."

Frank looked around. They were alone. He said, "How does that work? How do archaeologists protect the treasures they find? Who has ownership rights?"

"Well, it gets complicated, but generally the government of the country of origin and the country where it is found will lay claim. Whoever the parties are, it's usually settled in court."

The man Frank noticed at the little grocery store entered the tomb and was examining the artifacts like a tourist. Gently taking Abby by the arm, Frank led her back outside and down the path. "Sorry, I was getting claustrophobic." Frank glanced back at the tomb entrance. The man was still inside. Frank was probably just being paranoid, but in his previous life paranoia kept him alive.

From Tumuli Park, Abby took Frank to see tombs in Noso-dong. She explained that they were constructed between the 4th and 5th centuries. The subsequent excavations uncovered gold crowns.

After Noso-dong they got a cab to the tomb of King Muyol. As they entered the tomb compound, Frank admired a monument of a tortoise carrying dragons.

"It symbolizes the power of King Muyol's position," Abby said.

"What's the significance of the turtle?" Frank asked.

"Koreans believe that the turtle of the north is a shamanistic deity that guards the universe."

Frank nodded as though listening intently, but he had other things on his mind at the moment. He briefly scanned the area and mentally mapped out an exit plan in case he needed to leave fast.

CHAPTER ELEVEN
Seoul

As Mok Don finished up his call, he glanced up at Soo-man who stood in front of his desk, his head bowed in humility.

Mok Don hung up the phone. "What do you have to report? Hurry up, I'm very busy."

Soo-man nodded. "My man in Kyongju has been following the American. He's met a woman there. They stopped by an apartment for just a minute; when she came out, she was wearing a scarf. We traced the address and ran searches. Her name is Abby Sinclair. She's an archaeologist whose--"

Mok Don hissed. "He's with an archaeologist?"

"Auk-il overheard some talk of claims."

Mok Don stared at Soo-man, barely able to believe what he was hearing. "What do you know about her?"

"She studied archaeology at Oxford University in England. She's been assisting on excavations in Kyongju, but only assisting. Prior to that she worked in Israel, Turkey and Egypt."

"How do you know this?"

"We paid her dig director in Kyongju. He had her résumé and other information. She's a very delicious American woman, and he thought she would be easy. Instead she slapped him and quit because of his demands for special favors. He was reluctant to tell us, but we got it out of him. His dig has turned up some pottery and bronze artifacts, but he says no gold."

Mok Don shook his head impatiently. "What have they been doing?"

"Visiting archeological sights around the city. Auk-il's giving them a little room so they don't spot him."

"Room?" Mok Don's eye's widened. "Take her into custody, now."

"Auk-il overheard the American saying something about the Korean government and a court case."

Mok Don stood up and cursed. "Government involvement is the last thing I need. I want that woman immediately. Bring her to me."

"What about the fisherman?"

"Keep your man close by. I want to know everything he does."

"If Auk-il gets any closer, he fears the American will notice him. I've got a fresh face on his way there."

"Tell Auk-il if he loses the American I'll bury him in one of those tombs."

***

The restaurant was Abby's favorite. They sat on the floor across from each other. The table was half covered with a dozen side dishes of rice, salad, various kimchis, vegetables, sauces and others. The waitress, a middle aged woman, approached the table carrying a metal box of red hot coals by the metal handle with a double-insulated hot pad. She lifted the grill from the center of the table and dropped the coals down into the brazier. She replaced the grill and got a large plate of pulgogi, marinated beef strips. Then, using prongs, one by one, she placed all the pulgogi on the grill. When all the strips were barbecuing, she left them alone.

Frank took a sip of tea. "I'm glad Mr. Lee referred me to you. I have great respect for him."

"He's an inspiration to me," Abby said. "His mother is too. She's a great woman and close friend. Mr. Lee's very good to her." A slight sadness came over Abby. "She's had a hard life, but you'd never know it."

The waitress came back to the table with scissors and cut the sizzling pulgogi into thinner strips. Frank tried a piece of kimchi. "Mr. Lee tells me you know something of the Aleutians."

Abby's face brightened. "I've never been there, but years ago an Aleut fisherman gave Mr. Lee some artifacts. He gave them to me, and I did some research. I developed a theory linking ancient Koreans to the Aleutians."

"Now you've got my interest. What's your theory?" Frank watched her closely.

"It's obscure, really," she said. "There's archaeological evidence linking ancient Korean cave dwellers with the Eskimos of the eastern coast of Siberia. These original Koreans were driven northward around the third millennium B.C. by migrants from Central Asia--"

"Migrants?"

"Mongolian migrants--they drove Koreans out of their own land. Forced northward, the Koreans settled in Sakhalin, Kamchatka, and the arctic region. There are cultural similarities between ancient Koreans and Siberian Eskimos. Some of these Korean migrants eventually reached Japan. Archaeological evidence suggests man had already been in the Aleutians for thousands of years, but I suspect that some of these ancient Koreans migrated to the Aleutians in small numbers as late comers. There might have even been cases of earlier migration."

Frank kneaded his chin. "So your theory is that Aleuts were originally Korean?"

She shook her head. "Modern archaeological work in the Aleutians has yet to give a clear picture of the origin of the chain's population. The exceptions link Aleuts to northern Japan and the Siberian Pacific Rim; but ancient Koreans migrated to those same regions. After going so far, it seems to me, some would have sailed to Attu and other Aleutian Islands."

"Sounds plausible," Frank said. "Mr. Lee built up my curiosity, but I'm even more intrigued now. Perhaps if you had more evidence, your theory would find its way into history books."

A warm trace of hope simmered in Abby's dark eyes. She smiled as she looked at Frank. "Hopefully some day I'll get a chance to prove it. Of course, I'll have to go to the Aleutians." She lowered her head and sipped from her straw. Then her gaze returned to Frank.

He glanced toward the window, around the restaurant. Abby looked too. There were numerous long tables lined with men in dark business suits. The men were having a good time and talking loudly. At one table there was a family.

Frank leaned toward Abby and spoke in hushed tones. "Maybe you should. Have you ever heard of Kiska Island?"

Abby paused. "Yes, it's one of the islands in the Aleutians."

"That's right, and it's my home."

Abby's eyes met Frank's and she smiled.

The waitress returned and waved her prongs, indicating that the pulgogi was ready and they should begin eating. She handed the prongs to Frank; he thanked her and served the sizzling strips. Following Abby's example, he put a piece of pulgogi in a large lettuce leaf, followed by a bean paste and red pepper sauce.

"Why did you decide to live in the Aleutians? Kiska must be one of the most remote islands in the world."

"I guess I'm sort of a loner. When I was a crab fisherman, I took a liking to the islands. This pulgogi is excellent. How do they make it?"

"It's marinated in soy sauce, sesame oil, sesame seeds, garlic, green onions and some other seasonings." Abby spooned some koch'ujang tchigae, red pepper paste stew. For a while neither said anything. There was a lot of talking at other tables, dishes clanging, metal chopsticks tinging in bowls.

They talked about Abby's living on and off in Korea, her childhood, and how she had moved around a lot as a kid because her father had been in the military.

"My mother survived breast cancer and I can't take her for granted. When I'm not on a dig or a climb, I come here to visit her."

"Did you say climb?"

Abby explained that she was also involved with a group that organized mountain climbing expeditions to raise money for breast cancer research. They talked about her climbing for a while and how Abby was nearly killed herself on one of the climbs.

"You're a risk taker, aren't you, Abby?"

"As my grandmother always said, here today, gone tomorrow."

Abby told Frank about her adventures as an archaeologist. "Archaeology is often uneventful," she said. "I spend a lot of time between digs applying for grants and corresponding with some of my peers. I have contacts at several universities. I occasionally write articles for archaeological magazines."

"How about the digs? Are they dangerous?"

"Traveling in the Middle East is sort of a thrill. The digs themselves are . . . well, sometimes the greatest danger you face is the bugs. I never go anywhere without my insect repellent."

"Where will you go next?"

She thought for a moment. "I'll probably stay around here. This area is hard to beat if you're an archaeologist with an interest in the Three Kingdoms. Unless . . . a better opportunity came up."

As the evening progressed, the business men finished and left. Time was slipping away. It seemed they'd hardly arrived, and yet they were the last ones in the restaurant.

Afterwards, Frank was getting in Abby's car when he noticed a car parked a block away with two men inside. As they drove away, he watched, but the car didn't follow. He stared at the side mirror for a while. Then he said, "I'd love to go see some ruins tonight. Know of any good trails for a midnight hike?"

She turned the steering wheel and grinned at him. "Sounds like fun. I've got my work clothes in the trunk."

Later, Frank followed her on the moonlit mountain trails of Kyongju. Even under the trees, the moonlight filtered down, and often they crossed clearings where the vegetation was sparse. The hills were littered with shrines, rock carvings, statues, and other relics.

After a couple of hours, they took a rest near the ruins of a pagoda. They sat down on a couple of stone blocks. "Thanks for bringing me up here," Frank said. "This is one of the most memorable hikes I've ever been on."

"Oh, I'm so glad to hear you say that. How long are you staying?"

"Unfortunately, only a day or two."

"Then you'll have to change your plans. Kyongju is the best place in the world to learn about Korean relics."

"I wish I could stay."

"I do to. There's so much to see. You haven't even begun to see it all. Koreans call Kyongju 'the museum without walls.' I love Kyongju. Get lost anywhere in these mountains and you'll find one archeological gem after another."

Frank tried to smile, but looked away. He wished he could stay longer. He wished his life was simpler, but even these surroundings emphasized the urgency of his situation. He came here under the cover of a tourist, but he couldn't forget his real purpose. It was the Kiska treasure that he had to deal with.

He looked over at Abby and found her eyes beautiful in the moonlight. He smiled.

***

Abby slowed the car as they approached the hotel. It was three a.m.

Frank reached for Abby's hand. "Why don't you come by my hotel at ten for breakfast."

"I'd love to."

He watched her drive away. Then he saw a glimpse of the car he saw at the restaurant.

Following her—

And then they were gone. Out of sight.

Frank got his duffle bag and turned in his keys. He jumped in the first cab in front of the hotel. "Take me to the bus station," he said.

When they arrived, he told the cabby to wait for him. He put his bag in a locker and returned to the car. As the cabby pulled onto the road, Frank told him the name of Abby's neighborhood. A few blocks later, the man's cell phone rang. He grunted a few times and hung up. A few blocks later, he made a turn that seemed to take them the wrong way out of town. Frank protested, but the man pointed at a map and spoke in Korean with conviction.

"Who called you?" Frank said.

The cabby shook the map and said something incomprehensible.

"Stop the car," Frank said, pointing at the side of the road. "Now."

"Shillye hamnida," the cabby said, acting confused.

"Pull over!"

The cabby understood and did as he was told. The headlights of another car were now illuminating the side of his face.

As Frank looked back, the cabby jumped out of the car. Frank threw his car door open. He swung his legs out of the cab and his thighs flexed as he tackled the fleeing driver. The man's hand opened up and the keys slid on the pavement. Frank looked up, and the bright lights of the approaching vehicle momentarily blinded him. Light glinted off the keys. Frank sprung up and grabbed them. As the driver yelled and pointed, Frank kicked him in the groin. The man groaned in agony and curled on the ground. Frank heard the report of a gunshot from the approaching car.

He jumped in the driver's seat of the cab and started the engine on the first try. He stood on the gas pedal. The tires spun up a rooster tail of gravel at the crawling cabby and then tore away tread with a screech as they caught pavement. The transmission screamed in protest to the workload as the cab roared down the dark road.

CHAPTER TWELVE

As the cab sped away from the scene, Frank watched the rear-view mirror and saw the cabby get up on his knees. The approaching car veered off the road at high speed. The tail end slid sideways in the gravel. The cabby disappeared under the side of the car by the rear wheel.

Frank cursed. He pushed harder on the accelerator.

In the rear-view mirror he saw the car swerve back on the road and follow him.

He pushed the car harder. The speedometer exceeded a hundred. He didn't know where he was going except that he was heading away from town.

He was overtaking another car in front of him, but he couldn't pass because several cars were coming the other direction. The car behind him closed to within a hundred yards. After the oncoming cars passed, Frank swung the cab into the other lane and hit the gas again as he passed the slow-moving vehicle, almost forcing an oncoming car off the road. He gunned it and the cab leapt into a sprint, the speedometer climbing rapidly.

In the rear-view mirror, he saw the pursuing car pass a slow-moving vehicle.

Frank turned his eyes back to the road, which curved just slightly. He let off the gas a bit to let the transmission upshift. Then he poured on the power again.

The following car closed to within fifty yards.

The cab wouldn't go any faster. Frank heard a shot. The door of the trunk popped up, blocking his view. His reflexes caused him to swerve just slightly as his hands jerked at the steering wheel. The wheels chirped beneath him, and he felt a rush of fear in his stomach.

He looked at the side mirror. The headlights were within twenty yards. A burst of automatic gunfire slammed into the open trunk door, penetrating the metal and shattering the back window. Cold air blew in and chilled his face.

At the last possible moment, he swung the cab into the oncoming lane toward a multi-tiered pagoda off to the left. He turned the wheel harder. The wheels screeched. The back slid, but he turned into the slide and the rear wheels caught. The cab shot down another road that took a Y away from the main road. The following car didn't make the turn, but after Frank passed the pagoda, which was now off to the right, he passed another cut-off that connected with the main road. Two headlights announced trouble, and the following vehicle got sideways as it took the corner.

Frank hit the gas. Within moments the headlights were behind him again. Because of the wind, the open trunk thumped on its hinges, and Frank saw spears of light stabbing through the bullet holes in the trunk lid.

Trees flew past on both sides like pillars in a tunnel. The road split into three directions, and Frank held to the far left, pumping the breaks as he took the bend. The road curved to the right again, and Frank didn't see any lights behind him. The cab sped past a hotel, and as Frank went into the next curve, the lights reappeared in his mirror.

The next bend in the road came hard, and Frank slowed the cab. As he came out of the bend, his headlights flooded a large abandoned parking area. He turned the wheel and hit the breaks, causing the cab to slide sideways to a stop. He jumped out and ran up a mountain trail, hearing behind him the sound of a revving car engine and gravel crunching under tires. Light filtered through the trees until the driver turned them off. Frank was temporarily blinded by the sudden darkness, so he slowed to a jog.

His eyes adjusted to the night, and the trail soon opened up to what appeared to be a magnificent palace or ancient Buddhist temple built on a series of stone terraces in the treed foothills.

Frank was momentarily awe-struck by contrast between the peacefulness and quiescence of this place and the adrenaline jumping through him as he ran along the stone wall for a bridge stairway that led up into the old temple. They were coming for him, and he doubted that it was for fellowship.

The stairs led up to a door in a stone wall beneath traditional Korean structures of arched and curved tile roofs. The gate wasn't locked. He entered a courtyard. As he turned around to close the gate, he scanned the darkness, careful not to focus on anything but to rely on his peripheral vision. He saw two figures running up the trail. One of the men was large and muscular.

Frank turned and jogged through a court yard with two large, multi-tiered pagodas. He stopped by a thirty-foot pagoda and quickly glanced around. The courtyard was surrounded by stone walls, traditional structures, and covered walkways. He heard nothing, but he thought he smelled incense. He crouched down behind the pagoda and waited . . .

The faint sounds of feet climbing stairs gave way to silence. Frank's eyes were well adjusted to the darkness now, and peeking around the base of the pagoda, he saw a bald man slip through the main gate. The man stepped in the courtyard and stood with his back to the wall, scanning for movement.

The bald man began slowly walking through the courtyard. He crouched down low and his head shifted back and forth as he worked his way through the shadows. He clasped his hands out in front of him, and the outline of a pistol told Frank the thug had no intentions of worship.

As the man carefully approached the pagoda, Frank ducked around the backside and hid in the shadow behind the pagoda stairs. As the man came around the corner, Frank sprang out of the shadows and delivered a vicious blow to the mound of the radial nerve in the top of the man's forearm, causing him to drop his gun and yell in surprise.

Frank followed the initial attack by hammering his palm into the man's orbital bones. These bones communicated the force directly to the frontal lobes of the brain and the man buckled, unconscious.

Frank scanned for the man's pistol, but heard the fast shuffle of sprinting feet. He spun around as the hulkish man tackled him. The hit came hard and the brick floor even harder. Frank maneuvered just enough so that he didn't take the full brunt of the man's weight. As he scrambled up, he noticed some movement with his peripheral vision.

The big man gained his feet and slugged Frank in the chest. He stumbled backwards into the rock pagoda.

The killer grabbed Frank, throwing him down on the ground. As Frank got up, the big man drop-kicked him in the chest. Frank rolled on the ground. Before he could gain his feet, incredibly powerful arms grabbed him from behind, pinning his own arms and squeezing him relentlessly.

"Life is suffering," the man said in a raspy low voice.

Some alarm deep inside Frank told him that his ribs were not meant to take this kind of pressure. He couldn't breath. He suddenly noticed what the movement was that he had seen. Dozens of monks with shaved heads were now standing underneath the eves of the surrounding buildings, watching the action.

"Then start living," Frank said.

Using the back of his head, he delivered a solid blow into the killer's nose. The man's iron grip tightened. Springing his neck muscles, Frank delivered a second blow. This time the killer's arms lost their hold.

Frank whirled around hammered him under the chin with the palm of his hand. Some of the monks grunted in shock.

The big man wailed in pain. Frank delivered the next blow into his solar plexus. Then he dropped to the ground and whirled, kicking the killer's feet out from under him.

The big man hit the ground hard.

Frank spotted the gun, but was too late. The bald man got there first, scooping it off the ground. Frank ran around the pagoda as several shots ricocheted off the towering stone structure. The monks scattered for cover, and Frank sprinted down an alley between two buildings before leaving the monastery by a side entrance. He ran down the trail to the cab.

CHAPTER THIRTEEN
November 28th

Abby woke just before 5:00 a.m. She tossed and turned in bed and looked at her clock every twenty minutes. She kept rolling over as she anticipated her plans to have breakfast with Frank. Now she was checking her clock at ten minutes intervals. She wondered what the day would bring. And every five minutes she verified that it was still too early to get up. Her alarm sounded at 7:30 a.m.

She finally got up and attempted a letter to a friend in London, but was too preoccupied. She thought about Frank Murdoch and all the possibilities he was bringing into her life. She wanted to go with him back to Kiska Island to research her thesis. Maybe he would offer her the chance today.

Abby crossed her legs and leaned back in her desk chair. As usual she was ready to go anywhere anytime. A suitcase with its top flipped back sat by the wallboard in her bedroom. A backpack rested against the wall. The suitcase was half-full with neatly-folded clothes. Loosely-spaced clothes hung on hangars in the closet.

She thought about Frank. He was an attractive man with a rugged quality. She enjoyed his company from the start. And it didn't hurt that he was a friend of Mr. Lee's, a good judge of character.

When it was time to get ready, she got in the shower and let the warm streams of hot water massage her body. Minutes later she was still soaking when she thought she heard something. She turned off the water and put a towel around her. She opened the bathroom door and stood there. Water ran down her legs. Her heart rushed.

"Hello?" she said loudly.

There was no sound, no answer. Of course there wasn't. She walked through the bedroom and opened the door to the living area. She stood there and looked around.

"Hello?"

Silence . . .

Abby checked the other bedroom. Nothing.

She looked out the peep hole in the front door. Nobody there. The door was locked. She must have imagined hearing the noise. Back in the bedroom she dried off and decided on what to wear. After turning off all the lights, she stepped outside and locked the door. She checked her mail box and was surprised to find a letter addressed to Frank from Mr. Lee, which she pushed into her pocket. She was crossing the parking lot when she heard someone. She started to turn around but--

Someone grabbed her from behind. She started to scream but a hand came over her mouth. The grip was hard and it hurt her neck. The hand yanked her backward. Hurting her! A car engine started and tires screeched. A car door opened.

"Get in."

He was roughly pushing her in. She turned her head enough to see a Korean man. Again she tried to scream, but he only hurt her neck more.

"If you tell me where the treasure is right now, I'll let you go. Otherwise, this will be the last car ride you ever take." He loosened his hand on her mouth.

"What are you talking about?" she said.

The man shook his head. "Wrong answer. You tell me right now or you'll never be seen again."

Abby gasped. "I don't—"

The grip tightened viciously. The man violently forced her further into the car, punching her several times. Knocked flat onto the seat, Abby turned over onto her back. She kicked with two feet. Several kicks missed before she drove a kick squarely into his gut, making him gasp for air. The driver, leaning into the back seat, grabbed her around the throat and started choking her. Scratching his arms, Abby saw Frank come up behind the other one.

***

Frank slammed the car door on the kidnapper's legs. He heard a snapping sound. The Korean screamed in agony and sagged to his stomach on the car seat. Frank jerked the door open, grabbed the man, and drove an elbow into his jaw.

He was pulling Abby out of the car when the driver jumped out of the car and reached for the gun in his shoulder holster.

At the same moment, Frank leapt onto the trunk of the car, dove across the roof, and snapped off the car antenna. As the driver drew his gun, Frank skewered him through his cheeks with the antenna. The Korean screamed, dropping his pistol. Despite his shock, the man jerked the antenna out of his cheeks. Using the narrow rod like an ice-pick, he lunged at Frank, wailing from the depths of his gut. Using the V of his palm and thumb, Frank ensnared the man's stabbing arm in mid-strike. He rammed the fore-knuckles of his clenched fist into the man's throat.

The Korean stumbled backwards, collapsed to the ground, his arms covering his face and neck.

Frank saw Abby running down the street. He jumped in the car and sped after her, slowing as he drove alongside.

"Get in," he said. But she ran faster.

"Abby, get in the car. There may be more of them."

"Who are they?"

"Get in. I'll tell you."

The wheels screeched as they sped away from the scene in the kidnapper's car.

She gasped for breath. "He grabbed me, he grabbed me from behind-- Why?"

"I'm getting you out of here," Frank said. "We're going to Seoul."

"Who were they?" Abby said trembling.

"We were followed yesterday."

Her eyes opened wide and her mouth tightened. "What? You knew about them?"

Frank looked over at her, then back at the road.

"Why didn't you tell me? Why didn't you say anything last night?"

"He disappeared. After you dropped me—"

"Oh my God. I can't believe this. They were going to kill me!" Abby turned and looked out the back window for a moment. "That man said I'd never be seen again." She was breathing deeply and slowly. She kept remembering the strong garlic odor of her attacker's breath. She crossed her arms around her tightly and sank down into the seat.

Frank drove to the bus station and retrieved his bag. Then they were driving again. He said something to her, but she wasn't listening.

"How do I get to Seoul?" he demanded.

She looked over at him for a moment. "Take a right, I mean a left, up at the light. That'll take us north."

Neither of them spoke for a long time. Abby was feeling nauseated. She rolled down the window for fresh air, but it was too cold outside, so she quickly closed it. She squeezed herself as tightly as she could with her arms, but couldn't stay warm.

Frank turned on the heat. "What did they say?"

Abby uncrossed her arms, relaxing a little in the warmth of the heat.

"Tell me what he said."

"The treasure—they wanted to know where it is. What are they talking about?"

"I found treasure on my island."

"What?"

Frank shook his head. "I asked a colonel in Seoul to do some research for me. I can't believe he— I'm sorry I've gotten you involved in this. Right now the only thing that's important is keeping you safe." He looked over at her. "Are you hurt?"

"My neck is a little sore, but it's fine. I'm just shaken up."

The gravity of what happened was starting to sink in now. Frank had nearly gotten her killed—and yet he saved her life. She couldn't go home. If those men struck once, they would strike again.

As they traveled north, Abby felt dizzy. They drove for an hour and she said nothing more, neither of them did. She watched countryside speed past and felt as though Frank Murdoch and the treasure and the attack were all a dream. It must have been a dream and she was going to wake up . . . but then she fell asleep . . . She woke later feeling groggy and looked over at him. She was so tired . . . Who was he? . . . She was sleeping . . . She was safe . . . And she felt his hand gently tugging on her shoulder, nudging her awake.

"How far to Seoul?" he said, his voice strong, gentle, and comforting.

She checked the map. "Another hour and a half."

"You were out cold for hours," he said. "How do you feel?"

"I'm okay."

"You're sure you're not hurt?"

"I'm alright." She squeezed her sore neck muscles while directing him through the city. He kept looking over at her with a concerned expression on his face. "What now?" she said.

He turned and drove down a back street. "I want you to go back to Kiska with me till I can sort this all out."

"Oh, I don't think so."

"These people are professionals. They'll find you no matter where you go. We have to leave the country tomorrow."

"No, I'm going to my mom's."

"Abby, they will find you. You have to come with me."

She didn't say anything.

"We'll leave tomorrow. I have a couple of things I need to do in the morning. While I'm doing that, I want you to buy some clothes for our trip, and a camera to photograph the artifacts."

For a moment, she realized that she could take credit for the discovery. She thought about fame and riches and being sought after by universities and maybe even National Geographic. But then she remembered the danger they were in.

"Where will we stay tonight?"

"We'll find a hotel on the outskirts of Seoul."

Twenty minutes later, they found a small family-run inn and checked in as Mr. and Mrs. Park. This was a common name in Korea, but would also work for an American couple. That night they took a long walk along a country road. They stopped by a field of tiered rice patties.

"I'm scared," she said.

Frank found himself moved by her soft voice. As he stood there contemplating, she looked up at him, and he found himself pulled in by her dark eyes. "You have to stay with me. That's the only way I can keep you safe."

They walked back to the inn. Frank scoped the perimeter first. Once assured no new cars were in sight, they went inside. As Abby settled into the bed, Frank slumped in the chair near the door.

Suddenly a life of killing started reeling through his mind. He winced against the pressure of an oncoming headache. He felt the strangling depression crawling back over him. He saw himself tumbling backwards, falling back into a living hell of his own creation-- a dark existence of self-hate. He remembered looking death in the face and then making a wild promise that offered a ray of hope. It was gonna be a long night.

CHAPTER FOURTEEN
Kyongju

After shutting off the van and killing the headlights, Soo-man got out and went around back. In the pitch-black darkness, he couldn't even see the dirt road stretching from beneath his feet into the woods in either direction. The hinges creaked as Chull-su pulled open the back door of the van.

Soo-man looked into the back of the van at the body wrapped in bed sheets and duct tape. "We've got to do this quickly."

"You carry him," Chull-su said.

With his huge hands, Soo-Man pulled on his stocking cap. "Why'd Mok Don bother sending you down here?"

"After your screw up, you're in no position to ask."

Soo-man glared at him. "Be careful what you say." He tossed a clanging pillow case full of junk to him. "Bring the bag."

Soo-man lifted Auk-il's rigid body out of the van and over his shoulder.

Chull-su followed. He shined the flashlight ahead of Soo-man, illuminating the trail.

Half way to the mound tomb, Soo-man heaved Auk-il's body from his right shoulder to his left shoulder. The jolting caused Auk-il to struggle and moan, but the bedsheets and duct tape held fast. After what Auk-il had gone through, Soo-man was amazed he was still conscious.

When Soo-man stepped on the base of his dirt pile, he dropped the body onto the ground. "Get that sheet off him."

Chull-su cut it away with a razor knife. He pulled the sheet away and left Auk-il naked on the frozen ground, his face and head covered in blood, his cheeks swollen. He tried to open his eyes but they were swollen shut. Chull-su removed the gag. Auk-il moaned in agony.

"You piece of shit," Soo-man said. "All I told you to do was abduct the woman." He spit on him. "You screwed up, and I lost face." He rolled the body into the shallow grave in the side of the huge mound. He could smell the frozen earth. Auk-il gasped and moaned and moved around. Chull-su stepped up beside Soo-man and shined the light down into the pit.

"Get out of my way."

Chull-su stood back.

Soo-man took the bag from him and dumped the pillow case full of cheap relics onto him. Auk-il groaned when the objects hit him.

"Don't worry," Soo-man said. "Ten years from now, archaeologists will probably dig up your bones and pronounce you a Paekche King."

Soo-man took the shovel and started filling the hole. He shoveled fast. He didn't want to end up like this. He had to find the Americans.

CHAPTER FIFTEEN
November 29th

Mok Don stood gazing out the window of his office across miles of roofs into the haze. He heard the door to his office open and turned to see Soo-man.

The security director was dressed in a gray suit. He bowed. Mok Don walked over. Soo-man lay a clear plastic sandwich bag on Mok Don's desk. Through the plastic, Mok Don saw about two dozen blood-stained teeth. He picked up the bag, frowning. "Are they all here?"

"Yes."

Mok Don dropped the bag in his desk drawer. "Get back to work. I have meetings."

After Soo-man left, Mok Don returned to the window and looked out across the hazy city. He heard the door to his office open and turned to see Colonel Kim. The colonel bowed deeply, and Mok Don returned the courtesy.

"I'm delighted you were able to see me on such short notice, Colonel."

"The pleasure is mine."

"Take a seat. We have a shared interest in mutual profit. Please"--Mok Don gestured--"please take a seat, my friend."

The colonel sat down, and Mok Don walked over to his four-shelf open étagère, gesturing expansively with his arms: "Choson exhibition piece, crafted from a pear tree, I'm very proud of this antique. How do you like my gold treasures?"

"Spectacular," the colonel said.

Mok Don gestured to the second shelf. "A fifth century gold cup with an openwork stem from the Old Shilla Dynasty." He removed the gold cup with two hands and placed it on the desk in front of Colonel Kim.

"Ah." The colonel inspected the antique, nodding to show his appreciation. "Beautiful."

From the credenza Mok Don removed a dragon-shaped celadon wine ewer and celadon wine cup. "These, Colonel, are Koryo. I've heard a ewer such as this exists that is pure gold." Mok Don lifted the dragon ewer by the lotus-stem tail, and wine spilled from the dragon's mouth into the gold cup in front of Colonel Kim. "You are honored today, Colonel. Only I have used that cup, only I and Shilla royalty." Mok Don set down the dragon ewer in front of the colonel. "And now you."

After a nervous glance, Colonel Kim stood and bowed three times. He hesitated slightly, then poured wine into Mok Don's cup. Korean tradition dictated that it was rude to pour your own drink. Colonel Kim set the ewer down and bowed again. "Yes, Mok Don, I am honored, but I don't know why."

Mok Don smiled. "But you do," he said, nodding. "Let us drink."

The colonel's eyes were open wide as he took his seat and tipped the gold cup.

Mok Don drank greedily from his 12th-century celadon cup, savoring the aged wine. Then he placed the green ceramic cup on the matching-green companion stand. "I have followed your exploits over the years with affection, Colonel. You have a firm hand in dealing with North Korean defectors. You are right in thinking they must be dealt with severely."

"I deal with problems in a decisive and direct manner. I do what I have to."

Mok Don smiled. "I couldn't agree with you more. I've seen you on television, and we have some mutual friends. A man with your . . . abilities. I might have use for such a man one day. And if such an arrangement came to realization, you would do very well indeed. I remember my friends. Favors never go unanswered." Mok Don saw the reaction. The colonel straightened slightly and showed himself a trifle invigorated at the prospect.

"I've heard that an American is researching some antiquities. And you are helping him."

A severity overcame the colonel's aspect. His knuckles turned white as he gripped the arms of the chair. "How do you know about this?"

"I am a resourceful man. I know about the shipment the American is researching. And, were I to learn he has actually located this shipment, I would reward you generously. Why are you helping Frank Murdoch?"

"I . . ." The colonel shifted in his chair. "It's of no consequence."

"I happen to know, Colonel, that you paid a security guard to get into those archives. That leads me to believe this inquiry is more than frivolous."

The colonel shifted in his chair.

"Relax." Mok Don smiled. "I understand your discomfort. Bribes have become a serious matter here in Korea, and you're sitting with one of the few important men in Korea who hasn't been accused of paying any. Don't worry, Colonel. I didn't summon you here to be your judge. Nor do I intend to report this crime to the authorities. An action like that could jeopardize your career and subject you to public humiliation. I know that won't be necessary. And that makes me very happy, my friend. I have no desire to add fuel to their political witch hunt."

The colonel took a deep breath and sat back. He stared attentively at Mok Don.

"But I need answers," Mok Don said. "Why are you helping the American? Are you partners?"

The colonel raised his open hands. "I am doing him a favor, that's all."

"You are old friends then."

"No. Absolutely not."

"What about the girl? Is she the one who found the treasure?"

"What girl?"

"He is paying you for your services."

The colonel cleared his throat. "A soldier of fortune fights for the highest bidder. Or the strongest leader. Better to join the strong than perish with the weak. I have given these matters much thought."

Mok Don grinned. "If you assured me that the American had actually discovered this treasure, I would reward you richly."

"No. You don't understand. I can't get involved." He lowered his hands and touched the metals at his breast. "You speak of my future. If I betray the American, I'll have no future. He will kill me."

"What?" Mok Don hissed. "You're a colonel in the Korean army. You should fear no man."

"He will kill you, Mok Don."

Mok Don narrowed his eyes. "You must be joking if you think I'd let an American pig get in my way. There are few Americans who I couldn't buy and sell with my spare change."

"You don't know what sort of man you're dealing with here."

"Tell me."

"The risk is too great. I would be forced to leave the country. Go into hiding."

"If you don't cooperate, you may not be so fortunate."

The colonel stared at Mok Don. He shook his head, laughing. "The man you call Frank Murdoch, I know as John Blake. He's assassinated terrorists all over the world. You don't want to attract his attention. You may be famous and powerful, but that won't matter to a man like him--no more than it matters to a machine. Make one mistake and he'll bury both of us."

"He's a fisherman." Mok Don waved him off in disgust.

"He's your worst nightmare."

Mok Don squinted. "How is it you know so much about this man?"

"It's my job to know."

"And how did the American happen to contact you about this treasure?"

The colonel shifted toward the window, his body rigid. Mok Don was amazed at the colonel's outward display of pressure. He would have made a poor general.

"Many years ago, he was hired to train our special forces operating in the demilitarized zone. I met him then. And he remembered me." The colonel started to smile, but the corners of his mouth turned down quickly. "I never imagined I would betray John Blake."

Mok Don felt a vile impulse run rank in his body. "Relax, Colonel, you're going to pull the arms right out of my chair. Do you know what that chair is worth? Are you aware of the place such an antique holds in Korean history?" Mok Don rose quickly. "No! Because your loyalties are to foreigners. Just make sure you don't betray me, my friend. Or John Blake will be the least of your worries."

The colonel started to say something but stopped himself.

"My friend," Mok Don said, "my dear friend. I need to know more about this man. You're giving me generalities. I need specifics."

Colonel Kim's head was shaking even before Mok Don finished speaking. "I don't know any more. But there is someone else who can tell you more about Blake."

"And who is that?"

Colonel Kim winced, a contortion twisting on his face. A fatalistic sigh… "The President."

CHAPTER SIXTEEN

Colonel Kim's sleek black Grandeur approached the parking lot exit gate at DowKai International headquarters. Reflecting on the astounding meeting with Mok Don, Colonel Kim couldn't help examining the barb-wire fences surrounding the grim facility. Something about those barbed fences reminded him that he would have to face John Blake--no way out, the meeting was set.

He hadn't completely betrayed the man, but he pointed Mok Don in the right direction. He cursed in disgust. Who was he fooling? He betrayed probably the most dangerous man in the world. Now he had to face him and remain totally calm.

The colonel recalled his first meeting with Blake years before, ushering him to a meeting with a general in the Korean army. He was told who John Blake was and what it meant when the man showed up for a meeting. The explosive events that followed allowed Colonel Kim to surmise the rest. And they all went down. Only Blake vanished amidst the chaos.

The gate opened automatically, and he drove out of the parking lot.

First he would go to the National Museum, then back to the military base. The sooner he got this meeting over, the better. He headed south.

Three blocks behind the colonel's car, another car moved with the flow of traffic. Inside were the Park brothers, Chull-su and Hyun.

The taller brother, Chull-su, drove the car. He was an emaciated man in a wrinkled black suit. With a half-drunk can of warm beer, he washed down a packet of pills and tossed the empty can into the back seat.

In the passenger's seat, Hyun looked slowly up from his notebook computer. His goatee was impeccably trimmed, his hair slicked back.

"You look worse today," he said, tapping on the notebook computer in his lap with carefully manicured fingernails.

"Don't talk," Chull-su said, edging the car forward. He felt his anger creeping back upon him as he thought of his wife. Bonded under Confucian rule, she used to nurse him every morning as was proper-- until she read about the American women who don't submit to their abusive husbands. When Chull-su drank too much, his wife's eyes got black in the morning. Now she was threatening to leave him. He looked at his brother and said, "Where's the colonel?"

Hyun glanced at the laptop. "Right now, he's driving through It'aewon."

"Is he stopping?"

"Doesn't look like it." Hyun pulled his pistol out from his jacket and began polishing the weapon with a cloth.

"Just watch the computer. We don't want to make a mistake."

Hyun polished for several minutes before putting the gun away. Then he looked over at Chull-su and said, "What's wrong with you now? You look like you're gonna die."

Chull-su stopped the car and put his free hand to his stomach. "The pain will pass, always does. Just hits me in waves." He cursed and shook his head. He reached down and turned up the heat, eased his foot off the brakes.

"Mok Don praised your devotion to duty," Hyun said. "A high honor. I don't know how you keep going though."

"Obedience," Chull-su said. A ringing started in his head. His vision went white. Some seconds later, color returned. He didn't even know what his sickness was because he'd seen so many doctors and gotten so many different diagnoses. As long as he could serve the group, he didn't care anymore.

The group itself was made up of salary men divided into sub-groups. A good salary man imitated figureheads. Independent thinking was not wise, not tolerated, not desirable. All eyes looked up. Anyone with a higher position in the chaebol was an authority figure. Leaders were another breed. Mok Don was the supreme authority.

A salary man was at the beck and call of his leaders. It was an honor to work for a man of Mok Don's stature, an honor to work for a proud and successful chaebol like DowKai.

Each of the businesses making up DowKai was run independently by group leaders like himself. Group leaders were set for life. All he had to do was conform and adhere: Subservience to the boss, allegiance, blood loyalty, relationships dictating respect and authority throughout the organization, unquestioned obedience, a lifetime commitment.

The DowKai philosophy gave Chull-su internal peace, unity; it removed thought and decision from action. As long as he worked within the philosophy, Mok Don would be pleased. Chull-su slowed the car as they approached another traffic light.

Hyun scowled at the computer. "He's heading toward Chung-gu now."

"He's working for an American. The man has no loyalty."

"I've lost his signal. I think he's in the Namsan tunnel."

Chull-su reached down and fished around the ash tray for a butt. He lit up and took a deep draw. He rolled down the window and exhaled, flicked the butt onto the street. He coughed several times and said, "Americans are soft. The one Mok Don taped is a fisherman."

Hyun stared at his computer. "He's finished."

CHAPTER SEVENTEEN

The light on Mok Don's phone blinked. Rapidly he picked up the receiver.

"Mr. Don," his secretary said, "I have the President on the line. I'll connect you now."

Mok Don had long courted the favor of Korean presidents with his invisible contributions. After that, winning contracts was just a matter of listening to their threats and agreeing on a sum large enough to satisfy them. Chaebol leaders and presidents had long been partners in national economic development. Efficiency being the desired end, all moral aspects were irrelevant. You either played along or you were devoured by the bigger dragon.

The presidents always received Mok Don's customary contributions, but never from a source traceable back to Mok Don. As long as they knew Mok Don paid up, they were happy. When they handed Mok Don large market shares and lucrative government contracts, the gifts couldn't be traced to donations.

Unlike the previous succession of corrupt strongman presidents, President Paek Yoon-Ki won his office in fair elections. A representative from the military never came to DowKai for the customary visit. Mok Don knew President Paek from long acquaintance and detested him. The man was a new kind of president over whom Mok Don exercised no influence. A hero of the Korean War and well known for his fearless exploits, the old man was the toughest leader to ever occupy the Blue House. He was elected on a platform of reform. Unfortunately, despicably, he made good on his promises. The populace was like a hungry monster, and President Paek constantly fed it with indicted human sacrifices. A slice of the aristocracy was hauled off in chains.

President Paek was like an epidemic plague infecting the rabble. Publicly, the man was also one of the most eccentric president in Korean history. He was famous for actually having worked alongside the gardeners at the Blue House. This was disgraceful. There were photographs of him in the newspapers digging and raking around the grounds. The people loved him for his humility. They saw him as noble, but understanding of their struggles.

The man was an actor as far as Mok Don was concerned. The President understood public relations and was playing upon the sentiments of the masses who wanted fair distribution of wealth. The ignorant masses followed along like mules behind a hay wagon.

There was a pause and the connection was made.

"Mok Don," the President said, "I've been meaning to speak with you. It helps me to keep my finger on the pulse of the economy."

"Then perhaps you'll call off your police force and prosecutors. I'm growing weary of their harassment. They've been a nuisance for too long trying to uncover evidence of corruption. The economy suffers when I'm distracted from my work. When the economy suffers, so does your popularity."

"I didn't know they were still bothering you. I'll look into it. However, if they have good cause, there's nothing I can do."

Mok Don stabbed his desk with his pencil eraser. "It's harassment, they have nothing--" He cut himself short, vacillating. "Sometimes the innocent must be inconvenienced to bring low the guilty. Prior to this call, I held another press conference to voice my support of your war against corruption. Of course, I expect nothing in return, no favors. I'm just a humble citizen exercising my initiative."

"As you please," the President said. "Other chaebol leaders have exercised less discretion than you." There was a pause. "Or so it would appear. Anyway, as things stand, you've become a symbol of hope to our people with your moralistic press conferences."

"Don't forget, President Paek: The people need a morale booster. They need a reminder that there's one man who still plays by the rules and succeeds."

"I won't pretend I agree with that assessment, but justice has run its course."

"That's exactly right," Mok Don said, slapping his pencil down on the desk. "Justice is the word. By the way, this new ministry you've established governing marine affairs and fisheries is a great improvement. Upgrading the maritime police organization to a national agency will go a long way toward fighting piracy and smuggling in the West Sea. And I commend you for your fight against corruption at the highest levels."

There was a long silence . . .

"Before I hang up, Mr. President, there is something I must ask you about."

The President cleared his throat. "Fine, but I have just a minute. I have a press conference of my own to attend and time is running out."

"I was told that you know of a man named John Blake."

The pause was a long one. When the president spoke, his voice was hard. "What's this about?"

"An American politician told me you knew Blake. I suspect you wouldn't want to be linked to this character. From what I've heard, he's notorious. And your reputation is milky white. I assure you this call has nothing to do with your connection to this man. As far as I'm concerned there isn't one."

"There isn't," the president said. "Certainly, I know who Blake is. But why would that interest you?"

"I think he may be planning a trip to Korea. I've been informed that some of my foreign competitors want me dead and have hired him for the job."

The President hissed. "Then I'll send you flowers ahead of time."

Mok Don spent a long moment considering the President's reaction. "You sound amused."

"If Blake is after you, I wouldn't close your eyes for long. I heard he was expensive, but then you didn't have to worry about him botching the operation, causing embarrassment and political backsliding. He was dependable and deniable."

Mok Don picked up his pencil and tapped the desk. The satisfaction in the President's voice was starting to irritate him.

"The Israelis hired him to make key hits against Turkish terrorists," the President went on; "the Spanish hired him to stop gunrunners ferrying weapons to the Basques, ETA; the English used him to intercept IRA gunrunners; he executed several Chinese crime bosses and heroin traffickers in Hong Kong."

"He has a lot of blood on his hands."

"More than you know."

Mok Don pulled his tie loose and shifted in his chair. "Who does he work for?"

"He was a mercenary, a master assassin. Legend has it, he began with the CIA, but branched out and worked for numerous potentates and heads of state. World leaders brought him in when they needed a deniable operator. He was so efficient in North Korea that years later another administration hired him to train our elite special forces. Finally, they sent him north again. He killed nine men based on false intelligence. When he found out that his terrorist targets were actually members of the Christian underground who had intercepted an illegal weapons shipment from the South, he tracked down his employers and took out five men including a South Korean general. But every man has his limitations . . . I'm afraid, you need not fear. Blake is dead. He was killed while attempting to leave the country."

"Are you sure about that?" Mok Don asked.

"No body was ever recovered, but his boat was bombed while making its escape. So perhaps you don't have to worry about being killed, Mok Don. But just in case the report of Blake's death was mere propaganda, you might want to appoint a successor."

CHAPTER EIGHTEEN

After spending the morning at the inn with Abby, giving her explicit instructions on what to buy and where to meet him later, Frank went to work altering his appearance. He cut off the tip of a pacifier then cut the bulb in half. With his small finger, he inserted the pacifier into his nostril, which distorted the shape of his nose. Then he applied reddish-brown make-up over his face, hands, and neck. Next he got out black hair, fringe beard and mustache. Patiently, he parted his own dark hair and applied black dye with a sponge. Lastly he put in brown-tinted contact lenses. His identity disguised, he dressed in dark gray pants, sweater, overcoat, and black beret cap. He wore special shoes with a false heel that gave him a peculiar limp.

Only thing he couldn't disguise was his stony expression. He placed his make-up back into his pack and zipped up the pocket. Walking out of the bathroom, he put his pack down. He sat on the edge of the bed for a minute and rested his forehead in his hands, eyes shut. Then he got up.

He arrived at the National Museum before lunch. The wind blew steadily beneath a gray sky, and it was cold enough to make him regret having left his scarf in Alaska.

The museum was in the former Japanese capital located behind the old city gate. Intended as an insult against the Korean people, the building was purposely constructed in front of Kyongbok Palace: it blocked the majestic views of the palace with its gracefully arched and tiered structures. The building was formal and topped with an imposing dome. Built by the Japanese in 1926, they had attempted to imitate 19th century neo-classical style.

Frank knew more about Seoul now and its turbulent history, and he looked at the city gate and its traditional tile roof with interest as he scooted through the cold air and purchased a ticket to the museum.

Inside, the museum was magnificent, both palatial and stately. He spent an hour roaming around on five different levels packed with Korean artifacts. The Kiska treasures belonged in this collection; they were part of the same heritage, originated with the same dynasties.

While browsing, he studied the layout of the museum, the positions and moods of the security guards, and the exits. He scanned the museum employees and the patrons alike, looking for any unusual behavior. He decided to stick with the original plan. If anything went wrong, he had three back-up plans.

***

When Colonel Kim parked his car, Chull-su let Hyun off to follow on foot. Wearing his ever present surgical mask, Hyun walked five blocks and watched the colonel enter the old city gate and purchase a ticket to the National Museum. Hyun stopped at the old gate and waited. Hot breath under his surgical mask warmed his cheeks. The mask not only kept him warm, but also did a good job of hiding his facial features.

He reached under his silk jacket, tapped his pistol and unsnapped the thong. Entering the museum, he didn't see the colonel. He casually strolled through the first floor. No colonel. Hyun made his way back to the center of the museum. Climbing the stairs to the second floor he began his sweep.

***

At eleven-thirty, Frank began watching the front of the museum for any sign of surveillance. Nothing disturbed him. When the colonel arrived, he came alone and acted natural, although he appeared to be under stress. Seeing the colonel's lean face and thin eyebrows, Frank worked hard to relax. The colonel walked past him without acknowledgment or recognition and proceeded up to the cafeteria where they were supposed to meet.

Frank forced himself to watch the front of the museum for several minutes. Then he went up the stairs to the cafeteria on the second floor. The room was impressive with its hundred-foot ceilings and intricate neoclassical detail. Besides the colonel, there were only a few other patrons. He ordered a cup of coffee and a pastry. Then he approached the table of a surprised Colonel Kim.

Looking sharp in his uniform, Colonel Kim appeared to have aged since Frank last saw him. The lines on his face were deeper than Frank remembered. The thin eyebrows were almost gray now.

It's been a long time, Colonel." Frank set his coffee and pastry on the table.

Realizing that John Blake was the man standing in front of him, the colonel stood and bowed deeply.

Frank ignored the gesture and settled into a chair.

Colonel Kim suddenly looked back at the entrance, then around the cafeteria. Tension clung to his aspect. "You startled me," he said. "I didn't recognize you."

Frank took a long breath and his throat was tight. "I have one minute. What did you find out?"

"I brought you the documents we discussed on the phone." The colonel put his chin down to his chest. He reached into his overcoat and brought out a stack of folded papers which he shoved at Frank. "Very difficult to find. Took persistence and luck, and a lot of money, more than I expected."

Frank leafed through them casually. They were all written in Japanese characters. "Sum this up for me."

The colonel nodded quickly. He looked directly at Frank, an intensity in his stare. "According to the letter, Japan's governor-general obtained information on royal tombs. The information was given by an anonymous Korean, a former government official. The letter was a confirmation of another letter sent to Tokyo. According to the export papers, whatever they found in those tombs must have been a small fraction of the total shipment. The contents were shipped to Tokyo."

Frank again started leafing through the papers. Then he stopped and slowly folded them. He casually slipped the papers into his inside coat pocket. He withdrew an envelope and slid it across the table to the colonel, who surveyed the room again before picking it up. Two other patrons were leaving, a man and a woman. The colonel impulsively shoved the envelope into his lap where Frank couldn't see it under the table and started counting the hundred dollar bills.

"Do they give a location?"

"No."

"Who did you tell about this?"

The colonel's head twitched unnaturally. "I told no one. What is between us stays between us—forever. Now, I must get back. We're on special alert this winter due to infiltrators and provocative troop movements in the North. I leave now as your friend and confidant."

"In my business, I can't afford to let someone betray me and get away with it. You tell me who."

The colonel continued staring at Frank--glowering. "You should not have come back here."

"I don't plan to return unless I have to visit you personally. I asked you a question."

"Don't ever contact me again." The colonel slipped the envelope into his inside coat pocket. He rose and left the cafeteria.

Frank let him go. He sipped his coffee and thought about which exit to take. He looked around. A woman with two kids got up, and they all walked out. Frank was the only person left in the cafeteria other than the attendant. The silence eased his stress some. He reminded himself that his trip was nearly finished.

He stood to leave and lifted his coffee cup for a last sip. As the rim came to his lips—came the roar of a gunshot, and Frank's body jerked in reaction. The sound bounced around the museum like a ping-pong ball. Frank felt searing pain. Boiling coffee scalded his chest before the echo of the shot passed. He gasped as he threw his cup down and jumped up, glancing around the room. Nobody there, nobody at the entrance, the shot was in another room. On his way out of the cafeteria, he grabbed a fistful of napkins, and still gritting his teeth from the burn, carelessly wiped the coffee off his jacket and shirt. His ears were ringing.

He moved cautiously, yet quickly down the hall. A woman screamed. At the stairs he found Colonel Kim's body in an expanding pool of blood—surrounded by a snowfall of hundred dollar bills. Shot in the back, the bullet had exploded outward through his heart, ripping through the breast pocket where Kim had put the envelope of cash. Many of the bills were blood-stained. A man and a woman stared horror-stricken at the dead soldier. The woman was crying in a fit of frantic hysteria, clutching the man. It was the same man and woman who left the cafeteria minutes earlier.

Frank wanted to pursue the killer in full sprint, but knew how that would look. He didn't know which way the killer had gone and didn't want to be seen running through the museum right after the man he just met in the cafeteria was shot execution-style. Half way down the stairs, two security guards rounded the corner and looked straight at him, yelling something in Korean.

"Up there." Frank said with the feigned panic of a tourist. "Up there." He pointed desperately.

The security guard's confused expressions changed to determination and they raced past Frank and up the stairs. Frank continued on down and went straight out the front door.

Fifty yards ahead of him, a man was walking quickly through the old city gate. Under the gate, he hesitated and looked back. He wore a surgeon's mask that covered his face below his eyes. Seeing Frank, he walked faster. Frank took off running in full sprint. A black car stopped beyond the gate and the man quickly got in. The car left with screeching tires.

When Frank came through the old city gate, he slowed to a brisk walk as he took in the busy street with its hundreds of cars. At least a dozen black cars raced off in fast moving traffic. They were gone.

With a wave of his hand, a taxi pulled over and Frank got in.

He took a long slow breath. He looked out the window and slowly massaged his chin with his right hand.

Murdered a colonel of the Korean army--inside the National Museum. Frank would meet Abby and leave the country right away.

CHAPTER NINETEEN

Sitting at his antique desk with his elbows on his desk, Mok Don patiently endured Hyun's recount . . . When Hyun's disturbing explanation was over, Mok Don inspected his salary man in silence.

Hyun's hair was slicked back stylishly. His plaid sweater stood out too much, and his goatee was a flagrant example of western influence. His arms hung straight at his side, his chubby fingers touching his suede pants.

Mok Don returned to his file and resumed reading. He sifted through the pages, rapidly comprehending the information. Coming to the end, he laid the papers down.

"Where was the American?"

"He saw nothing. It was a clean hit. I turned out the colonel's lights and closed the door on my way out."

Mok Don's eyes narrowed. For several moments he considered Hyun. Finally he said, "The colonel knew too much. We've given the American a lesson he won't forget. When we meet again, we won't have to convince him we mean business. You will be meeting him again soon, Hyun."

Hyun bowed in gratitude, relaxed beneath the tension, breathed deeply, sighed.

Mok Don's eyes scrutinized him. "You've come a long way here at DowKai, haven't you?"

"I've risen to the upper ranks of the organization."

"That's because you get things done. You and your brother are hard workers."

Hyun stood up straighter. "Thank you. I've stopped at nothing to accomplish your goals. Chull-su and I are proud to serve DowKai, to serve you. We are grateful, honored by your confidence." Hyun bowed.

Mok Don said, "Honored? You've earned quite a reputation for yourself. And now you're taking bold steps to further it. Surely your actions will be on the front page of all the newspapers, on the news."

"All of our loyalty is with you, Mok Don. A clean hit, you'll see. They'll probably blame North Korean agents. My brother thinks they'll see the assassination as an opportunity for propaganda and feed the press anti-North Korean rhetoric."

On Mok Don's desk sat the gold Sarira Reliquary. He nodded toward the relic. "Do you know what that is?"

"A gold trinket box on a pedestal."

Mok Don smiled. "Not exactly. That's the Sarira Reliquary. Solid gold, yes. It's one of Korea's finest treasures. And it's mine." Mok Don reached down, removed the lid to the reliquary. "This is a miniature casket, not a trinket box. It's for storing sacred relics; however, since nothing is sacred, the reliquary remains empty." He replaced the lid. "How long has Initiative Three been in the code?"

"As long as I can remember."

"Sixteen years. That's a long time, isn't it?"

"A real long time."

"I would say, Hyun, the Sarira Reliquary is as close as you'll come to a sacred relic. There are others. For sixteen years I've been waiting to get possession of them. I've been patient. Tell me, did the American leave the museum?"

"Oh sure, he left, came out right behind me."

"You saw him leave?"

"I looked back and there he was, coming down the steps. I didn't stick around to chat."

"What would we have done if the American was taken into custody by the police?"

"That would not have happened."

"Oh?" Mok Don glared. "Why not?"

"He's just an American fisherman," Hyun said. "The authorities would not suspect him. There were witnesses to assure that. A Korean couple saw the hit, saw me. But I was wearing a surgical mask. They could not identify me."

"What if the police thought the American was involved? After all, he met with the colonel just minutes before the hit. There must have also been witnesses to that."

"They would not think he was involved. American servicemen often get blamed for crimes, but not tourists."

Mok Don gasped. *Bloody hell.*"

Fear on his face, Hyun stepped back. "How--"

"How," Mok Don yelled viciously. He stood fluidly and turned to the credenza backed up against the wall. He opened the black mother-of-pearl inlaid lacquer box and removed a white, jade-handled pistol. The .45 caliber weapon was a custom-made gift from a former Korean President. He walked around the desk to face Hyun. He stopped and smiled warmly. Calmly, softly, he said, "Did you ask me how?"

"No," Hyun said, stepping back. "Mok Don, what--"

"Open your mouth!"

"But--"

"Open the filthy bug pit!"

"Oh, no, please." Hyun's stumpy legs buckled and he dropped to his knees. "Please, please, please--"

"Shut up!" Mok Don slammed the muzzle of the weapon into Hyun's partly open mouth, violently shearing off teeth. "I said, open the bug pit," he shrieked.

Swallowing the steel, Hyun's eyes were terror-filled and wild. He whimpered.

"You could have ruined this entire operation," Mok Don screamed, his face clawed with wrinkles as he pushed the muzzle against the back of Hyun's throat.

Hyun choked and gagged on the muzzle. Mok Don jerked the gun out of his mouth, scraping exposed nerves of freshly broken teeth. Bloody cuspidal fragments tinged on the black marble floor. A front tooth bounced and skid.

Hyun screamed. He fell to the floor and writhed in agony, clawing at his face. He climbed to his knees, kissed the marble, whimpered, cried in torment. He sniffled several times and tried to pull himself together. He looked up at Mok Don, then retreated to the floor, only to try again to regain composure. Finally, he stood up, avoiding eye contact with Mok Don.

"Look at me." Mok Don slapped him across the face. Hyun's head snapped sideways. He forcibly turned his head back and looked at Mok Don, shaking his head, begging with desperate eyes. Tears streaked down his swarthy cheeks. He grasped his suede pant legs and squeezed.

Calmly Mok Don said, "Don't let me down again."

"I won't." Blood ran from Hyun's split lips, from the corners of his mouth.

"I want you to go to Dutch Harbor. The American's boat is there; sooner or later, he'll show up. I want you to snoop around, ask questions. The *Pinisha*'s first mate, Won-song, found the American's fishing boat, but I need to know more. Before Murdoch arrives, get us some hard information on him. Where does he live? Where does he go? Work with Soo-man, follow the American." Mok Don nodded.

"You may go. The next time you take independent action will be your last."

Hyun bowed and left the office.

Mok Don shook his head. There wasn't a good man other than himself in the entire DowKai organization. No matter. Hyun was an efficient killer. And Mok Don would soon have a job for him.

Mok Don called his head servant to ask how his daughter was doing. She was now taking drugs for her depression. Mok Don ordered his servant not to let her out of the house. He did this for her own safety and out of fear that she would confide in a friend. Mok Don could hide her shame. His daughter would not bring disgrace on his name.

He hung up, thought again about Hyun. Killing the colonel in the museum was nothing compared to what Soo-man did to Mok Don's daughter. Mok Don didn't believe that Soo-man forced himself on her without some encouragement. Soo-man was incredibly strong, but he wasn't so foolish as to intentionally rape Mok Don's daughter. Soo-man was one of the smarter men at DowKai.

Perhaps if this had been the first incidence, Mok Don would have believed his daughter's story outright. But she was a liar. No matter how much he cared for her, Mok Don knew she was morally flexible. She probably encouraged Soo-man's advances at first, and his lust got out of control. But for Soo-man to have scandalized Mok Don's daughter and his name—that demanded the severest punishment.

CHAPTER TWENTY

In the Lotte Hotel restaurant, with a view of the lobby, Chull-su finished his meal. After spending an hour mulling over the DowKai philosophy, he felt confused. The philosophy had always given him strength, unity, importance.

His brother was now missing several teeth because Mok Don slammed the muzzle of a pistol into his mouth. His brother deserved what he got. In killing the colonel, he acted independently, thought for himself. It was dangerous, foolish. A DowKai executive could wind up dead for a move like that.

But worse still, when Mok Don killed a man, he also killed any kin that might want retribution later on. Chull-su was kin. Nothing so blatant had ever been done by the brothers in defiance of Mok Don.

After an hour of mulling over the corporate philosophy, he couldn't find an answer to the dilemma, at least not one that gave him a way out if things got nasty. He'd always understood the philosophy and supported the articles. Relatives of victims, especially men, had to be killed. They posed a threat to Mok Don and DowKai. Chull-su and his brother had carried out executions. The philosophy guided all their actions. But never until now had Chull-su felt the teeth of the philosophy bearing down on him personally.

And there was nothing to do about his position. Nowhere to go. He was a DowKai man, part of the group, a link in the chain. He couldn't avoid the shame and dishonor caused by his brother's independent act.

What disturbed him most were the impulses that surged through him. In his shame, he *too* was having independent thoughts. Was he no better a man than his brother? But some part of him felt cheated. The system, DowKai, Mok Don, the philosophy--these are what he served, supported, lived for. Now, through no fault of his own, he had lost status. Could there be a flaw in the system? These thoughts were dangerous. Who was he to question Mok Don? All he could do was continue to follow orders.

Chull-su left the restaurant, stopped in the lobby, and called Soo-man. "Murdoch has not come back here. I'm on my way to the airport."

CHAPTER TWENTY-ONE

Together, Frank and Abby drove to the port of Puson, where they hired a fishing boat to take them to Japan. After a day at sea gliding over smooth waters, they arrived in Yokohama, Japan, and took the train to Tokyo. At the airport, they checked in their baggage and headed to the proper terminal for boarding. Frank didn't notice anyone following or watching, but people were swarming the wide corridors. When the terminal was in sight, he became extra cautious, but saw nothing of concern. He and Abby went straight for the ramp and boarded.

After taxiing and waiting, the plane rushed down the runway and lifted off.

Frank slept through most of the flight. As the plane touched down in Seattle, he felt a sense of relief. Seattle had once been his home. He thought about the summers he had spent on the Ballard docks doing ship repairs, preparation work, chasing down spare parts and supplies for upcoming crab seasons. He remembered having clam chowder on the waterfront with Melody, watching the boats together.

The Seattle layover lasted two hours, and then they flew north. In Anchorage, they transferred to a puddle jumper that flew them to the remote fishing village of Dutch Harbor. The small plane rattled in turbulence for most of the trip. Soon it dropped down through the white layer of clouds and landed on Amaknak, a small island connected to larger Unalaska Island by bridge.

Frank hired a mud-sprayed taxi.

The old fishing village was a former US Navy base the Japanese pounded with bombs in 1942.

Dutch Harbor was an isolated village, a watery place of bay views and snowy volcanic mountains swamped in the nothingness of overhanging gray clouds. The world seemed to blow past in the driving wind and snow. Rusted Quonset huts and snow-covered bunkers from World War Two peeked out from shrouded, snowy hills.

Prefabricated shells with ribbed metal walls and sliding windows endured the elements of the gusty village. It was a picturesque world of icicles, boats and docks, shipping containers stacked atop one another by dumpsters, and snow piled atop various heaps of fishing materials. Cannery workers walked briskly, leaning into the wind and snow.

The cab stopped at the Bering Sea Inn, overlooking the small boat harbor. Frank stepped out into the cold, inhaled the brisk, salty air, and helped Abby out of the cab, gathering bags from the trunk. It was starting to get dark.

The trading post would be worth a stop if there was time. You could never have too many supplies on Kiska, especially going into winter.

Time was critical, but there were certain things that needed doing. He wanted to get to his boat. But now he felt it was more urgent to stop by the Bering Sea Inn. Dutch Harbor was a small town. News traveled fast.

The structure was rustic and popular among fishermen. Frank and Abby passed through the lobby and went into the diner. There were people coming and going, chairs scraping, burly fishermen hunched over plates.

A large bearded man wearing a white apron walked out of the kitchen drying his hands with a white towel. He wasn't familiar. Probably new to town. Frank hadn't been in the Bering Sea Inn for months.

"Howdy," the man said. "Cold out there, ain't it?" When he saw Abby, his eyes opened wide, but then he caught himself and looked back at Frank. "Don't suppose you folks are lookin' for that fancy new chalet over on Margaret Bay."

"We're in the right place," Frank said. "Bentley Range in today?"

"Naw, Bentley's in the lower forty-eight. Visitin' family." The man finished drying his hands and tucked the hand towel under the strap of his apron.

Frank laid their bags on the floor and pulled out a chair for Abby at a table facing the harbor. Then he helped himself to a seat. "I've known Bentley for a long time," Frank said. "He's a good man. Didn't get your name."

"Wade. Wade Olsen."

"We could sure use a cup of coffee."

"You betcha." Wade got a pot of coffee and filled their mugs.

"How long's Bentley gone for?" Frank asked.

"Be back in a month, after the holidays." Wade returned to the kitchen.

People were talking and tinging silverware on dishes. A big Norwegian stomped by. Frank unzipped his duffel bag. After he and Abby changed into their snow boots, Wade rejoined them.

"I'll tell Bentley you stopped by. What did you say your name was?"

"Frank Murdoch." As the words left his mouth, Frank studied Wade's face for the slightest reaction. Frank Murdoch--the name appeared to strike a chord: Frank watched his eyes roll slightly as if he was wondering where he'd heard the name before. There were two possibilities: Bentley Range might have mentioned Frank's name, anyone might have. Frank had been around a long time. The fishing industry was small. The second possibility—

"Heard there was an Asian in town asking around about me."

"That's it," Wade said. "I knew I'd heard your name before. He was in here this morning. Said he was a friend of yours."

"What else did he say?" Frank asked.

"Wondered how he could get in touch with you. I told him I didn't know you."

"Short guy with slicked back hair?"

"Yeah, and a goatee. He showed up here right after that Russian ship docked. He a friend of yours?"

Frank shrugged. "Did he ask anything else about me?"

"Not really." Wade looked left and right. "I guess I better get back to work."

"I came here to ask Bentley if this Asian came around. Since Bentley's not here, I'd appreciate it if you'd help me out and tell me what you can about the guy."

Wade nodded. "Alright. He was unusual."

"What do you mean?"

"Well, he came on in here, a little short guy with stubby legs. I said hello and he didn't even look at me. I noticed strain in his neck like he was grimacing in pain."

"Grimacing in pain?" Frank glanced at Abby.

"No kidding," Wade said. "I know it's cold out there, but he was overdoing it. He pulled his scarf away and looked straight at me. That's when I saw his nasty fat lips and the blood seeping out of his mouth at the corners. I shuddered, but I figured, okay, he got his butt kicked bigtime."

Wade glanced fleetingly toward the kitchen. "So he sat down and ordered coffee. When he drank the coffee, he hissed like the coffee was really hurting his mouth bad. I went back into the kitchen and kept an eye on him to see when he was ready to pay.

"Before he left, he asked me if I knew Frank Murdoch. His English was hard to understand. When he spoke, I finally saw what all the hissing was about. The man's front teeth were shattered--most all of 'em. Just bloody stubs. The cold air on all those exposed nerves must have been agonizing. And the coffee . . . I felt for him. Anyway, I told him I never heard of you. Then he wrapped his scarf around his face and left."

"Did he come back again?" Frank asked.

"That was the last I saw of him."

"You said there was a Russian ship in town?"

"Yeah. The *Pinisha*. Flew a Russian flag. I never miss a ship coming through. Can't keep track of all the small vessels, just too many, but I rarely miss a ship. We get a couple freighter landings a week here: an import and an export, and of course the American President Lines ship. Crewmen usually come through here. The *Pinisha* was a general cargo ship. Showed up about the same time the Asian guy did. She was docked for most of the day. I never did hear what her cargo was. Anyway, she's been through before."

"What?"

"Yeah, a few months ago. I remember her captain. Ordered eggs and bacon for dinner. Drunk. Wouldn't quit talking. Said if there was ever an opening in the crew mess, I was his man. Lot of foreigners come through here: Japanese, Russians, Koreans—but this guy was something else. Spent all of an hour braggin' about his glamorous lifestyle on the *Pinisha*. Being a bit of a ship buff, I listened, though he was laying it on thick. Struck me as funny that a Korean commanded a Russian ship."

"He told you that?"

"Oh, yeah. Said the ship was registered with Russia for convenience. Then he left me a twenty-dollar tip for a twenty-dollar meal."

Frank looked at Wade for several moments. "Did you say registered with Russia for convenience?"

Wade nodded. "That's what he said. Tell you the truth, I'm glad he didn't stop in this time."

"Well, that's—" Frank paused and stared at Wade. "What company did he work for?"

"Wait a minute." Wade walked into the back. When he returned, he was shaking his head. "The man gave me a card, but I lost it. The writing was in English, but I can't remember the company name. I never considered going to work for him. In case Bentley asks, he has nothing to worry about. As I said, there aren't many secrets around Dutch Harbor, and there's only a few restaurants, so I hear things. Most folks passing through stop off for a bite. The burgers are worth a long walk."

"I'll vouch for that, and I appreciate the information. Do you have a number where I can contact Bentley? It's important."

"Wait a minute." Wade left and returned with a piece of paper which he handed to Frank. "Here you go."

"Bentley's lucky to have you working for him."

"Happy to help, you being his old friend and all."

Frank laid cash on the table to pay for the coffee, plus a twenty-dollar tip. He stood up and lifted their bags. "If anyone else comes around asking about me, I'd appreciate it if you'd say you don't know me and haven't seen me."

"No problem. Ma'am, you come on back, you hear?"

Frank left the bags in the lobby, and they went up to the second floor. They walked slowly down the hall. Twice Frank looked over his shoulder. The hall was empty. The boards creaked under their feet. He knocked on the door.

CHAPTER TWENTY-TWO
November 30th

The door swung open.

Frank's trail boss, Brian Nash, craned his long neck out the doorway, glancing down the hall. He said, "Come on in. We're just playing rummy."

Frank made introductions and explained that Abby was going to Kiska.

Clay Krukov got up from the table, his long black hair brushing his shoulders. He looked at Abby with his narrow dark eyes. Clay was like a brother to Frank. They fought together in the jungles of South America long before Clay ever worked on Frank's crab boats. After Frank sold his fleet, Clay stayed on as a ranch and boat hand.

Frank said, "I have to tell you something important."

Brian leaned against the wall. The sleeves of his checkered shirt were rolled up, and he crossed his arms. "This have anything to do with an Asian askin' all over town about you?"

Frank looked at Brian for a moment. "What did he want?"

"Asked where you could be found. I saw him board the *Pinisha*."

"What did you tell him?"

"I didn't know you," Brian said.

"How about you, Clay?" Frank said.

"Same." Clay had his brown fingers half buried in his caribou-fur pants. "I've got my reputation to consider. Nothing personal." He grinned.

Frank raised his eyebrows. "What was up? Really."

Clay said, "Didn't seem like a friend. Gave me a bad feeling."

Frank noticed Abby was watching Clay closely with her lips compressed.

He walked over to the window, pulled back the curtain and looked out. The snow was coming down hard outside. It was getting dark. Below a couple of crab fishermen walked by. Someone with their back to Frank was walking over to the small boat harbor.

Frank let the curtain fall and turned back to the others. "Either of you familiar with the *Pinisha*?"

"I've seen her in the Shelikof Strait," Clay said. "But that was a few years ago."

"Not me," Brian said.

"I've seen her out there too, " Frank said. "She's probably a tramper." He walked slowly across the room. "I went to Korea because I found a few artifacts that I wanted to investigate." He stopped and faced them.

"I didn't tell you the whole story. I didn't want to say anything until I got all the facts. But now I think someone's following me."

Brian craned his neck slightly forward. "What are you talking about?"

Frank hesitated, rubbed the back of his head, nodded slightly. In a hushed voice, he said, "A fortune in Korean gold relics on Kiska Island."

Clay stared blank-faced at Frank.

Brian squinted, and his atom's apple moved when he swallowed. "You kidding us?" he said. "On Kiska?"

Frank said, "I didn't give the location to anyone I didn't trust. A couple people knew I was researching a shipment of gold that disappeared during World War Two, that's all. Unfortunately, I made a mistake. I paid a man to buy access to classified government archives in Seoul." Again Frank lowered his tone of voice. "That man is now dead."

Clay looked down and whispered to himself.

The lines on Brian's forehead became deep wrinkles. His crossed arms dropped to his sides as he stood up straight. "My God, who are these people?"

Frank started to speak, but Brian cut him short, stepping forward. "My wife's alone on that island--"

"So are Luke and Ingrid. I don't think they're in immediate danger. The shipment of treasure I tracked was presumed lost at sea. Whoever these people are, I don't believe they know where the gold is. Still, we can't take chances. We have to leave immediately and see that we aren't followed.

"Regardless of what happens, if we're in danger--Brian, if our families are in danger--it's because of the gold. You're my friends, you've both been loyal to me, and I trust you. Whatever happens, I want to cut you both in on a share, but I can't cut you in until I know I have a share to cut you in on. I've got to arrange a deal with the Koreans. It's complicated; that's why Abby's coming along. She's an archaeologist."

Clay glanced at Abby, lowered his head.

"I'm more concerned about Karen than any share of gold," Brian said.

"Once we get out of town, we'll all be a lot safer. Meet me at the *Hector* in thirty minutes, but watch your backsides getting there. Make sure you're not followed. And stay off the radios."

CHAPTER TWENTY-THREE

Frank and Abby caught a cab to Red Claw Seafood's dock. Frank told the cabby to wait for him. Bud Galer, an old friend, was the foreman at the cannery. Bud was holding the supplies Frank ordered from ACME, including Christmas presents.

Before Frank went into the cannery office, he hesitated and glanced down the dock . . . No one around. Nothing out of the ordinary. He entered the office behind Abby.

An Aleut woman with thick glasses and a friendly grin greeted them at the desk.

"I'm here to see Bud."

"He's not here. He'll be back tomorrow."

"My name's Frank Murdoch."

"Oh, yes, Mr. Murdoch. Bud said you might stop by. I'll have our forklift take the supplies out to your boat." The woman got up and disappeared through a door leading into the cannery.

Frank and Abby walked back out on the dock, which was covered with packed snow. Numerous boats lay idle across the water, crab boats lined up at piers. A few purse seiners and trawlers who called Dutch Harbor home slept with their hawser lines secured to bollards. Across the harbor a single-engine seaplane floated in the cold pulsating water. Just down the dock from Frank, a sheet of ice covered a stack of half-ton crab pots. Here and there, halogen lights lit up snow flurries.

A fork lift rolled down a loading ramp and swung around Frank's way with three loaded pallets. The bleary-eyed driver stopped by the *Hector*. He got down and they boarded the crabber. Frank opened the door to the accommodations and showed Abby to her cabin.

"I've got to help this guy. Why don't you make yourself at home."

Abby sat down on the berth.

Frank walked over and put his hand on her shoulder. "Everything will be alright," he said. "We'll cast off within the hour. After that, we'll be lost to the world. After I go out, I want you to lock your door and keep it locked. I have to take care of a few things. We'll be out of here real soon."

"Frank, I'll be fine."

On the foc'sle deck, Frank climbed into the crane operator's cabin. With the fork lift driver's guiding hand on deck, Frank removed the hatch cover with the crane, onloaded twelve pallets, and closed the hatch again. Frank thanked the man . . . who was happy to assist and would return to help cast off.

Down on the weather deck, Frank paused and took a deep breath of the fresh Alaskan air. Fog floated overhead and snow blew down and added to the dusting on deck.

He left his bags in the wet room, climbed three decks to the wheelhouse and started the big marine diesel engines. In his office he unlocked the top drawer of his desk and withdrew his .357 magnum handgun. He made sure it was loaded. He stopped to check on Abby again before he went outside.

"Did your father teach you how to shoot?"

"I'm pretty good with an M-16."

"Are you serious?"

"I used to go with my dad to the shooting range."

Frank handed her the .357. "Hold on to this. I don't think you'll need it, but I'll be gone for a little while. Whatever you do, don't shoot Clay or Brian. They'll be arriving anytime."

With the *Hector* warming up, Frank returned to the dock, and the cab dropped him at the Russian Orthodox Church. Standing there, he beheld the tired old historic structure with its onion-dome cupolas and crosses looming in the night. He went inside, finding the pews empty. It occurred to him that he might be the person who could pay to have this old church renovated and restored to its original splendor. He dropped to his knees.

"Blessed Father, I . . ." He trailed off. Indecision gripped him and he remained at the pew for some time. Finally, he stood up. He had to go. Shouldn't have come here. Walking out of the church, he felt stress spread from his heart into his shoulders and neck, his temples and eyes.

Back at the *Hector*, numbing wind blew a thick screen of snow through the boat's halogen mast lights as water lapped up against her hull. The acrid smell of diesel fumes from her rumbling engines permeated the air.

Brian and Clay were ready to go. The fork lift driver returned and threw off the *Hector*'s three-inch hawser lines. As the boat pulled away from the dock, Frank waved to him. Below on deck, Clay was prepping the *Hector* for open seas. Beneath Frank's guiding hands the black-hulled crabber wound through the harbor, set out upon the open sea where wind howled through her rigging as she pushed through eight-foot swells, and began a 800-mile journey across the expansive Aleutian Island chain.

Frank was greatly relieved to be at sea again. He felt confident they were now beyond the reach of trouble. He engaged the autopilot and went down into the hold to make sure the lashings on the cargo were holding. He was thankful that the refrigeration unit was operating. On the way back, he was crossing the weather deck when a wave broke over the gunwales and sent him rolling under a freezing whitewater froth. Frank cursed his carelessness. On his second try, he made it to the wetroom, shivering and tasting salt in his mouth. When he walked into the galley, Abby was sitting there having coffee. She looked at him with raised eyebrows. Frank met her warm gaze. In that moment, as he stood there freezing, something soft and silent passed between them.

Abby got up and came to him. "Frank, what happened to you?"

"A wave got the best of me."

She squeezed his arms. "You're freezing."

"You been out there yet?"

"No, and from the looks of you, I'm not sure I want to."

"You're safer in here until the ocean calms down and it probably won't. If you fall overboard, the life expectancy in these waters without a survival suit is ten to fifteen minutes. If there's an emergency, you've got a survival suit under your bunk. Get it on quickly, because it's the only thing that can save your life out here. I'm not anticipating any problems, but you need to be aware. Let me show you where it is."

In the small room they brushed against each other.

Frank looked at Abby and felt a moment's temptation.

Abby said, "You're shivering, you better get some warm clothes on."

"Yeah, I'll be back in a few minutes."

Frank dried off and changed his clothes. When he returned, Abby had coffee waiting for him in the galley.

The door down the hall slammed. Clay came into the galley and brought the smell of oil with him. "Engines sound good."

"What's that you're wearing?" Abby asked.

Clay looked at her suspiciously. "A gutskin parka," he said. "It's a sort of raincoat."

"Really?" Abby said, fascinated. She reached out and felt the material. "How did they make all these tassels and loops?"

"I made them by twisting and braiding sinews and hairs and sewing them into the seams." He frowned. "To you archaeologists I guess I'm a sort of living time capsule."

"You are to me," Frank said. Now to Abby: "When we get to Kiska, don't be shocked if you see a frozen walrus head on top of his cabin."

Abby's eyes opened wide. "Really?"

"Sure," Clay said, "instant protein."

Abby sat back looking embarrassed.

Clay started searching the shelves. Frank said, "Sorry, Clay, we were in a hurry. The pancake mix is still packed in the crates."

Clay's shoulders sank and he turned around with a pitiful expression on his face.

Frank looked at Abby. "Clay once hiked forty miles over moving ice flows just to buy flour for pancakes."

"Worst part was I forgot the maple syrup," Clay said. "I wonder what the anthropologists would make of that." He walked out saying, "I'll be in the engine room."

Abby shrank down in her chair, her face flushed.

Frank shrugged his shoulders and sipped his coffee. "Don't mind him. Different universities have sent archaeologists to the village he's from. They stirred up trouble among his people. Don't take it personally."

Abby shrugged.

Frank took a deep breath and said, "I'm afraid I've caused you a lot of trouble. I meant it when I said you may not be safe in South Korea anymore. I want you to know I'll pay to get you set up in a new apartment somewhere. Helping you out is the least I can do. Later on, when things settle down, I'll pay to move your things."

She nodded and looked at Frank. "Thanks. Actually I don't have much stuff. I live out of a few suitcases and backpacks. With all the excitement, I almost forgot about my apartment.

"Frank, I've been thinking more about your discovery. I meant it that your claim is uncertain. In America, archaeological discoveries on private property are often beyond governmental control, but that's no guarantee. Every state is different. And with something this important, anything could happen."

"That's not acceptable. I'm not fighting this in court--any court. I've got leverage and I'm not giving it up." He slowly took a sip of his coffee and set the cup down as a wave doused the porthole. He bunched his shoulders and shivered. "We know the Korean government will want the artifacts for their museums. I'm not opposed to that, but it's not that simple, either. I want you to call up the head of the Seoul National Museum and present them with an offer."

Abby said, "Better yet, why don't I give your terms to an international antiquities lawyer I know in the Netherlands named Dane Leisbeth. He can mitigate a settlement out of court better than I can, and you'll still be anonymous."

Frank nodded. "That's a good idea. Let's call him right now."

Abby looked at her watch. "With the time difference in the Netherlands, he should be in his office."

For the next few minutes, Frank explained his offer to her. Then Abby got the address book out of her purse, and they went up to the wheelhouse.

"You remember what to tell him, right?" Frank said.

She smiled. "You'll arrange for a foundation to take possession of half the treasure and orchestrate a ten-year world tour. The rest of the treasure you'll withhold as a good faith measure. If the Koreans interfere or assert a claim during this ten-year period, they'll never see the missing treasure. All profits from the exhibit will be directed to a charity of your choice. After ten years, all the treasure will be returned to South Korea."

"What if they want assurance the missing treasure will be returned?"

"If you didn't want to return the treasure, you wouldn't be calling. They either play along or they'll never see anything. You're very generous to return this treasure. Cooperating with you is the least they can do. They'll never know who you are because the officers of the foundation won't know who you are. You'll remain totally anonymous."

Frank turned to the assigned frequency on the single-sideband radio and had his call relayed to Dane's office.

While Abby spoke to the lawyer, Frank wandered over to the radar screen and quickly lost track of Abby's conversation.

The three pips on the radar spoke of trouble. With the lights off, the radar's rotating azimuth cursor swung its 360-degree arcs in a glowing pool of cathode-green. With each pass the cursor illuminated pips of the following vessels. The digital readout on the color radar unit showed the closest vessel was trailing at 12 miles. The other two boats followed 26 and 31 miles behind. Frank punched a series of buttons establishing an alarm range. If any of the three boats came within five miles, the radar alarm would sound. Probably crab boats, he thought, yet it was a time for caution. He glanced at the anemometer; the wind velocity peg hung at thirty-two knots. He punched a new course into the automatic pilot and let it take over as the *Hector* moved westward through the Bering Sea.

Frank was still watching the radar ten minutes later when Abby walked over and stood next to him. "Dane says to call him in a couple of days."

Frank looked up from the radar and made an effort to nod appreciatively.

Abby looked down at the radar, then quickly back up at Frank. The excitement on her face was suddenly gone.

CHAPTER TWENTY-FOUR

Driven by her huge twisting single propeller, the blue-hulled cargo ship *Pinisha* splashed through the rough seas of Unimak Pass along the Great Circle shipping route. Her white bridge and accommodation superstructure rose high above her green decks.

Leaning over the chart table on the bridge like an eagle peering down upon prey, Shipmaster Chung put a position on the paper map, a standard precaution he took every thirty minutes in case of equipment failure.

"Shipmaster Chung."

Chung flinched and spun around with anger in his eyes. He found himself startled by Soo-man's intimidating presence. Chung felt like an eagle picking at a deer carcass when the bird was surprised by rouge bear.

"Knock before you enter the bridge," Chung said. "I thought that door was locked."

"No."

"What do you want?"

Soo-man curled his over-developed arm and looked at his watch. "Our signal is moving."

Shipmaster Chung adjusted his captain's hat. "I know that. Hyun left the receiver here. We're just keeping our distance and waiting for Mok Don. He'll arrive in the morning."

"I just wanted to make sure you were after our signal."

"Of course. What the hell do you think we're doing here? We're following outside of radar range."

Soo-man turned to leave.

"Hold on," Chung said. "There's a problem with your transmitter aboard the other vessel."

Soo-man slowly turned back around. His steroid-filled body moved like a side of beef swinging on a hook in a butcher's cold locker. "A problem? The signal is clear enough, isn't it? What problem?"

"Whoever designed these tracking devices never intended them to be used aboard ships."

Slowly Soo-man crossed his arms and glared at Shipmaster Chung. "They were designed for auto and ship surveillance. What's the problem?"

Chung turned and walked to the helm consul, his spit-shined black shoes clicking on the bridge floor. From his high perch on the bridge, he scanned the forward decks and noted a flock of seagulls circling a floating object in the water off the port bow. He turned back to Soo-man. "What frequency do your receivers operate on?"

"That's a stupid question."

Chung motioned towards the Loran-C receiver. "They operate at 100 Kilohertz. Look at this."

Soo-man joined him in time to see the numbers scramble and then right themselves. "What does this have to do with my receiver?"

"This is a Loran-C navigator. You'll find one of these on nearly every large boat in Alaskan waters, including, no doubt, the boat we're following. It works at 100 Kilohertz. Your transmitter uses the same frequency; and for some reason it's scrambling our Loran-C every six seconds. It may be doing the same thing to the Loran-C aboard the other boat. They'll probably try to locate the source of the problem— and they'll find your transmitter."

Chung shook his head in disgust. He stalked across the bridge, but he hesitated and turned back. "Not to mention we'll lose our signal. They might even guess what's happening without locating the transmitter. This puts Initiative Three in jeopardy." Chung watched him with a look of cold indifference that masked his secret pleasure at this screw up.

Soo-man stared at the receiver. Sweat beaded on his forehead as he watched the receiver scramble time and time again. Fear crept onto his face and penetrated his eyes. Then he walked out.

Shipmaster Chung shivered and grinned at the same time. Soo-man gave him the creeps. Chung ran his own show. He didn't like Soo-man wandering the passageways day and night. Chung was comfortable at sea. He was free to make his deals and sail from one port to another. He didn't like extra eyes onboard.

Now he had Hyun aboard, too. With Soo-man it was security, protecting the group. Business was business. But Hyun was demented. And soon his brother Chull-su would be joining him onboard. The sooner this operation was over the better. Then he could get these ghouls off his boat and get back to business. Already he'd postponed a heroine deal when the market in America was booming. Who else would Mok Don bring?

CHAPTER TWENTY-FIVE
Kiska Island

Karen Nash stepped up on the covered porch and went inside Frank Murdoch's log home, entering through the front door. She pulled back the blue hood and ran her fingers through her red, curly hair. Earlier, on the single-sideband, Ingrid said to let herself in.

Ingrid stood near the rock fireplace. She smiled and said, "That's quite a fog bank moving in."

"It's cold out there," Karen said. "How are you, darling? You see that red fox down on the beach?"

"He's been around the last few days, always at the same time."

"We've had a few foxes down our way lately. He's eyeing that emperor goose."

Ingrid moved to the window. "There it goes. The fox will have to find his meal somewhere else."

"He will. The foxes are eating the newborn lambs before they even shed their afterbirth. Brian is mad."

Ingrid put her palms on her cheeks. "It's a good thing we have the sheep dogs, or the foxes would get all the lambs."

"Those dogs may keep the foxes under control, but they scare me. Lately they've been hunting foxes in a pack. Brian says if he can't control those dogs, he'll have to shoot them and get new ones." Karen unzipped her jacket and handed Ingrid the saddle bags. "Here's the powdered milk you wanted."

"Oh, yes, thank you, we're all out until Frank gets back. Luke gets into everything in sight. I can hardly wait until the pantry is full." Ingrid walked over to the kitchen, where she busied herself with pouring tea. She looked out the window for a spell. "Luke runs off every time I turn around."

"I saw him down the beach."

Ingrid returned with the tea, setting it down on the table.

"Thank you," Karen said. "Any word from Frank?"

"He said if things go well, he might come back early, but I think it's too soon."

Karen nodded. "Did you see that crab boat out there this morning?"

Ingrid glanced out toward the water. "They dropped anchor. I saw two men working on deck."

"I expect they were doing repairs of some sort. Ingrid darling, you must have second thoughts about working in such an isolated place."

"I get lonely sometimes."

"So do I, but I have Brian."

"I guess I'll return to Switzerland one day."

"Guess?" Karen was watching Ingrid closely. "I just hate to think you'll be leaving some day. But at your age, you need some excitement in your life and you surely won't find any around here. Not for a thousand miles. Isn't that right?"

Ingrid shrugged. "I think I'd miss Kiska as much as Switzerland."

Karen raised her eyebrows. She was quiet for a moment, then she looked out the window at the beach and said, "That boat out in the bay this morning was a Japanese crab boat, wasn't it?" Karen said.

"Looked like it."

"I didn't see them dock."

"They minded their own business," Ingrid said. "They didn't call on the radio, either."

"I wish Brian or Clay would have stayed here. It scares me being out here all alone."

CHAPTER TWENTY-SIX
North Pacific

For two nights and days the *Hector* sailed westward at ten-knots pace along the sweeping arc of islands that stretched a thousand miles, from the Alaska Peninsula to Russia's Kamchatka Peninsula.

After passing Bogoslof--a volcanic island that had cooled enough so birds, sea lions, and fur seals took to the shores--one of the pursuing boats broke off to the north into the vast Bering Sea. Probably hunting king crab. With that pip off the radarscope, it left two for Frank to watch. Early that morning the two remaining vessels veered south toward Adak Island and also disappeared from radar. Probably hunting brown king crab as Frank often had in Adak's raging seas and shrieking wind-tunnel passages.

With the *Hector* rolling in the cold gray sea and moaning wind, Frank became obsessive in his reading. Twelve hours out of every twenty-four was spent with some philosophical manuscript in hand. He poured over six volumes, finishing with *The Confessions of St. Augustine*. Frank felt good to think that a sinner like Augustine could change and become a saint, but he was also disappointed. His own sins were worse and his own reality was different. He was no angel and never would be. He had a lot to make up for. His past was · complicated, and it would not just go away.

During a reading break, he stepped across the dark wheelhouse to check the glowing radar. He looked out at the ocean as the *Hector's* bow, illuminated by halogen deck lights, scooped up tons of ocean and shed a phosphorescent flood through the scuppers.

After checking the gyro compass and their position, Frank strolled over to the chart desk, turned on the reading lamp and measured distances with a pair of dividers. He knew the course well, and the autopilot was all right. Things were looking brighter. Perhaps the *Hector* slipped out of Dutch Harbor undetected. He thought about the weather fax and brought out the log book, noting their position, course, and last barometer reading.

Brian Nash arrived in the wheelhouse. He walked to the window and said, "I'll take over for Clay. He's been out there breaking up deck ice for quite a while now." Brian laid his gloves on the control consul.

"Good idea," Frank said, closing the log book. "A cold Bering Sea pressure system is headed our way. Might bring some of the worst storms in years. The good news is it won't arrive for three days. We'll be home by tomorrow."

Brian wrapped his scarf around his neck. "No tellin' when that front might show up. The forecasts are usually wrong. Noticed the barometer's been dropping. Those boats show up again on radar?"

"I think we've seen the last of them. You find any problems with the Loran-C receiver?"

Since leaving Dutch Harbor, the Loran-C navigator had been experiencing consistent pulses of static energy. The old Loran-A systems operated near 2 Megahertz, a frequency plagued by atmospheric noise and interference from foreign broadcast stations; Loran-C, however, operated at 100 Kilohertz, where static noise was limited, radio propagation was good, and interference from foreign broadcast stations was virtually non-existent. Frank was perplexed. At first he wrote the interference off as random airwaves of some kind, but it continued for two days in regular, methodical pulses.

"No problems I could see," Brian said. "Looked normal."

"You sure? It isn't acting normal."

"I know. Bill Gains once told me about a similar problem with the Loran-C on his boat."

"What was wrong?"

Brian shrugged. "An old unit. He got a new one and that was that."

Frank nodded. "I thought the Loran-C was malfunctioning, but bearings match the satnav and all functions and interfaces are working properly."

"Clay checked it out, but came up empty. As far as I'm concerned, if Clay couldn't find anything, it's faulty equipment."

Frank nodded, hoping it was that simple. But he wondered if the Koreans might have found his boat. The short guy asking around about him sounded persistent. The woman at Red Claw didn't say anything about anyone snooping around the *Hector*. There was no way to know if someone boarded unseen during the night. The alarm didn't go off. Equipment was always malfunctioning.

"All right," Frank said. "Let's get home, then. We'll deal with it later. You're probably right, it's probably a malfunction, but I'm gonna keep watching this anyway."

"So we're heading straight back to Kiska?"

Frank walked to the radarscope. What was he so worried about? Nobody was following on radar anymore. "May as well. I was thinking of ducking into a cove if necessary, but since those other boats went away, I don't see any reason to stall, especially with the mother of williwaws bearing down on us."

Brian zipped up his jacket and slipped on his gloves. He turned and started out of the wheelhouse. "I agree. I don't like leaving Karen alone for this long."

The *Hector* plowed through ten-foot swell that sprayed over the bow and froze on deck. In the wheelhouse, warm air circulated. The autopilot clicked two notches to starboard. At the chart desk, Frank booted up the laptop and satellite weather tracker. An image formed on the computer screen of a huge storm, a turning cyclonic mass. Longitude and latitude overlays, coastlines, their current position--it looked closer than three days off.

He was feeling grungy, so he changed into his other jeans that had dried. Back in the wheelhouse, he ambled over to the view seat and sat down, felt a crunch beneath him. He reached into his pocket and pulled out an envelope--the letter from Mr. Lee. Frank had forgotten all about it. He reached up and turned on the overhead reading lamp. He opened the envelope and unfolded the paper.

Frank:

My associate dug up a couple extraordinary facts about the lost shipment of treasure. A Captain Yokota and his crew mysteriously disappeared at sea prior to the disappearance of Musashi Maru--*the ship carrying the treasure back to Japan from Russia. What's striking about this is Captain Yokota and his crew were the ones who originally transported the treasure out of Korea. They were due for reassignment to Iwo Jima when they disappeared at sea. There was speculation Yokota and his renegade crew plundered the* Musashi Maru *and then sailed for Argentina. The entire crew was disgraced by the Japanese Army: they were listed as deserters, but were never seen again. The freighter in question was carrying the missing shipment I told you about.*

My diligent associate's other discovery is even more striking: a 1,000-pound, golden "turtle-ship replica" was among the cargo!

Lee

Frank stared at the letter in amazement. The Korean treasure was pirate treasure.
He found Abby down in her berth with well-fitting pajamas accentuating her soft feminine figure. She was sitting on her bed Indian-style writing a note.

Frank stepped inside the cabin and closed the door. He handed her the letter. "It's from Mr. Lee."

And after she read it, she looked at Frank and said, "This is amazing. Is it true? Is the turtle ship really on Kiska?"

"I didn't see it. There was a carving of a ship on the cave wall."

"But it might be there?"

Frank shrugged. "It was dark. I inspected the cave pretty quickly. I suppose it could be buried in the treasure mound."

"Really."

"We'll check it out when we get there, but it would've been hard to miss something that big."

Abby's smile faded momentarily, but then her face brightened again. "It's still exciting just to be on the trail of such an amazing artifact. The very existence of something like that would make every Korean dream." Then her smile faded. "Oh no."

"What is it?"

"This doesn't help your position at all, Frank. This golden turtle ship would entice a national outcry. It would probably be considered Korea's single greatest relic. Koreans are very patriotic. And the turtle ship symbolizes what's probably the most glorious chapter in Korean military history. Its legacy is a source of tremendous pride. Admiral Yi Sun-shin, who created the turtle ships has often been compared to Sir Frances Drake and Lord Nelson of England."

"That's high praise," Frank said.

"My father claims Admiral Yi was better. Once after a great naval victory over the Russians, a Japanese admiral said, 'Compare me with Lord Nelson if you like, but Admiral Yi was too remarkable for anyone.' The Korean Navy even has a special unit whose sole commission is to search for sunken relics from Admiral Yi's turtle ship." Abby handed the letter back to him. "I called Dane back."

"And . . ."

"The Koreans want all the treasure returned, and then they'll decide on your reward."

He shook his head. "That's not what I expected. I thought they'd accept my offer."

Abby sighed. "You don't want to go to court, but what else can you do now? I mentioned the United States Code before; it's really an echo of the Federal Antiquities Act. You didn't think the President would exercise his privileges under those laws. I still don't understand why you say that, but I understand there are some things you can't talk about."

Frank nodded slightly with a stony face. He certainly couldn't mention that he assassinated terrorist leaders for a former president, and that the CIA was in the dark. He couldn't mention that he knew ruinous secrets about many politicians. No, the President wouldn't stir up trouble, but Frank couldn't elaborate.

Abby watched him carefully, waiting for a response. She said, "Luckily, the United States is one of the few countries in the world which doesn't carefully regulate archaeology. Many archaeologists consider the Federal Antiquities laws to be virtually unenforceable. Most of the state laws are fashioned after the federal laws and have an equally slim chance of being enforced. Alaska would fall into that category under normal circumstances. But we're not talking about arrowheads and pots here."

A long roll of the boat disintegrated into a rumbling shudder and a wave splashed against the port hole.

Abby watched the ocean play through the glass.

Frank sat down on the edge of the bed and put his hand on her shoulder. "Litigation is a minefield that I won't go through. We'll call Dane back later and tell him I've decided to keep the treasure for my personal collection. That should get their attention."

"I don't know, Frank. Even if they go along with your proposal, contracts aren't honored in Korea the way they are in America."

"Who says contracts are honored in America? As long as they think it's in their best interest to do so, they'll honor the contract. I have no intention of giving them a choice in the matter."

Abby sighed.

Frank folded the letter and pushed it into his pocket. "I have to get back up to the wheelhouse. Autopilots can't be blindly trusted." He started to get up--

"Frank, I don't mean to be rude, but I don't understand why you just don't give them what's rightfully theirs? Why are you insisting on taking the treasure on a world tour?"

He sat back down, uncomfortably aware that Abby was very close and very attractive. "This is just something I need to do. I can't explain it all to you now. I hope someday you understand. I really have to get back to the wheelhouse. I need to check the radar for other vessels. If we have a collision out here, we're in big trouble."

Frank was in the wheelhouse for only a few minutes when Clay arrived with his journal under his arm. His hair was white with frost. His face glowed red from the bitter cold. He was rubbing his hands together vigorously. He stood at the chart desk, facing the computer.

"How are icing conditions out there?" Frank asked.

"Not good, but manageable. I should have done this sooner."

"Done what?"

"Tracked down the *Pinisha* on private computer networks."

Living in the remote Aleutians didn't isolate Frank and Clay from the information age. Utilizing the *Hector*'s microwave uplink to orbiting communications satellites, they could interface with virtually any computer or network tied to the worldwide Internet. Clay was far more proficient in exploiting these resources than Frank was. A year before, just for the challenge, Clay developed a program that identified secret access codes, and he was gifted at navigating computer networks and their diverse software.

Clay entered a number into the communications software and placed a call with the punching of another button.

Topside a parabolic antenna—3 feet in diameter—locked onto a communications satellite that was in a subpolar orbit twenty-three thousand miles overhead. The dish was installed on a gyroscopically stabilized platform to prevent ship movements from interfering with its auto-tracking mechanism. To protect the satellite tracking dish against the harsh sea environment, a protective fiberglass radome fully covered it.

Frank crossed the wheelhouse and watched the bow climb a big swell. As the *Hector* pushed on at 10 knots, the bow fell into the trough that followed, plowing into the next wave and drenching the decks with a cloud of spray.

Below on deck, Brian was a dark, sinewy figure breaking up ice by lifting the long crowbar and letting the pointed end drop back down to chip away frozen chunks. After making some progress, Brian picked up the snow shovel and threw the ice overboard. Frank wished he was the one getting the exercise on deck, but knew his shift would come soon enough. He looked down at the radar glowing in the darkness. No other vessels.

Even with the lights out, a gentle electronic radiance filtered through the darkness, and Frank glowed in the radar's green halo. There was also the green glow of overhead VHF and sideband radio displays, the glass ball of the gyrocompass, and numerous other instruments. Multicolored depth sounders illuminated the consul near the captain's seat along with satellite navigation displays. The automatic pilot clicked to starboard . . . starboard . . . starboard . . . holding her preset course against drift from current and waves. Clay was bathing in an effulgence behind the laptop at the chart desk. When Frank rejoined him, Clay said, "I've logged onto a computer network at Lloyd's of London."

"They still in business?"

"Yeah, and I've found a syndicate with the *Pinisha* on their register. Just wait a moment, here. . . . There it is." Clay pointed to corporate name on the computer screen. "Sampoon Corporation. Owner of record."

"That was easy."

"What's all this? . . ." The file on the screen was scrolling down.

"A lot of technical information about the *Pinisha*'s capabilities," Frank said.

"Looks like more carriers listed here."

"Maritime insurers normally share the risk."

"I could get into their databases."

"More of the same. Any other options?"

Clay downloaded the file onto a disk and printed the file.

As he rerouted the terminal, he said, "*The Korea Herald* is an English newspaper. Their website might have references to Sampoon in the business section. Here we go." He did a headline search. Nothing came up for Sampoon. "Odd."

"Maybe not," Frank said. "All fingers point to Korean ownership and operation, but the *Pinisha* is a Russian-registered vessel."

"I have an idea." Again Clay accessed the Lloyd's syndicate. He opened the *Pinisha*'s policy and scrolled through documents, freezing the screen on Sampoon's corporate address. "There it is: a post office box in Vladivostok. Uh-huh, Vladivostok is also the Port of Registry."

"Interesting." Frank turned and while pacing across the wheelhouse, he said, "There's a flourishing Mafia-run black market in Vladivostok."

Clay said, "While we're in England, let's stop in at the Baltic Exchange."

"You can do that?" Frank walked back to the chart desk and leaned toward the monitor. The Baltic was a membership of brokers who specialized in finding cargoes for ships and ships for cargoes. Brokers on the floor of the Baltic represented practically all the tramp-ship owners in the world, as well as principals seeking tonnage for their goods.

Clay paged through his journal and found the code he was looking for. He logged onto the computer network at the Baltic and accessed transaction files on the *Pinisha*.

"So this is how you keep up on the price of wool?" Frank said.

"One of many ways."

"Might pay to look at Sampoon's options and charter-parties. Be interesting to see who signed them. Negotiating charter-parties usually involves telephone negotiations confirmed with faxes and telexes. See if you can dig up fax and telex copies."

"This may take a few minutes, but I think I can manage it."

Frank wandered back to the window. Brian was chipping fervently at the thickening ice buildup. A lot of ships sank in the Bering Sea from excessive ice buildup. As the *Hector* plowed through successive swells, nets of spray puffed over her bows. She rose and fell . . . rose and fell. Faint voices broadcast over the single-sideband radio, the usual fishing chatter. Wind howled. Diesel engines grumbled.

"Frank, take a look at this." And when Frank joined him, Clay said, "I ran a historical on the *Pinisha*: three years worth of information on cargoes and principals. This has charter-parties, cables, faxes, telexes, wire transfers, e-mail, you name it."

"Let's take a look."

Clay scrolled down pages by the dozen, alternately stopping at names and signatures. All references were to Sampoon. Signatures were M.D.

"Nothing helpful in any of this stuff," Frank said. "These guys are good."

"Not so good."

"What do you mean?"

Clay pointed at the screen. "Look right there. We have a fax number."

"What will that do for us?"

"Give me a minute here, I've already downloaded, and it's time to beat a retreat." Clay rapidly punched at the keyboard as varying displays flashed on the screen.

Frank strolled across the wheelhouse and looked at the latest hour-by-hour meteorological report from the automated data system. An adjustment was posted. Serious weather was coming their way. Extended forecast looked even bleaker. The arctic pressure-system was now forecasted as two days away. He walked towards Clay, who looked possessed as he tapped the keyboard at a furious pace.

"Just entered the central switching station of the telephone company and reprogrammed it," Clay said.

"You did what?"

"You heard me."

"How did--" Frank hesitated. "Is there anything you can't do with that computer?"

"Can't smell the sea air with it, can't dip your hand in mountain streams, can't listen to spirits upon still waters."

Clay rapped away at the keyboard. Melting ice was dripping from his fox-pelt hat and onto his face. He said, "You may as well know, this is considered access-device computer fraud. That puts us under the jurisdiction of the United States Secret Service and the FBI. They probably have a legal attaché in Korea who'll cooperate with the local authorities."

Frank stared at Clay with his mouth half open, waiting for him to go on. Some impulse born of uncomfortable silence overpowered his patience and he said, "I'm guessing you can cover your tracks, right?"

"I'll run a herd of electronic caribou over those tracks. They'll rake the tundra."

"What does that mean in layman's terms?"

"The caribou wipe out my electronic footprints."

He typed another command which brought up the message: Initiate Stampede--Enter Password. He typed the password. Bullets appeared on the screen: [*****]

"We're lost among the herd," Clay said, his fingers pounding the keyboard. "There they go." A world map on the screen dissolved to a herd of running caribou. He waved his fist. "Go get 'em." The caribou slowly dissolved. Clay exited and logged out. "You know, the authorities would impound every piece of electronic equipment on this vessel for what we've done tonight. Might even impound the *Hector*. They don't take this stuff lightly. But fortunately, my friend, our tracks were lost among the herd."

"I'm not following you. What's this about reprogramming the telephone switching station?"

"Not the whole station, just the fax number." Clay opened the shelf beneath the printer. "We should be receiving a fax anytime that will identify the real owner of the *Pinisha*. You see, I just call-forwarded the fax number we picked up at the Baltic. Any faxes to that number will come here instead."

"In that case, we won't be waiting long," Frank said. "Shipping companies are deluged. Paperwork feeds through their faxes constantly."

CHAPTER TWENTY-SEVEN
December 3rd, 1:50 A.M.

They waited only five minutes for the fax. Clay broke into the telephone station again, switched the number back, scrambled his retreat, and logged out. Frank glared at the fax. The content was illegible, encrypted in characters of the Korean han'gul alphabet. Top of page-two, in standard business format, the name, address, and phone number of the receiving party was printed, also in Korean.

He found Abby in her bathrobe getting ready for bed. "I need to know who this fax is to," Frank said, handing her the paper.

She looked at the fax and said, "Heaumoi, I've never heard of them." And she spelled it out on the fax.

Frank returned to the wheelhouse. Clay was in the view seat, sharpening his hunting knife.

"Got it," Frank said. "Let's track her down."

Clay returned to the chart table and routed his laptop to the *The Korea Herald* site. His search didn't reveal a shred of information about a company called Heaumoi. Before long he was searching files at Bureau Veritas, the French equivalent of Lloyd's of London. Over the next three hours, Clay returned to the Baltic and Lloyd's of London; he broke into the computers of half a dozen marine underwriters; Shipping Administration in Vladivostok; Korean Register of Shipping; Korean Ship Owners' Association; Port of Inchon Management

Corporation; Port of Puson Business Association--nobody had any record of a company called Heaumoi.

"We may be tracking a ghost," Frank said.

Clay nodded. "I'm getting the same feeling. They may have their own caribou."

"I think I know how these people operate, Clay. Their herd of caribou is a dense onion shell, ten- or twelve-layers deep, of bogus companies and fake holding corporations registered all over the globe. While diverting that fax was resourceful, tracing the number won't work, either. I'll bet that fax machine is in a safe house under a false name. We're into it, all right--Korean Mafia. Their paper and electronic trails are painstakingly covered. There are times when the simplest methods are the best. We just have to go after their weak spot."

"What did you have in mind?"

"The gentleman I met at the Bering Sea Inn in Dutch Harbor, Wade Olsen was his name. He gave me an idea. You see, he's been working at there for three months. In that time, the *Pinisha* made two stops in Dutch Harbor. Once, the captain stopped by the inn. He was drunk and talkative and spoke freely about the *Pinisha*. Even gave Wade a business card, though he no longer had it. The captain is our weak link. He has a big ego and a big mouth when he drinks. I have a hunch that wasn't the first time the *Pinisha*'s captain went to the Bering Sea Inn. Tramper or not, the *Pinisha* frequents Alaska waters. You mentioned seeing her a few years back, and I have, too. It's time to call Bentley Range. Should have called him a long time ago."

Frank walked over to the captain's chair and sat down. He dimmed the lights in the wheelhouse, reached up, took the mike for the single-sideband radio, and turned to the assigned frequency. He had a private operator relay his call to the number where Bentley Range was supposed to be.

A deep voice came over the radio: "Frank Murdoch, where have you been, partner?"

"Stopped in at the Bering Sea Inn two days ago."

"That's what Wade said. What's going on?"

"I need to ask you about something. You aware of a ship called the *Pinisha*?"

"Painfully. Her Korean captain tends to stop by the Bering Sea Inn after he's good and drunk. Comes through every few months flapping his gums. He's different. Gets offended if you call him a captain. Demands to be called Shipmaster Chung."

Frank noticed that Clay was watching him.

"I'm trying to track him down," Frank said. "He ever mention the company he works for?"

"And then some. DowKai--the power brokers of the Far East, he calls them. Talks about a CEO named Mok Don as if the man could walk on water, then calls him a vulture."

"How do you spell DowKai?"

Bently told him.

Frank jotted the name down on a sheet of paper. He noticed Clay do the same, and the clicking started up again over at the computer.

"He say anything about this Mok Don character?"

Bentley snorted. "Says Mok Don is the greatest man in all Korea. Referred to him several times as a genius of massive stature. Said we Americans could learn from Mok Don, but could never be his equal. He was drinkin', all right."

"You've been a great help, Bentley. Appreciate it."

"Glad to help. Stop by when you're in town and bring your boy. Apple pie, on the house."

"Thanks, Bentley. I'll do that. Happy Holidays."

"Same to ya. Merry Christmas."

Frank hung up.

Clay said, "Got it, right here."

Frank stood up and walked over to the chart desk.

"*The Korea Herald* web page. I found an article on DowKai. One of Korea's top industrial giants. An international conglomerate, or *chaebol,* comprised of dozens of varied businesses. They're among the few chaebols that came out of the slush fund scandal unstained. Their international businesses include shipping, transportation, and electronics manufacturing."

"Can you download and print?"

"Done."

"Chaebol . . ." Frank mumbled. "That blows my Mafia theory."

Clay looked up from the computer with an air of skepticism. "They couldn't be connected and keep it a secret. Maybe that guy in Dutch Harbor was just a passenger on the *Pinisha*. Some of those ships carry ten or twelve."

"I know. And you're right. Those chaebols have thousands of employees." Frank shook his head. "Then again, so did the Korean government and look what happened with that slush fund scandal. Charges were filed against two ex-presidents and dozens of chaebol leaders--everything from graft to murder. As I recall, a lot of them ended up in jail."

Frank took a deep breath and said, "Maybe they can't keep it a secret. Maybe their time is just running out. What if only a select layer of people at the top know what's really going on. A secret elite within the chaebol participates and conspires to commit international crime. Most DowKai workers wouldn't even know their proud chaebol is an international crime syndicate."

Frank walked across the wheelhouse, stopping at the window. "I'm still curious about their government links in Vladivostok." He walked out, expediting down to his office, recovering his phone book, and regaining the wheelhouse.

"What are you going to do with that?" Clay asked.

"Sending a fax to Mr. Lee. I want to find out what DowKai's links are to political figures in Vladivostok--if any. Mr. Lee dabbles politics these days, and he might be able to help. I also want to find out more about Mok Don."

CHAPTER TWENTY-EIGHT

The *Pinisha* crawled westward at 10 knots. On the bridge, Shipmaster Chung stood at his perch at the windshield gazing out across an expanse of ocean. Chung walked over and checked the radar. He looked over at Won-song, the first mate, who was studying the electronic chart like an admiral combing over his attack plan.

Chung straightened his posture and said, "We have two radar pips, Mok Don and his crew arriving in helicopters."

"The men are looking good," Won-song said. "Spit and polish."

Shipmaster Chung peered at him coldly. "They better look sharp, or I'll have them licking the chrome off the taffrail."

"How many men is Mok Don bringing with him?"

"Forty." Chung watched him carefully and noticed his look of surprise.

Won-song looked at Chung with and adjusted his narrow, red-rimmed glasses. "Why so many? I haven't gotten used to having Hyun on board yet. The little creep was shooting seagulls off the stern this morning. Had a pile of dead birds on the deck."

"I know, he threw bread to attract them."

"He must have killed a hundred."

"So what if he killed some seagulls. You're talking about a man who blew up a family and bragged about it."

"You see what I mean? We have a bunch of sickos on board."

Chung leaned over the radar. "And here they come. Mok Don and forty more creeps."

"I'm serious--why so many?"

"Mok Don said he had his reasons. Probably using the situation as an opportunity to promote internal cooperation. You don't know how lucky we are to work at sea. Out here we're insulated from all the politics. Except right now our luck is on hold." Shipmaster Chung reexamined the radarscope. They were almost on top of him. He lifted his binoculars. There they were—two birds heading straight for the *Pinisha*. As they approached the *Pinisha*, the noise got loud. First one, then the other, landed on the aft helicopter pad. After dropping twenty men, the first helicopter lifted off again and sped towards the horizon. The second set down on the pad. Twenty-one men unloaded. Mok Don was the last.

Every six seconds, timed bursts of radio energy shot from the hidden transmitter aboard the *Hector*, traveled at a constant velocity of 300 million meters per second across a hundred miles of Bering Sea to a receiver in the wheelhouse of the *Pinisha*. Each train of pulses was coded so receiving equipment could identify the transmitter from which the code originated.

Shipmaster Chung stared down at the receiver which showed the position of the *Hector* as a red, flashing light. Mok Don stood next to him.

"There she is," Chung said. "A hundred miles due west."

"Incredible," Mok Don said, wetting his lips with his tongue, leaning forward for a closer look. "DowKai technology at its finest."

Shipmaster Chung looked away, embarrassed. His face twitched from tension. Finally, he said, "The uh . . . technology is excellent, Mok Don. The only problem is that it was intended for automobiles."

Mok Don glared at him. "Automobiles and boats. Is there a problem with its performance? It appears to be working beautifully."

"Take a look at this." Chung led Mok Don to the Loran-C receiver. They watched numbers scramble.

"That's Japanese technology," Mok Don said. "I don't see how this relates to DowKai surveillance equipment."

"The surveillance equipment operates on the 100 Kilohertz frequency. Choosing that frequency was a poor choice. It's the same frequency as Loran-C. That's why you're seeing the Loran-C receiver scramble. It scrambles with every pulse sent out by our transmitter aboard the *Hector*. I wish I'd have been consulted on this matter before the unit went into production."

"You weren't consulted?"

"No."

"I ordered Soo-man to get your approval. This is security equipment. I specifically ordered him to do that."

"Never heard a thing."

Mok Don gasped. "But it still works?"

"Yes, but I suspect our receiver is also scrambling the Loran-C unit onboard the *Hector*. It could raise suspicions with the Americans."

"So you're telling me our surveillance has been compromised as a result of this blunder."

Shipmaster Chung frowned.

Mok Don turned and walked across the bridge. As he turned and walked back to Chung, his face transformed to a platter of contained fury. "Once again Soo-man has screwed up. Where is he now?"

"The exercise room."

Mok Don stared at Chung. "He's exercising? Do you mean to tell me, Shipmaster Chung"--Mok Don suddenly began screaming--"that DowKai is crumbling beneath his colossal blunder, and his only concern is exercising."

"It would appear so."

Mok Don chuckled slightly and shook his head. "Shipmaster Chung, you're a history buff, aren't you?"

"I read history, but I've yet to find your equal, Mok Don."

Mok Don solemnly bowed his head just slightly forward. He slowly rolled his head on his shoulders. He thought for a moment and said, "Historically, what would you say is the harshest form of shipboard punishment? Something that would impress upon the men with the importance of diligence, loyalty, and efficiency."

***

Lying on his back, fully pumped with Deca-Durabolin steroids, Soo-man heaved at his fourth set of 240-pound bench presses. Sweat dripped from his entire body. Forcing one rep after another, he grunted and strained. Veins swelled in his arms.

And then the message commanded over the ship-wide intercom system: "This is Mok Don speaking. All hands on deck. All DowKai personnel on deck. Everyone will be present for the keelhauling of Soo-man."

The barbell slammed down on the supports with a loud clank and rattle.

Soo-man sat up. What was a keelhauling? He reached for the white towel and wiped the sweat off his huge muscles. Keelhauling . . . He wasn't even summoned for an explanation.

He had a good idea what this was about, though. Mok Don found out about the problems with the receiver. It wasn't Soo-man's fault. Sure, Mok Don had told him to run all the specifications by Shipmaster Chung and other DowKai captains. But at the same time he demanded an unrealistic completion date. Soo-man, not wanting to be blamed for pushing the project beyond its completion date, gave his approval. It was a lose-lose proposition--and he was the loser. His one hope had been that DowKai's engineers would get it right—without glitches. What kind of engineers were they? Or did Mok Don find out about Soo-man using his daughter?

Soo-man stood and slipped on his sweats. He left the exercise room, descended three stairwells and stepped into the bitterly cold wind on the main deck. The sweat covering his body began to freeze, and he began shaking.

The crew was conglomerating on deck. He saw the little Hyun next to
Chull-su. Mok Don's forty DowKai soldiers were standing around on deck, all wearing their blue DowKai jumpsuits. Several looked at him. Seamen rushed around preparing for the keelhauling. And there was Shipmaster Chung, supervising the operation.

"Man the crane on thwartship track," Chung yelled, swinging his arm around. "Get into that nest now."

A seaman up on the crane deck climbed into the crane operator's cabin.

Shivering harder now from cold sweat, Soo-man approached Shipmaster Chung. "What's going on? What's a keelhauling? This your idea?"

"Mok Don's orders." Chung said it with cold indifference.

The words sank like daggers, the reality of them cutting deep. The crane hummed and the boom lowered. The cable and hook dangled over the starboard rail. Soo-man examined the hook's position in terror. What on earth did they have planned for him? Never mind that. He was disgraced before the group. He wouldn't squeal like those cowards he dropped overboard last year. He would maintain his personal honor by showing courage. With his arms crossed he dropped to his knees, the rail providing some shelter from the glacial wind.

Looking forward, he saw four sailors running toward him along the rail on his side. They carried the end of a cable that ran over the side, into the icy sea--and under the *Pinisha*. Soo-man wanted to scream. Where was Mok Don? His head darted around. Nowhere. He looked up at the wheelhouse. Behind the window, a black figure loomed ominously. The men with the cable stopped in front of Soo-man. It felt like a rock turned over in his stomach. He would face it, whatever it was, like a man, without protest. He began to crumble inside, but he got up on his feet.

"No," he mumbled. "Not the sea." The faces of dead men raced through his mind. Men he had dropped overboard were laughing at him. "No," Soo-man yelled.

Twenty DowKai soldiers encircled him; behind them, stood Hyun, Chull-su , and several seamen. Realizing he was under the eyes of the group, he fought to control his emotions. Shipmaster Chung stepped forward, his shoes clicking on the steel deck.

"Tie lines around his hands and feet," Chung yelled at two seamen holding loose rope.

The seamen, wary to go near Soo-man, edged forward.

Chung shouted, "Move it or you'll be next."

The men rushed forward and bound Soo-man's extremities. He didn't struggle. He would submit to Mok Don's will.

***

Shipmaster Chung looked on Soo-man's humiliation and downfall with pleasure. The executioner would finally get what he deserved.

The hook lowered from the crane aloft and stopped over Soo-man's head. Chung motioned to the men with the cable over the side to move closer.

"Hurry up," he said. "Soo-man is cold. You gonna make him wait all day?"

The men struggled fiercely against the current. The cable ran under the keel of the ship and up to the heavy lift derrick on the port beam. They fought against the friction of the *Pinisha*'s ten knot clip.

"Fasten those hooks," Shipmaster Chung squalled. The men with the cable threw its hook over the ropes binding Soo-man's feet.

"Get his hands over that hook," Chung said.

Honorably, Soo-man lifted his own arms over the crane hook. With that done, his courage failed him. "No," he yelled, "you'll rip me in half." Terror gripped Soo-man's face. "Please, please, please."

The crane hummed a high pitch, the hook leapt upward. It jerked Soo-man five feet in the air; the sea friction--from the cable hooked to his feet--yanked him to angling astern.

Soo-man screamed incoherently. He thrashed like a fish on the end of a line, his massive hulk of flesh flailing about. Screams, cries, squeals--he maintained not the slightest vestige of honor as he swung out over the frigid Bering Sea.

Shipmaster Chung smirked. "Down crane--up winch," he yelled. Hydraulics whined as Soo-man dropped, thrashing all the way into the icy, sub-polar ocean. As the crane hook dropped, the winch took in the slack at his feet and dragged Soo-man into the freezing chop against the *Pinisha*'s ten knot running speed. He quickly disappeared with the crane line in tow. His bound hands entered the water last.

Shipmaster Chung watched his first keelhauling with a thrilling adrenaline high. The savagery of the punishment startled him. Purely barbarian. Pulling Soo-man thwartwise at ten knots would force-fill him with sea water. Shipmaster Chung could only guess at the violent forces tearing at Soo-man under keel.

"Halt crane--halt winch," Chung said. With Soo-man dragging crosswise under the keel, the cables stopped. Chung felt goose bumps rising on his back. What impulse of cruelty made him prolong the demonstration? He felt powerful. Sexy.

Fifty cold, numb men lined the starboard rail, silenced by shock. The crane hummed, but lay idle. Wintry wind broke across the deck. Hyun laughed quietly.

Someone said, "You're going to kill him."

That's right, Chung thought.

Then Mok Don's voice thundered over the loudspeaker. "Proceed. I want him alive."

"Down crane--up winch," Shipmaster Chung yelled.

The pitch of the hums changed, and the cables started moving again. In unison the crew moved across-decks to the port rail, where the winch and heavy lift derrick reeled in the cable. At first, a form emerged beneath the dark surface. Then the cable gave way to shoes and muscular, blue legs with sweats bunched up around the knees. As the cable lifted him by his ankles, his thick trunk emerged followed by blue arms and hands. A dozen crew members groaned in disgust. In two minutes, Soo-man's appearance had altered radically. His skin was pale with a blue tinge. Blood seeped from beneath the ropes at his hands and feet, also from his nose. He looked like a corpse being pulled out of a freezer. The water instantly froze on his skin.

The derrick swung aft and dropped Soo-man on the steel deck like a cold slab of meat.

CHAPTER TWENTY-NINE
December 4th, Evening

The barometer hung at an alarming low. Frank made an entry in the log book. Then he took over the helm from the autopilot. Kiska Island lay dead ahead. They'd spent three days on the Bering Sea--a vast arctic desert of a million square liquid miles. A gray zone of water, sky, and light that cast its leaden gloom on the *Hector*, camouflaging the old crabber, leaving the boat a tiny gray world apart from other people, places, and all sense of civilized reality.

An hour later the *Hector* idled into Opelia Harbor channel, and for the first time in days, the view offered more than gray. Icy, black water reached inland two miles. Slow moving ice chunks bobbed in the chop. Birch logs from Kamchatka, brought by the Japan Current, littered rocky, black-sand beaches. Jagged lava rock walls rose behind stretches of black sand, where seagulls screamed and seals played.

Startled by a sound, Frank spun away from the helm and reached for his shoulder holster. Recovering from the surprise, he let his hand fall to his side.

"Relax, man. It's just me."

Brian walked into the wheelhouse to the port-side consul and set down a cup of coffee. He stripped off his gloves and looked at his hands. They were white. He tried bending the fingers, but movement was restricted.

"Good to be back," he said. "I've got a lot of work to do." He lifted a mug of coffee with both hands and squeezed it. Finally he took a long sip.

Something banged against the hull. Frank glanced at the fathometer. It was high tide and plenty deep.

Brian walked to the side window and looked down. "Just a small chunk of ice," he said, rotating the steaming cup in his hands, squeezing it from all different angles.

Frank looked back at Opelia Channel unwinding before them. Black water curved between jagged crags on either side, giving way to stark, rocky hills and rolling tundra.

Brian sipped his coffee and looked down the channel. Frank edged the wheel to port and watched the fathometer. He had to keep a

safe distance from a rocky ledge that reached out into the channel up
ahead. He glanced over at the barometer, which was still dropping.

On his way out, Brian said, "I'm going on deck to get ready for
docking."

Frank navigated the *Hector* for another half mile before he
reached into his pocket and pulled out the little old bottle he'd brought
up from his office. He looked into the old bottle at the seed. What a
simple thing it was, a little brown seed. He jingled it around a couple
of times to a chime. He dumped the seed into his palm, set down the
bottle, and looked at the seed. It was amazing that a little seed could
grow into a huge tree. Frank could not pay the seed to grow. He could
not threaten it. All he could do was plant the seed and believe in it.
Faith was a simple idea in a complicated world. It seemed almost naïve
in some circumstances while logical in others. Frank felt detached
from simplicity. The world pulled him in another direction. The kind
of men he'd often dealt with in the past could not be trusted in to do the
right things. They had to be bribed, blackmailed, or threatened. What
kind of a man had Frank become? A man who dealt with reality
perhaps.

For years he had studied histories of Machiavelli, The Corsican,
Hannibal, Clausewitz, Plutarch, and the others. He'd saturated his
mind with a range of philosophies. But now, he was worn down by it
all. A whisper calmed him. He wanted to live peacefully and simply.
He wanted to sleep soundly at night. But, he still lived in a very
complicated world, and he had to deal with situations in a realistic way.
Frank dropped the little seed into the antique bottle and shoved it into
his pocket.

Misty Butte rose broad on the port beam, her high peak lost in
gray cloud cover. Dead ahead, a wide swath of shoreline separated
Brian and Clay's log homes at the end of the protected harbor. Behind
them, the Snowy Mountain Range rose like the teeth of a saw, two-
thousand feet, to dramatic, stark peaks and serrated ridges. Fresh snow
dusted the mountainsides, frosting them white at the upper reaches. On
the starboard bow, at the foot of gentle hills of brown tundra sat Casa
del Norte, the home he built for Melody and his son. All this he

absorbed with exhilaration, and yet he found himself gripping the helm tensely.

Karen Nash greeted them at the old wharf.

Brian and Clay manned the deck; Frank, the foc'sle crane. Working together they offloaded the pallets of supplies onto the dock and hand carried the boxes into the wharf shack. They were finishing up when Abby climbed onto the dock, her hair pinned up in a bun. Frank introduced her to Karen, and they talked for a while. Finally, Clay slung his caribou-hide backpack over his shoulder and started down the beach.

With darkness setting upon the island, Brian threw off the hawsers, and water churned as Frank eased the *Hector* away from the pier.

Came a dusky stretch tugging along the shore under shadowy silhouettes, tugging across the calm, protected harbor to the landing pier at Casa del Norte. Luke and Ingrid were waiting in the dim of nightfall to belay the lines.

Luke's white stocking cap covered most of his brown hair. "Who's she?" Luke said, staring at Abby. And Frank made introductions.

"It'll be good to have another woman on the island," Ingrid said, her blue eyes sparkling in the dock light. "How long will you be staying?"

Abby looked up at Frank. "I don't know yet. But after that boat ride I'm glad to have my feet on solid ground."

Frank took her by the arm. "Let's go on inside."

The warmth in the log house was a welcome greeting. Frank was relieved to be home, relieved that everyone was safe. Still, his mind tormented him, and he was filled with turmoil. He could not allow his comfortable life to lull him into complacency. The coffee was already on and Ingrid poured. Frank stoked the wood stove to roaring and stood close by, absorbing the warmth. His trip to Seoul, Korea, already seemed distant, like he'd barely left at all. Except, he did go, and a man was dead to prove it.

"Why don't we sit down?" Frank said. "Luke, put some wood on that fire."

Luke added three logs to the coals in the fireplace. The flames took instantly.

They talked about the trip for a while. Then Frank said, "Abby's here to take a look at some artifacts I found. She's an archaeologist."

Ingrid was curled on a chair and she leaned forward.

Luke looked at Abby as though he couldn't believe it. "You're an archaeologist?" Abby confirmed it and Luke said, "Have you ever seen mummies?"

"I've seen them in a few countries," Abby said, crossing her legs.

Frank clasped his hands. "Luke, why don't you go get the wooden box under my bed. Bring the sword, too."

Luke got the box and set it down on the coffee table. He held the gold sword and slowly pulled it from the sheath. Frank told Ingrid about the discovery, and her blue eyes opened wide with amazement. They all stared at the sword. Ingrid and Abby's gaze moved to the box. Abby took a deep breath. Ingrid looked over at Abby.

Frank said, "Ingrid, Luke . . . nobody off the island can know about the discovery until we take measures to safeguard the treasure. That much gold would put us in great danger if it became known. Mentioning this over the radio would be a death sentence." Frank paused.

He reached into the box and removed a gold crown. Seeing the relic again reminded him of crowns he'd seen and read about in Korea. Five columns with onion-dome tops rose like trees with branches from the round band. A dozen green curved jades hung from each column.

Six pendants dangled along the front of the gold band. The ends of the outer pendants were bullet shaped; green, curved jades fell at the ends of the inner two. The gold crown was glittering and elaborate.

Abby, who was staring silently, finally drew a breath and said, "This is Three Kingdoms treasure, alright." She ran her finger up one of the tree-like columns and said, "Notice the embossed dots lining the edges and the intricate gold spangles surrounding the jades." With her index finger she gently swung one of the pendants. "The pendants are made of spangles attached to twisted gold wires. Fabulous."

Ingrid mumbled something in French. And then in English, she said, "It's beautiful."

Abby was wondering at the crown now. "It's in perfect condition. This is amazing."

"That's a real crown," Luke said. "I think a queen wore it." Luke placed the gold sword on the table.

Abby smiled. "You're right. What you're looking at is from the Shilla Dynasty, probably 5th or 6th century. Other crowns like this have been excavated in Korea. The intricacy of detail here is meticulous. The curved jades are splendid, and none missing. The pendants are so delicately crafted, and yet, after all this time, their integrity is uncompromised."

Frank set down the crown. He reached into the box and withdrew a gold, dragon-shaped wine ewer. The dragon's head was the spout. A fin-shaped tail was the cover. Below the cover, large fins reached up and out.

Abby scrutinized the piece. "I've seen something like this from the Koryo Dynasty of the 12th century, but never in gold. What I've seen was celadon pottery. Korea is famous for their celadons and bluish-green glazes." She reached out and accepted the relic for closer inspection. She held the piece up slowly. "The incising of the bones, scales, and wings on the body is wonderful. Look at how Korean artisans utilized twisted gold flower stems reaching across the back to form the handle. And notice how flower pedals in relief form the base. I can't be sure of the origin." She passed the gold dragon to Ingrid, who inspected it carefully. "But the piece definitely resembles Koryo."

Ingrid put the wine ewer on the table and glanced over at Frank.

Frank reached in the box and pulled out a gold ostrich egg, a gold turtle, a gold cup with an openwork stem and seven spangles dangling below the rim. Each piece was crafted in intricate detail. These he set on the coffee table.

Then he reached in the box and withdrew a gold necklace of exquisite intricacy and beauty which he handed to Abby. She was silent at first, examining it seriously. Then she began talking: "This is amazing. Hundreds of granulated gold-leaf and teardrop spangles soldered to twisted gold wire." She swung it around slowly. "The detail is like a Hawaiian lei dipped in liquid gold. And, of course, the green curved jade at its lower extremity is the only non-gold link. You really save the best for last, don't you? I mean best from the perspective of painstaking craftsmanship, anyway. The attention to detail is divine."

"Ever seen anything like it?" Frank asked.

"I have and it was 6th-century Shilla. Frank, do you mind if I take some photographs?"

"Go ahead."

Abby got her camera and shot two rolls.

"Save some film," Frank said. "This is only a sample of what's to come."

After she put her camera away, Abby pulled the pencil out of her bun, and her hair tumbled down. She took careful notes on a pad.

The night was growing late. Ingrid, looking rather tired, excused herself for the evening, and left like a floating feather.

Luke said, "What are you gonna do with all the treasure, Dad?"

Frank was quiet for a moment. "There are some things I should have taken care of years ago. Maybe now is the time."

"What kind of things?"

"Well, I want to help some people with it."

"Like who?"

"I'm thinking about widows in North Korea."

"Why do you want to help widows, Dad?"

"Somebody's got to." He didn't like being evasive with his son, but he knew how to evade like some people knew how to breathe. This was not the time to explain that he had personally created many widows in North Korea. It was not the time to explain that he carried guilt. He hoped the right time for that discussion would never come.

"Are we gonna keep any?" Luke said.

"I've been thinking about that, and I've decided that you can keep the gold sword."

Luke sat up in his chair. He looked at Frank curiously. So did Abby.

Frank told Luke about the disappearance of the renegade crew of Japanese sailors in World War Two and the subsequent disappearance of the *Musashi Maru*.

"You mean it's pirates' gold?" Luke asked.

"My guess is a lot of people have died over that treasure. I also plan to renovate the old Russian Orthodox Church in Dutch Harbor."

Luke sighed.

"Frank, what about those men who attacked me?" Abby said. "What if they find out where you live?"

"Only a few people in Dutch Harbor know I live on Kiska. Others think I live in Seattle. If these Koreans try finding us in Seattle, say through the phone book or tax records, they'll come up empty-handed. The island's under a land trust and they'll never trace it back to me."

Despite their anonymity on the remote island, Frank locked the doors that night.

He dreamt about the little brown seed. He planted the seed and the seed grew into a great tree. And Frank was the tree, and the tree was good. But then the old man came and hewed the tree down.

Frank awoke and walked to the window. In the darkness, he stared out across the water and listened to the waves breaking on beach. The rumbling was getting louder. The storm was coming . . . but it would wait until tomorrow.

CHAPTER THIRTY
December 5th

Frank woke Abby at 5 a.m. and built a fire. Abby came out wearing a sweater and riding pants. The riding pants reminded Frank of his wife, and he remembered the happiness of taking trail rides with her long ago. For years now since her tragic death, Frank rose and had coffee alone. He tried to put it all out of his mind.

"I'm glad you're here, Abby, I really am."

"Me too, I'm excited. When are we leaving?"

"Soon." His wife always liked to go riding early in the morning.

They drank a cup of coffee together and walked through the early morning's calm chill to the *Hector*. In the glowing wheelhouse, Frank read the latest hour-by-hour meteorological report from the automated data system. He sat at the computer and brought up the satellite weather tracker's on-screen image: a turning cyclonic storm advancing with a violent front. It seemed to breathe and gyrate.

"Maybe a day off," Frank said. "There'll be hurricane force winds."

"I can't believe it," Abby said. "It's been blowing since we got to Dutch Harbor."

"Welcome to the Aleutians. These islands have been called cradle of the storms. Sometimes we get this pacific stillness with dense fog. But there's always another bluster moving in."

Frank kneeled down and opened up the cabinet under the chart desk. Two pages lay in front of the fax machine. He read the first one and handed it to Abby. "Looks like your lawyer friend Dane Leisbeth came through for us. The Korea National Museum has agreed to our terms."

Abby looked at the fax carefully and smiled. "That's wonderful."

Frank gave her a hug. "Thank you."

"I'm eager to see the treasure and begin the recovery project." She smoothed her hair back. "I can think of half a dozen magazines that'll be fighting for first publication rights of both the story and the photographs."

"There'll be a lot of interest. Revenues from the exhibit should be substantial." Frank was looking off to nowhere, envisioning a better future. He suddenly glanced down at the other page.

"This is from Mr. Lee. Says to call immediately."

Frank placed a ship-to-shore call to Seoul.

"I've got information about Mok Don," Mr. Lee said. "He's a famous man in Korea. A powerful man."

"What'd you find out?"

"Do you recall my telling you about comfort women?"

"They were the women who the Japanese rounded up and forced into prostitution during World War Two."

"Yes, that is right." Mr. Lee was silent for a while. "My mother was a comfort woman. They ruined her life. I've been in politics for three decades trying to combat the wrongs done to her during the war. It's been difficult. Certain Japanese politicians are patiently waiting for the comfort women to die of old age and take their shame and accusations with them to the grave."

Frank was silent. He waited for Mr. Lee to continue.

"During World War Two, Mok Don's father worked with the Japanese. He delivered Korean women to Japanese brothels. He provided other services for the Japanese, as well. He was an enemy of the people, a traitor; and Mok Don surpassed his example, darkly overshadowing him. You asked me to look into Mok Don's ties to Russia. Mok Don is known to have business ties with Surikov."

"Felix Surikov?"

"Yes, a famous man, but he's not in politics anymore. He and Mok Don make a bad pair. In one of their joint ventures, they smuggled Russian women into Korea with promises of high-paying jobs, then sold them into prostitution. We know this goes on, but ties to Mok Don cannot be proven.

"He and Surikov have publicized a joint venture shipping reindeer antlers and Alaskan bear parts to South Korea, where they are valued for medicinal and aphrodisiac qualities.

"Mok Don's most recent venture is marketing discount food. After many children in India developed tumors and a monstrous list of side effects, accusations were waged that the food was treated with nuclear waste, a process called food irradiation, which kills microorganisms and extends shelf life. Mok Don swore in public he hasn't irradiated Korean food, but admits to using the process in India. Either way, we suspect he and Surikov have been involved in nuclear proliferation.

"Mok Don made his fortune selling heroin. He organized his cronies into a crime family based on Confucian principles. He's founder of the DowKai group, one of Korea's largest and most respected multinational conglomerates."

"You say he sold heroine?"

"That's how it all started. Raw materials and cheap labor made China the natural place to manufacture the drugs; then the product was shipped to either Korea, Vietnam, or Japan. Today, America is his biggest market. Back in 1991, North Korean elite began the cultivation of opium poppy in a bid to earn foreign currency. Mok Don was their biggest customer. The Korean Peninsula is flanked by 3,400 islands. Meetings took place on these islands between DowKai people and North Korean Mafia. Contacts were made using civilian pleasure boats and luxury yachts.

"Drugs were only the beginning for Mok Don. Later he bought into different branches of the transportation business that he needed for his smuggling operations: fishing boats, trucks, small airplanes. As his business expanded, he moved into black market arms trading and cargo ships.

"Today his businesses include accounting, construction, and electronics manufacturing. Publicly, he's known for his legitimate business interests. There is no proof of his illegal activities. Mok Don is careful. And he's a powerful man. His businesses flourish in large part through contracts and favors from high ranking officials in the Korean government. His bribes to ex-general presidents bought him military contracts and protection. He's someone I would stay far away from."

"Thanks for the information. He won't find me. I'm invisible to the world and plan to keep it that way."

After Frank hung up the mike, he and Abby went to the barn and saddled the horses. He helped Abby up into her saddle and gave her the reins. "He's an easy horse. You shouldn't have any trouble with him."

"You're sure he isn't one of those wild horses you have on the island?"

"He was once, but he's tame now. Come on, we have a long ride ahead of us."

The high trail took them above the ocean along the steep and rocky shoreline. They rode in and out of dense fog banks for over two miles.

"I hear something," Abby said at a wide spot in the trail. She rode up next to Frank and grabbed his sleeve. "That sound. What on earth is it?"

"Nothing to worry about, " Frank said. "You'll see for yourself a ways up the trail." They rode for another half a mile until the sounds were loud and fiendish.

Frank smiled at Abby and said, "A stellar sea lion rookery site. You're hearing the wail of 2,000-pound bulls. There's another rookery several miles north of here at Lief Cove. I'll show you another time. We have to keep moving."

From the rookery at Cape St. Stephen they rode for hours through the tundra and muskeg bogs of the bleak tablelands. They stopped at Gertrude Cove and admired the *Borneo Maru,* one of the Japanese shipwrecks.

"The tsunami moved her fifty yards inland," Frank said.

"You're kidding," Abby said. "That's a big ship."

"There's lots of shipwrecks on Kiska," Frank said. "Mostly from World War Two."

They rode past Kiska Harbor, the streams, the lakes, the airfield built by the Japanese in World War Two. They rode by Musashi Inlet and up the Volcano Tundra Trail.

Along the way Frank did some hard thinking about Mok Don. What kind of man committed such horrible crimes against humanity?

He closed his eyes and shook his head. The truth never went away. Hadn't he himself killed for money? What kind of a man did that?

When the legal process of extradition and trial were impotent-- Frank was not. He showed no tolerance for foreign obstructionism. When terrorists blew up women and children and brazenly took credit for it, he went in and saw to justice.

He specialized in intercepting and neutralizing terrorist gunrunners and drug smugglers on the high seas. Terrorists played with death for money, and Frank's team crushed them on that basis. He gave no more consideration to their phony causes than they did.

In addition to the millions he accumulated in fees for assassinations, the profits he garnered selling confiscated vessels proved equally lucrative. After the crew was neutralized, the predetermined buyers dropped a new crew by helicopter. All the details and doctored paperwork were handled in advance right down to the time and position when the vessel would be under control.

Frank charged a $200,000 retainer plus expenses, all paid by direct transfer into one of his Cayman Island accounts. At the briefing, if he decided to go ahead with a job, a full fee was agreed upon, described as a consulting fee.

Elite government operatives in foreign countries moved money through their bureaucracies using dummy corporations and bogus contracts. Frank was paid a consulting fee for deep-sea salvage operations or whatever was appropriate. Large sums of money were laundered through such shrouded government manipulations.

A day came when huge fees blinded his judgment on which contracts to turn down. He became a pawn, manipulated by powerful forces to questionable ends. And he made a decisive hit on a terrorist cell that sparked retaliation. More innocent women and children lost their lives when terrorists detonated a car bomb in a crowded Tel Aviv shopping district. Frank sometimes counted himself indirectly responsible through cause and effect. In his gut he knew it wasn't his fault, but nothing was clear anymore.

He thought back. Like yesterday . . . Frank and Melody were riding horses on the Big Island of Hawaii, following a dirt road down a long gradual slope to the ocean. He could almost reach out and touch her soft warm shoulder. He could almost lean over and kiss her. "Hey you," he said with a smile.

The warm Hawaiian sun shining on them, saddles creaking, Melody in her riding helmet. She smiled at Frank with her innocent eyes. He felt such love for her that the rest of the world didn't matter. They had each other and that was all he wanted. Her smile touched him with happiness. He wished the day would never end. He wished he could freeze that moment in time forever. She said, "Maybe when we're old--"

The crack of gunfire-- The bullet grazed his cheek-- The world spun and he hit the ground hard. And then he saw Melody. "No," Frank screamed. "*No.*"

His love was gone. He would never get her back because of the life he chose for them, because she trusted him. Now the moment was indeed frozen in time forever in his mind. There was no escaping that day, no escaping himself--either on Kiska, or the South Pole. He couldn't hide from truth in the most remote corner of the earth.

His horse nickered. Hooves thumped on the ground. Frank looked over at Abby.

Kiska Volcano loomed like the shadow of a dark monstrosity in the still, cold, pre-dawn darkness. At the deadfall they turned inland and ground hitched the horses by the crater. Carrying a flashlight, Frank scaled the rock ramp and helped Abby down into the crater. Tendrils of steam curled out of the cave, and Frank noticed the sulfur smell. They followed the flashlight beam through the warm steam, their feet splashing in the millimeter-deep stream of water that ran down the cave floor. The sounds of water dripping from the ceiling echoed. Scattered gold artifacts glimmered under the light's beam in the first chamber. Frank could tell that Abby was fascinated by the bones and skulls, but the turtle ship carving loomed ominous. She spent several minutes examining the petroglyph and some of the artifacts. Then Frank led the way down the lava tube.

Entering the treasure chamber was like having a recurring illusion. Artifacts and gold treasures rose in a glittering subterranean treasure mound that inspired silence. Frank fought fleeting impulses to keep it all for himself and his son.

"I always wondered how a moment like this would be." Abby paused and took in the sight. "It's better than I imagined. The ancient Koreans were absolute masters in metallurgy. One glance and I can tell you many of these pieces will rank among Korea's finest antiquities. They're as noble as anything excavated there."

"What do you think the whole hoard is worth?"

Abby smiled. "Including the Japanese skeletons?"

"I think we can exclude them."

"To make an estimate, we'd have to weigh everything, multiply total tonnage by the current market price of gold, and multiply our sum by ten for the adjusted value of rare artifacts. But I can tell you there's a variation in the quality. I can spot several pieces that are worth no more than their weight in gold. Others are as good as the pieces you showed me last night. They're worth a premium. I wish I could start photographing and cataloguing immediately."

"After the storm, we'll come back. What do you guess it all weighs?"

"Hard to tell by looking, but I suppose I could make a crude estimate." She silently appraised the hoard, making calculations in her head. She picked up a few ceremonial objects and examined them carefully, intuitively gauging their mass. "Well, considering gold weighs twelve-hundred pounds per cubic foot and allowing for all the molding and crafting done in the foundry; also considering gold is a heavy metal, three times heavier than iron, they'd probably have to cast and hammer out two tons of gold to replace this collection including the crate in the passage. I'd say we're looking at roughly $250 million dollars worth of gold artifacts."

Frank stared at the treasure speechlessly. He looked over at Abby and sensed her amazement was as great as his. Finally he said, "With this storm coming in, we have to get back. I just want to dig into this mound and see if it's concealing the half-ton golden turtle ship." Frank moved some bones out of the way and then started moving relics. He put the objects aside quickly as he burrowed down into the hoard.

Abby stiffened. "Be gentle. After all, these are priceless artifacts, some of the great treasures of the world."

"I'll be more careful." Burrowing down a couple feet into the treasure mound took only minutes.

"A half-ton turtle ship would be at least the size of a table," Abby said. "It can't be under there or you'd have already found it."

Frank backed away from the hoard, carelessly stepping on and breaking a bone with a snap.

Abby cringed. "My colleagues would have a heart attack if they could see this."

Frank was still curious about the missing turtle ship, but anxiety about the storm was building within him. Even in the freezing cold he began to sweat. He'd pay for that on the way back.

"Come on," Frank said. Leaving the chamber, he stopped and turned again to look at the cache. Abby stood next to him without saying anything.

Frank felt a breeze chilling the sweat on his neck. When sweat freezes, a man loses body heat. In extremes, that could be fatal. Conditions weren't extreme yet, but soon would be. As he stood there hesitating, wind passed through the stillness and seeped down under his collar over rising goose bumps.

A breeze in the stillness.

He flashed his light abruptly against the cave wall. The breeze was coming from a shadowed nook to his left. The nook looked innocent enough. Except the wall at its back wasn't solid and consistent like the lava tube. Broken lava rocks rose in a crumbled pile from floor to ceiling, giving the appearance of a cave-in. The breeze was coming through cracks in the pile.

Frank said, "I think we've just found a concealed passage that branches off from here. Looks like the passage was concealed with these lava rocks. There must be a hidden cave system."

"Really?"

Frank nodded. "Come on, we've got a six hour ride ahead of us and we've got to get back before that storm hits. We'll explore this later." He strode out of the lava tube with Abby right behind him. He helped her out of the entrance crater and pulled the ground hitches. Abby mounted up, and Frank swung onto the saddle. "Let's go. Ya!" They rode long and hard, and the weather deteriorated with the hours. They were within a mile of the ranch when they heard the first gunshot.

CHAPTER THIRTY-ONE
Evening

The snow blew down thick in the rising blizzard. Frank drew rein and sat stone-still for a moment. Although they'd been riding in the snow for some time, he suddenly felt cold. Even from a mile away, he could tell the difference between an M-16 and an AK-47. There was no question that the report had come from an AK.

"What was that?" Abby said.

Frank quickly turned to her. "I want you to turn around and follow our tracks back to that animal shelter we passed a ways back. Wait for me there." Then he gave her instructions on what to do if he didn't return within two hours.

Realizing that Luke and Ingrid were all alone, Frank ran his horse toward Casa del Norte. As he approached the ranch house, he slowed the horse to a walk. He was hoping Brian had come around and shot a fox—or maybe even one of the dogs. And indeed, as he approached the house, he saw a dog sprawled and bloodstained. But it was Luke's dog! The animal was harmless. And then the sight of a landing craft on the beach shocked him.

Steam whisked from the wound on Luke's dead dog. And then came a scream from inside the house. Frank drew rein at the front door where he was looking down the hollow end of an AK-47.

"Get down," the Korean said. "Get inside."

Frank swung out of the saddle and walked inside out of the blowing snow. Ten Koreans were standing around the living room. In a glance, Frank sensed they had just arrived. Standing by Ingrid, Luke looked scared, but defiant. Tears streamed down Ingrid's face. Her shirt was nearly torn from her chest. Brian Nash sat on the ground with smeared blood on his badly swollen face. As he looked at Frank, a flood of painful emotion filled his eyes.

Ingrid hurried to Frank and clung to him.

"They killed her," Brian said. "They killed Karen!"

Adrenaline and shock and rage surged through Frank's nerves. When he spoke, he felt like he was listening to someone else speak, but the voice was his own. "Then they'll kill me too if they know what's good for them."

With an AK-47 suddenly at his back, four Koreans closed on Frank to suppress him. Ingrid was roughly pushed away. The first punch Frank took in the stomach. Restrained, he absorbed a half-dozen more to the face and body. With his adrenaline level, he could have hurt all four Koreans, but restrained himself for fear of immediate consequences to the others.

When the punches stopped, a skeletal man with an emaciated face and dark bags under his eyes walked in front of Frank carrying an AK. Ingrid was crying. Luke looked scared. Contempt swept over Brian's bleeding face. The man spoke in English.

"Tell me now. Where's the gold?"

Frank met his stare. That worthless cadaver killed Karen Nash. Frank's breath hissed through his teeth; his chest rose and fell. He tasted blood in his mouth from his bleeding lips. He began to shake from tension in every muscle intensified by suppressing his rage. He thought of the kind of scum that killed his own wife years ago.

One of the Koreans said something to him, calling him Chull-su. The man glared at Frank.

"Where's the gold?"

Frank said nothing.

Chull-su lifted the butt of the AK-47 as if to slam the weapon into Frank's head. "Tell me now."

"I don't know what you're talking about," Frank said. If he told them the location, the Koreans would kill them.

Chull-su turned his gun around and pointed the barrel at Frank's forehead. "I'm not playing," he said.

"Who are you? Why are you here?" Frank said

Chull-su slapped him. "You think I'm playing games?" he yelled. "You want to die, you decadent pig?" His yelling gave way to violent hacking and coughing. Everyone in the room stood by as Chull-su coughed. In between coughs, he darted baneful glances at Frank. Finally, he caught his breath for a moment.

"Get them out," he screamed at his men. "Lock them in the barn with the other animals--" His voice gave way to more uncontrolled hacking. "Call Mok Don for instructions."

The other Koreans roughly tugged Brian, Ingrid, and Luke up. All three, along with Frank, were hustled out the door into the fanning snow squall. Luke and Ingrid weren't wearing coats, and the temperature was near zero. Four Koreans escorted Frank and the others to the barn and locked them in the tack room. The solid door slammed shut behind them, and the Koreans bolted it from outside with a hefty exterior bolt lock.

Ingrid was fighting back tears. Frank took her in his arms and stared at Brian over her shoulder. Frank wanted to say something to Brian but couldn't. He didn't have the guts. He looked away, then turned back to him. "I'm sorry," Frank said, shaking his head. "I'm so sorry."

Brian sniffled hard. He took a deep hard breath. There were tears in his eyes as he spoke. "They raped her. Clay heard the gunshot then took off."

Frank winced. He helped Ingrid to sit down, then walked over to the window and looked out. Two Koreans were pushing off from the beach in a landing craft. Snow was driving down almost horizontally. Wind was starting to howl. Frank put his hand on Luke's shoulder.

Ingrid wiped her eyes with her sleeve. She turned to Frank. "Where's Abby?"

"Hiding nearby." He turned away. Karen's death was his fault. His carelessness got her killed. Not only had he gotten his own wife killed, but now Brian's. He would've welcomed death at that moment. A rod of heavy blackness ran through him like poison. He put his hand on his forehead. He grimaced and pinned his eyes shut tight. His attempt to earn forgiveness seemed hateful at that moment in time. He was already in Hell. He opened his eyes and returned his gaze to the beach. The landing craft was racing out around the point and heading up Opelia Harbor Channel; the *Pinisha* was probably anchored offshore beyond the mouth.

He had to stay calm. Like a machine. No emotion. Just think and act.

He turned and looked the room over. He walked to the closet and opened it. Numerous heavy old woolen sweaters and shirts hung there as well as windproof trousers and parkas. He pulled a woolen sweater out of the closet and gave it to Ingrid. He removed more clothes which he handed to Luke and Brian. A large, walnut storage chest lay in the corner of the room by the wall. Frank opened it. The chest was filled with old cold-weather clothes including thermal underwear, woolen socks, scarves, woolen balaclavas, woolen mittens, hoods, Caribou Sorels and mukluks. He pocketed a couple of small snow garments and turned to the others.

"Go through the chest, find what you can to stay warm. Dress for blizzard conditions and dress loosely."

Brian and Ingrid glanced questioningly at Frank then followed his order. Frank handed a sweater to Luke. "Put it on."

Frank was already warmly dressed from his morning ride. He looked at the wall dividing the tack room from the work room. At waist height the wall was lined with saddle racks. Blankets were thrown over the saddles. Apparently the Koreans hadn't looked the room over carefully. Frank grabbed a roll of duct tape off the shelf.

"Don't make any noise," he said. "Just wait here. Get dressed. Quickly."

The three looked at him. He got down on his hands and knees and crawled under the blankets draped over the saddles. Behind the blankets, under the saddles, a big dog door was installed for Taiga, who occasionally bunked down in the tackroom. One room was too confining for the big dog. Crawling on his hands and knees, Frank passed through the dog door into the tool room, letting the door swing gently shut behind him. The tool room door had a window. Frank stood back and looked out. A Korean was guarding the tackroom door. It was the one who battered Ingrid in the house. Frank pulled away and shuddered with disgust.

He closed his eyes and took several deep breaths.

Be a machine. A machine.

Again he looked out the window. The Korean man guarding the tack room door had an AK-47 slung over his shoulder and was pacing back and forth trying to stay warm. As the man walked by the tool room door, Frank stepped out, grabbed him from behind, and twisted his neck sideways till he groaned a cry of distress.

"You speak English?" Frank said.

"Yes," the man snarled through gritted teeth.

"Good," Frank said beneath gale winds singing a dirge around the barn. "You ought to do your homework before you come on my ranch and start killing people. You know who I am?"

"No," the man rasped.

"Well, you ought to since you're killing my friends." Frank slapped duct tape over his mouth and wrenched his arm until his right shoulder popped out of joint. The man cried out in pain, but the duct tape muffled his scream. Frank hammered him at the base of the neck, and he collapsed unconscious. Without letting the man fall to the ground, Frank dragged the body across the barn and dropped it in an empty horse stall, slipping off the AK-47 as he did so. He took a horse blanket from the nook between the stalls. Realizing that he'd lost his edge, he threw the blanket over the man and looked back. He stood there for a moment, hesitating. In the past he would not have hesitated to kill the man. Frank didn't have to kill the man. He just hoped he didn't live to regret his mercy. He closed the stall door.

His own horse, Cimeron, was in the next stall. They'd put him there without removing the saddle. Steam was rising from his back after the long ride across the island.

He walked to the barn door and looked out. The snow was blowing down so heavily he couldn't see the house. He opened the door to the tackroom. Brian, Ingrid, and Luke looked at him wide-eyed.

Frank said, "We have to get out of here immediately. Ingrid get the horses saddled up. Luke, help her. Do it now!"

"Where'd you get the gun?" Brian said.

Frank glanced down at the AK-47. "They left a guard and I took care of him. They'll kill us all if we don't get out of here. Get the horses saddled up."

Ingrid nodded in submission and walked into the barn. Luke followed her, staring back at his father as she led him out. Brian stayed behind as he saw Frank doing the same.

"Give me the gun, Frank. I'm going back in there alone."

"You're coming with us."

"Give me the gun!" There was a wild look in Brian's eyes.

"You want to give them what they deserve?"

"Damn right I do."

"Going back in there ain't gonna do anything. You'd be lucky to kill two of them before they blew you away."

"I don't care. Give me the gun."

"You come with us. I need your help or those dirtbags are gonna kill Luke and Ingrid and Abby, too. Is that what you want?"

Brian didn't say anything.

"Once we get the others to a safe place, we can come back and then I don't care what you do. I'll help you. We'll take out all of them."

Brian stared at Frank, then slowly nodded. "Alright, what are we gonna do? Ride out through the Tablelands?"

"Way this storm is picking up, we'd never make it through Bluster Pass."

Frank walked over to the window and looked out. Whiteness. Speeding swirling whiteness. He returned to Brian. "I think the *Pinisha*'s at the mouth of Opelia Harbor. Since I've no idea what's waiting for us, I don't want to try taking the *Hector*. Too risky. We could outmaneuver a large vessel in a surprise chase, but they'd probably spot us on radar coming up the channel. That or the ones in the house might find us missing and radio ahead. Either way, I don't see us making it out of Opelia Channel. No, it's risky, but we'll take the windward route. We can go to the emergency bunker at the base of the volcano. But first I have to get Abby. And I have to get to the *Hector*. You take Ingrid and Luke and make your way towards Foggy Butte. Abby and I will catch up."

Brian looked out at Ingrid and Luke, then nervously back at Frank. "Those murderers inside can still radio ahead. And if there's a ship out there, the windward route'll lead us right by her. What if they put ashore an ambush party?"

"You're gonna have to trust me. That's why I have to get to the *Hector*. We're wasting time."

They stepped into the main barn. Four horses stood saddled. Ingrid was putting a bit in the mouth of the last. Brian walked to the saddled horses and tightened the cinches. Frank walked to the barn door and looked outside.

Heavy snowfall howled past the barn in a blizzard. The house lay far beyond visibility. Frank walked back to Ingrid.

"I have to go to the *Hector*. You and Luke are riding out with Brian. I'll be a few minutes behind."

Ingrid glanced at him with fear in her tear-reddened eyes, then nodded and looked over at Brian.

Brian finished buckling on chaps and spat on the ground. "I'll take care of them."

Frank nodded and handed the AK to Brian. "Get them out of here."

Brian zipped up his coat and slung the rifle over his shoulder.

"It's a whiteout," Frank said. "So move fast and take advantage of the cover. Snow should cover our tracks before they can follow."

Frank took down his snowshoes from a nail on the barn wall. He hesitated, then grabbed an old bear trap from another nail. He walked to his son. Luke stood by Cimeron, watching his father with hollow eyes. Frank spoke as he tied the snowshoes to Cimeron's saddle.

"Luke, I'm counting on you to take care of Ingrid. And do whatever Brian tells you."

Luke looked up at his father and nodded, his lips quivering. Frank patted him on the back and helped him into the saddle.

He walked to Ingrid. Tears streamed down her cheeks. "You have to go now." He helped her into her saddle.

Brian swung onto his horse. As Frank opened the doors, a cloud of snow rushed inside.

"Get going," Frank said.

The three rode out into wind so strong it tilted them in their saddles. Twenty feet outside the barn, they disappeared into the storm. Frank opened the stall door and saw that the guard was coming around. He duck-taped the man's arms to his sides. Given that his shoulder was out of joint, he cried in agony while Frank bound him. Frank got a rope and bound his feet, then dragged the man out into the main barn area. He heaved the rope over a beam in the rafters and hoisted the man, who swung by his feet.

Frank grabbed the pommel, swung into his horse's saddle and rode out into the blizzard. With visibility at twenty feet, only his intimate knowledge of the terrain led him to the docks. Snow swirled over the bulwarks on the *Hector*'s deck like dust from the bed of a speeding truck. Wind screamed in the rigging. Frank whipped the reins around the hitching post and boarded the *Hector*.

Even in the protected harbor the boat was tossing against her buoys. He crossed the deck, entered the superstructure, and took the stairs down to the engine room. From a high ledge, he retrieved two keys. The locker door swung open, and Frank pulled out a brown, camouflage duffel bag. He then withdrew a large, white, empty duffel bag. After putting the brown bag into the white bag, he zipped it shut and went topside again. Carrying the duffel bag on deck, he hiked against the wind, climbed onto the dock and swung into the saddle.

It took some twenty minutes to get to Abby at the animal shelter where she was waiting. Together they cut behind Frank's home and forded Icy Creek. As Frank's horse gained the opposite river bank, a gunshot sent a bullet ringing past his ear.

"Come on, Abby." They dug heel and their horses bolted into the storm. They were quickly lost to whoever shot at them, but now had another problem. The Koreans would pursue. If they guessed correctly that their escaped prisoners were following the beach, an ambush party would lie in wait. Since the coastline of Opelia Harbor was fenced in by a devil's backbone--The Snowy Mountains--they could be trapped between an ambush and a pursuit party.

It was cold riding. Frank had lived in cold country a long time and was a fair judge. Temperature was below zero and dropping--unusually cold for the Aleutians--and a lot colder if you figured in the wind chill factor. The Siberian wind was blasting in bare and raw off a million square miles of uninhibited Bering Sea.

Frank shielded his eyes and angled towards the shore. He didn't know if there were any Koreans that far from the ranch, but didn't think so. He dug spur and the buck rose to a steady gait. Abby rode close behind. They were riding into blindness, but would soon come upon the shoreline, assuming Frank hadn't lost his direction.

Whiteouts were extremely dangerous and a man could easily lose his way and freeze to death. No man alive knew that land better than Brian Nash, not even Frank. But cold of such severity along with a whiteout and gale winds could dull a man's perceptions.

Following his instincts, Frank continued toward the channel over frozen muskeg and tussocks of snow-covered grass. Coming finally upon the igneous palisades lining the channel, he could hear big surf pounding the rocks, which was uncommon in those protected fjord waters.

He spurred the buck to a gallop, and the shoulder band of the heavy duffel bag dug harshly into his neck. Suddenly, he and Abby caught up with the others.

Frank drew rein and yelled to Ingrid: "You holding up alright?" She nodded.

"You need a snow mask. Put this on." Frank turned to his son. Luke's face was already covered with a thick woolen snow mask. Goggles protected his eyes. He was okay.

"Brian."

"Yeah?"

Frank unzipped the white duffel bag, then the brown one inside it. He pulled out a Winchester Model 12 combat shotgun and handed it to Brian.

"They know where we're headed and have time to put ashore an ambush party. With luck, we'll slip by them, but you know how narrow it gets up there.

"If we run into trouble, that's one of the best combat shotguns ever made. Doesn't have a trigger disconnector, so you can fire shells as fast as you can work the fore-end while keeping the trigger depressed." As Frank spoke he pulled a set of saddle bags from the duffel and slung them over Brian's saddle. "They're filled with paper-hulled double-aught buckshot loads holding nine pellets."

Brian took the weapon without objection, looked the trench gun over carefully, and passed the AK to Frank.

Killing a man--any man--was a hell of a thing to have to do. To his shame, Frank was no stranger to dealing death. But he wasn't about to sit back and let Mok Don's henchmen kill innocent people.

Frank slipped the AK in the bag and removed a Sig-Sauer P228 Night Stalker hand gun, strapping on the side holster.

He removed an AR-15 assault rifle, a semiautomatic version of the M-16. This he laid across his saddle, holding the gun tight against the wind. He removed a second saddle bag which fastened to his Western-style saddle. Frank zipped up the white bag and again slung the strap over his shoulder, now feeling less weight against his neck.

Finally, he pulled a jar of petroleum jelly out of his pocket and handed it to Brian, who smeared it all over his face to protect his exposed skin from frostbite.

Half hour later they were approaching the point. The blizzard was holding vision to fifteen feet. If there was a ship offshore, Frank couldn't see her lights. Suddenly, he drew rein and raised his AR-15 assault rifle. Something moved at the edge of visibility.

Chull-su shook violently as he spoke into the walkie-talkie. Ten of his men, also shaking, huddled around. Their clothes flapped in brutal winds and the bitter, hypothermic wind-chill factor.

Even with the speaker to his ear, Mok Don's voice was barely audible: *"Where are . . . ?"*

"We're along the inlet," Chull-su said. "We can't see anything. The men are freezing to death here."

"I don't want to hear about it."

To the walkie-talkie Chull-su shouted, "Nothing we can do until the storm passes. Request permission to return to the house and wait for them there . . ."

"No," snapped back. *"Find them. I'll personally shoot . . ."* The wind gusted and Chull-su couldn't hear. *". . . returns to the house . . . men lying in wait at the point . . . have them trapped and . . . wait out the storm . . ."*

Chull-su put the walkie-talkie in his inner pocket. As he did so, wind forced its way down inside his jacket. Wearily he dropped to his knees. The coughing started again and continued in a violent chain. He was bitter cold and his world spun. Bolts of pain shot through his head. He got out his flask and washed down a packet of pills. He coughed for several minutes more.

They were all dressed for the cold in thick, fur-lined jackets, but not all were prepared to weather a severe storm. Chull-su's gloved fingers were numb, so were his toes, but the pain inside his body from the sickness was unbearable. Mok Don had ordered him to proceed. He got up and led his men into the howling, freezing storm.

Not five minutes passed when he found the men Mok Don had spoken of, two men in the cruel, howling wind. When Chull-su's flashlight beam landed upon their faces and heads, several in his party gasped in horror.

"What happened to them?" This from a young killer named Jin-ho.

"Shut up." Chull-su fumbled in his jacket for the walkie-talkie. He removed it and pushed the speak button. "Mok Don ..."

"This is Mok Don. Have you got them?"

"No, we've found our men. They're dead."

"What?"

"They've been scalped."

"Speak up."

"Hair carved off their head."

Mok Don thundered back in a fit of rage, *"I'll do worse than that to you if you don't find them. Get busy. Bring them in alive. You. . . ."* The transmission was drowned out in speaker vibration and shrieking wind.

"Yes, Mok Don." Chull-su put away the walkie-talkie. "Head out."

CHAPTER THIRTY-TWO

Clay Krukov followed only forty feet behind the Koreans who pursued his friends on foot. Wind howled like a freight train. Occasionally, boulders or chunks of driftwood flew or rolled by in the puffing chaos. He struggled to keep his balance. At times he moved within fifteen feet of the Koreans, and with such poor visibility, only then could he see their black human forms in the night. He watched for the straggler to prey on.

In the scree of the mountains, one of the men began to fall behind. Holding his big hunting knife, Clay, under the cover of the storm, crept only ten feet behind the man. As Clay moved in, the Korean spontaneously looked back, and even in the howling darkness, Clay saw terror seize the man's face when he realized he was being stalked. The man never got off a shot or a yell to alert the others.

***

Leaning into the wind, Frank and Luke led their horses through the pounding cold. Brian followed behind Abby and Ingrid, who were also on foot now. The horses doggedly toiled in the traces behind hills and through the low valley without slowing. Against nature's fury they persisted across the snowy terrain. Finally they arrived at the igneous rock formations at the base of Kiska Volcano's west slope.

At the base of the volcano, long octopus tendrils of hardened magma reached out across the blanket of snow, piercing the blizzard and providing long, layered bulwarks of natural shelter against the wind.

Frank led them along the base of a twenty-foot high volcanic wall. The meadow covered ninety-plus acres and was surrounded on three sides by ten- and twenty-foot volcanic walls. They passed numerous lumps and heaps that conglomerated along the west wall-- wild horses and Casa del Norte sheep who frequently retreated to these wind-sheltered meadows during heavy weather. While ears were perking by the dozens, only a few of the untamed horses even bothered to rise and run.

At the far end of the meadow, Frank's supply bunker was built into the lava.

They all dismounted, and Frank opened the steel door to the dugout. "Bring the horses in."

After getting a fire going, Frank lit up an old oil lantern for additional light.

Exhausted, Luke and Ingrid wanted to sleep.

"Not now," Frank said. "Get warmed and dried first."

He surveyed the bunker in a glance. There were two cords of dry firewood stacked along the bunker's lava wall, as well as a month's supply of food stored in air-tight tin canisters. A long time ago he prepared the bunker in case of an emergency.

The containers held supplies such as freeze-dried food, cocoa, coffee, a coffee pot, and matches--all of which Frank removed and laid out. He piled more wood onto the fire and turned off the lantern to save fuel. The smoke funneled out through the chimney. In the coffee pot he fetched water from a stream that ran down off the volcano and through the meadow. This he hung on a spit to boil. After Brian finished tending to the horses, they all sat around the fire.

They waited without saying a word. Outside the wind moaned ghostlike.

***

Clay trailed the Koreans for quite a while before one of them slipped and fell into Louise Creek. The man went into shock from the cold. The group carried him for a while but he slowed them down. Finally, they panicked and left the man behind, left him huddled behind a rock. Clay came up behind him and easily jerked the rifle from his frozen hands. Then he came around and looked straight into the man's face. The Korean, suffering from hypothermia, was shivering violently beneath frozen clothes. He stared in shock at Clay, fear of the hunter overcoming fear of the cold.

"You're going to die, just like you killed the woman." Clay grabbed him by his hair waved his hunting knife in the man's face.

The man tried to flee, but found himself incapable of coordinated movement. A few minutes later, Clay spirited out of the area.

***

The fire did a poor job keeping them warm . . . They were all shaking . . . eventually their clothes warmed and dried. They bundled up in sleeping bags from the bunker.

Brian was devastated. And Frank wanted to roll up into a ball and hide from reality. He had actually hoped the Kiska treasure would allow him to help people. What a fool he had been to think redemption was for sale, or that he could live in peace. Evidently if he wouldn't fight evil, then hell would find him. Frank lay down and closed his eyes. He covered his face with his hands.

***

Clay caught up again and followed the criminals. Out of the violent blackness of cyclonic night a runaway log rolled right over one of the Koreans in an Aleutian gust that seconds later lifted Clay off his feet and slammed him down on the ground. The killers regrouped to examine their trounced comrade. Not thirty feet away, Clay lay camouflaged by darkness and a cape of Aleutian mayhem. Ice spicules flew in like projectiles that nearly drew blood.

The Koreans tried to help him, but their resolve was weak. Tempers started to flare. Finally, they seemed to agree there was nothing they could do. They quickly left him behind. A few minutes later, Clay got close enough to see bone sticking out of his leg. He kept after the others.

Finally, as the men crossed Bluster Pass, Clay, who was following at fifteen feet, got down on one knee. The rifle leapt in his hands one time, and a black form dropped in the darkness. Gunfire erupted in every direction. Fleeing on his hands and knees, Clay escaped into the blizzard.

***

Knowing they were being stalked from behind, Chull-su led the pursuit party. He held his AK-47 ready for action. His fingers were numb, but still functioned. His face was numb. The storm was relentless.

He stopped and turned to the others. "Come on. All of you. Keep up."

"We need shelter."

"Shut up, keep going. Mok Don's will." Chull-su saw who was speaking so boldly.

Jin-ho said, "We've got to stop or someone else will die."

Chull-su wanted to agree. Street murder, disposal, and planned killings--with those he was familiar; with guerrilla warfare and deadly storms he was not. But Jin-ho was attempting to usurp his authority.

"I'm warning you, shut up," Chull-su said.

"There's only five of us left. We have to make our own decision."

"Shut up or I'll kill you," Chull-su said. "We must obey Mok Don's orders."

"Dead men don't . . . ." His voice drowned out by the wailing wind.

"There's a bonus for . . ." Chull-su's voice disintegrated off his lips.

Jin-ho started to argue again.

"Get to the back of the line or I'll kill you myself."

Chull-su slammed the butt of his gun into Jin-ho's chest, knocking him to the ground.

Jin-ho moaned in pain. Slowly, holding his chest, he struggled up and fell behind the others.

"Anybody else complains and I'll kill you." Chull-su took point and led them on into the storm.

The wind was rancorous and made of ice so strong he could lean into it without falling. Every inch of loose clothing flapped furiously. All they could do was move forward.

As Chull-su trudged on, he felt pain spreading within him. He coughed almost constantly. Without slowing he withdrew his flask and sucked down a shot of rum. He started putting it away, but thought of the men who'd fallen . . . He reopened the flask and took another.

Something slammed into him and he was tumbling on the ground. When he came to a halt, he strained to see the others. They were scattered around on the ground. A strong gust had leveled the whole group. The wind came in so hard it was difficult to stand up, but he did. Soon they regrouped and Chull-su once more led them into the tempest. He knew they were no longer hunting the Americans, but simply trying to survive.

They humped through the tundra forever. As they followed a narrow trail that allowed passage between two steep land formations, Chull-su heard a clank and a *scream* right down the back of his neck.

He dove forward and hit the ground. He saw the man who'd been following him was thrashing on the ground and screaming like a wounded pig.

The men closed in around him. Chull-su got up and went over to see what happened. Terror worked its ugliness on several of the men's faces, and Chull-su felt his numb lips open with a guttural sound.

"He's caught in a trap," someone said. "A bear trap."

"It's broken. Oh mother, it's broken!"

"He can't walk. He's finished."

"Don't leave me, no, no, please, I'll die!"

"We've got to get out of here."

"You can't leave me, you can't--"

"Let's go," Chull-su said.

"We've got to get out of this storm," Jin-ho said. "We'll all die."

"Get moving." Chull-su motioned him ahead with his AK. "Over there."

CHAPTER THIRTY-THREE

Fire logs burned in the dimness of the bunker and slowly turned to coals. Frank piled more wood on the fire and kept it burning. He made instant soup which he gave to the others. Abby drank hers slowly as she watched the steam rising from her cup. Luke drank a few sips and poured the rest out. Ingrid wouldn't look at hers. Brian declined. Nobody said a word. Frank got back in his sleeping bag and lay awake.

All night long the storm wailed like a thousand crying wolves. Frank couldn't sleep. He sat by the fire, staring at the flames . . . sometimes closing his eyes and burying his face in his hands. He and Brian took watches every four hours.

Near morning, Frank was staring trance-like out the look-out slash when Brian came over.

"See anything out there?" Brian said.

Frank nodded slowly with heavy eyes and a numb frown. He kept his gaze on the bleak meadow. "Just snow and horses. Haven't seen an ear perk."

"What am I gonna do without her, Frank?"

Frank shook his head. "I wish I knew what to tell you. I'm sorry. I just don't know."

For a long while they both stared at the sinister land and the blustering sky play. Finally Brian said, "You figure they'll find us here?"

Frank nodded.

"Well, I'm ready for 'em."

"I know you are," Frank said. "We don't have any choice, we can't stay here. They outnumber us. If they got us, Abby, Ingrid and Luke would be alone at their mercy."

"Mercy? They ain't got no mercy. And they sure as hell aren't gonna get any from me."

Frank stared at Brian, too ashamed to respond. He could offer no hope, no peace. He said nothing, and he felt like a sand crab with no shell to hide his face in.

He said, "When the storm lets up, we'll do what has to be done."

"It's about time." Brian scowled. And then he leaned toward Frank and said, "What happened when you scouted for that ambush party?"

"I found them," Frank mumbled.

"What did you do?"

Frank's eyes shifted towards the fire. The others were still sleeping. He was almost whispering when he said, "I found them, already dead, by Clay's hand."

"Clay's--"

"You heard me."

Brian grimaced. "I thought--" He shook his head. "I take back what I thought about him deserting before."

Frank nodded and patted Brian on the back. "I'll take a look from the perch." He went outside.

Beginning at the ground level around thirty yards from the bunker, the ledge angled up over the bunker, jutting out three feet, a natural path up the face of the lava wall. Frank followed the path up over the the bunker. From this lookout spot, he could see a long ways, but no sign of the Koreans.

The storm wailed for two days and two nights. The watches never stopped, and the fire never burned out. By the early morning hours of the third day, the storm was dying down. Frank told Brian to feed his horse; they were leaving. Then two hours later, just as daybreak rose on the islands, Frank added more wood to the fire and whispered in Abby's ear, "I have to go."

She turned and looked into his eyes. "You're blaming yourself for this. I can see it on your face. What they did isn't your fault, and nobody blames you."

Frank nodded and turned away.

"Don't go," Abby said. "Maybe they'll just leave. Please, don't go. There's too many of them."

Frank resisted the urge to look back at her. He walked over to Luke who'd been withdrawn for two days and barely said a word, who now sat by the fire, staring into nowhere with anger etched on his face. Frank sat down next to the boy. He sat there for several minutes watching the fire. Finally, he turned to Luke and said, "I have to go now. I have to stop those men. "

"I want to go with you."

"No. I need you here."

Luke nodded.

"Whatever happens, Luke, there's something I want you to know. I've made mistakes in my life, bad ones. I wish I could take them back, but I can't. Whatever happens, don't ever forget that I love you."

Tears filled Luke's eyes. He grasped Frank's arm. "You're coming back, right?"

"You take care of the women while I'm gone."

Luke nodded and let go of his father.

"And don't forget what I showed you."

"I won't," Luke said, his voice shaky. He glanced at the pistol and then back at Frank.

Frank nodded and stood. Brian was attending to the stock, buckling a saddle bag. Frank walked over and peered outside again. Daylight was near.

Brian handed him reins and led his own horse outside.

Frank followed and stopped in the doorway for one last look. They sat mournfully in the dimness crowding the fire. The picture froze in his mind. Would he ever see them again? He turned and walked out into the bitter cold of early morning. The storm was over, and the wind whispered softly.

For a long spell of silence, Frank stared off into the gray sky that stretched from horizon to horizon. Finally he looked over at Brian and said, "I don't want you to come. I work better alone."

"Don't give me that. I have to . . . for Karen."

Frank grimaced. "I want you to stay and protect the others. We can't leave them alone."

"No way I'm gonna sit around and wait. I've waited long enough. I'm going with or without you."

Frank grasped the pommel, slid his foot into the stirrup, and swung onto the saddle. "Mok Don's men couldn't have survived the storm without shelter. If they're alive, my guess is we'll find them holed up at the Rat Lake cabins; that, or they're still back at Casa del Norte."

Brian mounted up and they started riding.

As they moved through the sheltered meadow, dozens of longcoats rose and ran. Galloping spiritedly, nearly a hundred of them beat hoof in backtrack and came to rest near the bunker.

Frank carried the Arctic Warfare counterterrorist sniping rifle across his saddle. Using European countersniper ammunition, the gun's long-range capability well exceeded a thousand meters.

Side by side, he and Brian pressed on. Visibility was poor. While the storm was over, the air chilled them as they left the protection of the massive lava tendrils and set out upon pure white plains. They passed the salt water lakes in the low valley, drove hard across a vast expanse of snow. As they rode along the beach of the smoky sea, sets of seven-foot waves roared out of the fog and thundered upon the shore. Inland, obscured mountains loomed frosty in the river-rock gray clouds. Frank guessed ten degrees, still cold for the Aleutians. They rode in the lows near the foothills, going well beyond the cabins and checking for sign.

"A herd of vermin came through here," Brian said.

"Those are fresh tracks."

"Looks like they're heading over Middle Pass toward the air base. Let's get after 'em."

"How many you figure?"

Brian studied the tracks for a moment. "Four or five. Rest of them must have stayed back at the ranch."

Frank skewed his eyes toward the mountains. He said, "We'll head back to the bunker. Following their tracks is too dangerous. From there we'll take the volcano tundra trail through the valley to the east shore. We'll see if we can head them off."

"No chance, Frank. We're right behind 'em. We go back that way, we'll be lucky to catch 'em before tomorrow. I ain't running scared. I'm going after 'em now."

Frank was about to insist on his plan, but he knew Brian wouldn't listen. And he couldn't hardly blame his friend. He thought of Karen, and he couldn't-- He didn't like being pushed into a dangerous and reckless situation, but at that moment, recklessness seemed almost justified. Besides, he was just as anxious as Brian to see to some justice.

Following tracks, they rode through Middle Pass. In all directions, rugged, precipitous mountains reached skyward into ashen clouds. Snow and blue-white ice coated the rocky palisades. At one point they heard the snap of a gunshot in the mountains ahead. Half hour later they found a dead Korean with a frostbitten blue face.

"Looks like they put him out of his misery."

"Foxes won't go hungry today," Brian said. "Neither will the dogs."

"Must have had a rough night."

Brian spat. "Their day's gonna be worse. We're gaining on 'em."

Frank glanced down at the tracks, which were looking fresher all the time. Kiska Harbor wasn't far off now. He said, "We're going on foot from here on out. The horses make too much noise."

Brian spurred his horse on. "Maybe when we get closer; they're still too far ahead."

They rode on and dropped down into the foothills above the harbor into thick fog, eerily still. They passed the old Japanese Shinto shrine and went down to the abandoned submarine base. The Koreans seemed to have conglomerated by one of the dilapidated two-man submarines left by the Japanese to rust through the decades. From the derelict, the traces turned north, parallel to the beach. Frank and Brian more or less followed Trout Lagoon Road past the wharf and the old sea plane ramp. They moved through the mist of North Head past Junior Lake and Fox Lake.

"They're down by the air field," Frank whispered, looking into clouds.

"Probably searching out the ruins."

"Lot of tunnels in this area. They could hide almost anywhere."

"Yeah, but their tracks are fresh in the snow. We know where they're going."

Frank looked at the tracks disappearing into the fog ahead. "Wait a minute," he whispered.

"I see 'em," Brian said, looking down at the sign. "There's fifteen or twenty now. They met up with another group."

"Yeah . . . and we're too close. They may have heard us."

CHAPTER THIRTY-FOUR

Frank and Brian sat on their horses in the still mist, listening. "Sounds like a ship," Frank whispered.

He turned and looked toward the water. The harbor itself was shrouded in fog. He sat motionless for several minutes until the veil of fog pulled back just slightly, unmasking something in the thick, misty vapor.

"I see it. There's its anchor," Brian said.

They were both staring at a big chain reaching down into the water when a shot rang out.

Frank's buck rared up on his hind legs. Another shot sounded.

The horse came down and Frank dug heel. Both his horse and Brian's galloped into a long natural trough between snow dunes and followed the trough till it leveled. They bolted into the open momentarily before disappearing into an old airplane hangar, the last one still standing on Kiska. Rusty fighter wings and aircraft parts were strewn along the walls.

They quickly dismounted.

"Stay down and back from the doors," Frank said.

Brian pumped his shotgun and ghosted for cover.

Frank ran to the far wall and spied a look from where he'd taken cover by the door behind an aircraft engine. White mounds rose here and there of icy, snow-covered ruins and wreckage approaching the old airfield--a white expanse. To his left, in front of the hangar, he saw snow-covered heaps lumped up at various distances.

"Tracks," Frank said.

"Let's get 'em," Brian said. "They're here somewhere." He was lying down opposite Frank past the other side of the hangar door.

"Get behind something solid," Frank said. He scanned the area. A blanket of snow reached into the distance where it dropped off into

Salmon Lagoon. Nearby stood a dilapidated structure that looked like a frosted rib cage looming in the fog.

"Get back," Frank said.

Brian sank low. A man rose from behind a crest of snow and dove for shelter behind a closer one. The boom from Brian's trench gun announced a hit as the man buckled in mid air and landed a twisted heap.

"Come on," Brian said. "Come and get me." He pumped his gun and shot the downed man a second time.

A dozen shots clattered out in a matter of seconds. A second wave of gunfire spewed forth, then a third. Dozens of icicles fell and stabbed the earth along the front of the hangar. Bullets rattled new holes through the hangar's siding. Icicles blew up. Rust fragments rained down as the wall took on the porous appearance of Swiss cheese.

Despite the storm of gunfire, Brian returned several shots through a hole where rust had eaten through the ribbed aluminum.

"Brian," Frank yelled. "Get cover."

Frank folded down the bipod on his Arctic Warfare counterterrorist sniping rifle. He rapidly flipped up the scope covers and zeroed in on a snow mound that was producing a lot of gunfire. His shot hammered home. Working the bolt action while sighting, he shifted his weapon rapidly and efficiently--blasting through hummocks of snow and ice where he saw movement. Visibility was poor, and a thick fog bank was slowly overtaking them.

A shot suddenly rang out from the rooftop of the old mess hall; Brian jerked. "Aah! They got me!"

"Roll away," Frank yelled. "Now. Get back."

Blood was gushing out of a chest wound near Brian's heart. He tried to roll, but was too slow. A burst riddled him, and Brian jerked and twisted under deadly fire.

"No!" Frank said.

In a desperate attempt to save his friend, Frank zeroed in on the rooftop sniper with his scope. He was about to squeeze off a shot when a human form covered in animal hides rose behind the target with a spear and harpooned the sniper, who flailed desperately against the stabbing prongs. A shot rang out, striking Clay, who spun and fell through the old roof and out of sight.

Abandoning his weapon, Frank ran and dove across the open doorway.

Brian was twisting against the wall and mumbling incoherently.

Seven or eight bullets had struck him. He was gulping for air. Frank could see him fading, blood flowing from mortal wounds. Brian drew in a ragged breath. Life departed from him in one long gasp.

"Brian . . . What have I done?" Frank said. He drew a deep breath and air hissed through his teeth.

The gunfire thundered and Frank watched bullets chew up a line toward him. He slapped his hand down on Brian's trench gun and ran toward the rear of the hangar while the barrage of gunfire erupted behind him. The horses reared up on their hind legs while Frank gathered up reins and calmed them. Gunfire continued to roar in through the front of the hangar and ricochet off old wings and fuselages. Frank led the horses to the shadowy rear.

Icicles lay on the ground, and Frank shoved a few into saddle bags with the ammo. He moved between the two horses who were calmed by his presence. Grabbing a saddle horn with each hand, he kneed the horses in their bellies. They exploded into a gallop with Frank hanging between them; they cleared the rear hangar door and fled out into the vaporous fog. The Koreans, seeing only the horses in flight, continued to direct their barrage on the hangar.

* * *

From behind a crest of snow and ice, Chull-su unloaded his automatic weapon into the front of the hangar. Fog was thick and he was numb all over. He tried to home in on where he'd heard the Americans yelling. He ducked down low, inserted a new magazine, and chambered a round. Taking advantage of the cover, he crawled to the old building. When he saw the horses run from the old hangar, he knew the Americans were trapped.

He crawled into the old building looking for the Aleut. He knew the Aleut was shot and fell through the roof. But he didn't see the body anywhere. He only saw the dead sniper. Chull-su got up and moved from room to room, very carefully, ending up beneath the hole in the roof. He leaned over and picked up a leather bag. He opened up the bag and looked inside.

He shrieked. The bag fell to the floor next to a scalp of black hair.

"Damn it," he said. "I'll kill you."

He went outside and took cover behind a berm.

The gunfire died down to occasional shots.

"The Aleut escaped," Chull-su yelled. And shooting erupted again. He hoped it was at the Aleut. When the shooting died down again, he yelled, "Some of you, work your way around the back of the hangar and take the Americans from behind."

Twenty minutes later, shots were fired. Yelling forewarned that Chull-su's men were coming out and not to shoot. Shortly, three men stood in front of him.

"Who'd you get?" Chull-su demanded.

"The blonde one."

"Get the others. Now!"

Stiff with internal pain, Chull-su got up onto his feet and nervously looked around into the fog. He could see some of his men crouched behind heaps of snow. Voices carried through the fog.

"Spread out," Chull-su yelled. "Find the others. Shoot the Aleut--but bring the American alive." Chull-su paused. "You hear that?" he yelled, hoping the American could hear him. "Give up now and nobody else gets hurt. You'll only make things harder on yourself by resisting."

Then he heard a faraway voice in the fog. "I'm waiting . . ."

Chull-su yelled, "Bring them to me and we'll see how impudent they are on their knees. Follow their tracks. They can't get away in the snow. Whoever brings them in alive will be honored."

***

After fleeing the airplane hangar into the fog, Frank galloped for a while but slowed his horse when he realized the Koreans were still shooting at the hangar. He hung forward in the saddle, hugging the back of his horse's neck.

He listened to the shots. Sounded as if when lone Koreans, masked by fog, shot at the hangar, the others assumed it was enemy action--and gunfire sparked more gunfire. The same kind of confusion in the fog had cost many American soldiers their lives during the Battle of Kiska during World War Two.

Frank quickly took advantage of the blunder. While the Koreans shot at the empty airplane hangar, he rode his horse and led Brian's alongside, laying two sets of tracks that rounded the perimeter of North Head, a stubby peninsula on the north shore of Kiska Harbor.

That done, he threaded erratically between a few of the numerous lakes that saturated the terrain. When the shooting stopped, he was running the horses through the low valley to the south. He let Brian's horse go, creating a separate set of tracks.

When Chull-su was ordering his men to take the hangar from the rear, Frank didn't slow down. When Chull-su was yelling, Frank answered without slowing as he continued to lay haphazard tracks all the way to Trout Lagoon and back around to a collapsed depression with easy access for his horse.

There were dozens of caves in the soft conglomerate rock around Kiska harbor. Frank had explored several of them. Leaving his horse, he went to a cave he'd been in before. The cave was about ninety feet deep, well built with solid shoring to support the walls and ceiling, and about seven-feet tall. He followed the cave past old stocks of food, medical supplies, equipment, box springs, Japanese shoes, partial bed springs, bed matting, pipes, and bomb fragments.

This cave was also stocked with old hand grenades and anti-personnel mines--unstable hazardous junk. He picked up an old box with Japanese writing on the side and carefully put several mines and grenades inside. He looked for anything else that might be of use, spotting a few coils of wire and white pipes, which he added to his collection. He continued searching while he weighed his circumstances.

When he allowed Brian's temper to stampede him, he'd made a mistake--and now Brian was dead. It didn't matter that his guilt over Karen Nash's death overpowered his common sense. They were both dead. Both of them. And Clay was hit.

Frank dropped to his knees and buried his face in his hands. He remembered Luke and Ingrid and Abby and knew that even now their lives depended on him. He had to get himself together.

Old days, whether Frank was leading third-world guerrillas on jungle raids or mercenaries on missions of terrorist cell annihilation-- understanding the men and discipline comprising the force was critical. War was a killing business and there was no place for half-measures, no place for kindness towards the enemy. In battle, one man was the difference between victory and defeat. One man meant everything.

They had to be stopped.

In Vietnam, Charlie dreaded South Korean soldiers for their cruelty. If a South Korean soldier ever drew his knife, he couldn't put it back in the sheath without blood on the blade. If there was no enemy, they cut themselves. Charlie stayed away.

Frank knew these Koreans were former soldiers. In Korea, military service was not optional. These men were used to guns and violence.

He moved down the tunnel to the entrance and froze before the wall of fog. Out there in the fog he heard movement. Someone was approaching the cave. Frank set down the box out of sight where it had ballistic protection. He lay down at the foot of the portal, elevation and angle providing him with ground cover, and sighted the trench gun. He waited . . . And a body emerged from the mist with an AK-47 leading the way.

Target acquired.

The report dinned home with thunderous kaboom. The man lifted up off his feet and dumped onto his back. Frank descended on him. The man was conscious, but in sad shape.

Frank took his AK and found three extra magazines in his
fatigue jacket. Frank said, "Sorry, mister but you're hunting out of
season." He retrieved the box and hurried to his horse. He put the
debris in saddle bags, mounted up, and rode out.

***

Moon-gon wiped his glove across the ice on his mustache as he
moved stealthily through the snow and fog--his Automat Kalashnikov
assault rifle ready for action, the selector on rock-'n'-roll. Carrying his
rifle like that, he was aware that someone might get hurt. Accidents
happened. He tongued his frozen mustache.

Like many of the other men, he was humiliated by the failure of
the DowKai soldiers during the storm. Fresh off the boat, he and the
other reinforcements would get the job done properly. Better men were
on the job now, and they'd already shot two out of three.

Moon-gon hoped to find the American himself. Bringing him
in alive and wounded would win favor with Mok Don.

As he moved out into the fog, his comrades were some twenty
feet apart. Somehow the Aleut had vanished. Nobody understood how
he got away without making tracks. They were making a clean sweep,
casting a net, but after a while, the others strayed and he no longer
heard their voices. Moon-gon was excited when he picked up tracks
that emerged from a tunnel entrance and trailed blood. This would be
easy.

Whatever trick the Aleut used, Moon-gon was on his trail now.
And then a gunshot cracked like distant thunder . . .

CHAPTER THIRTY-FIVE

When Abby heard shooting in the valley below, she considered turning her horse around and riding back to the bunker. Frank and Brian would have no chance against all those Koreans.

She kept going, riding her horse through the snowy mountain pass.

The dead man was a grisly sight. She stopped her horse. The twisted body looked like it was frozen solid. She squeezed the horse with her knees and rode on.

Why was it so quiet now?

Slowly, Abby rode down through the pass toward the coast.

***

Moon-gon followed the Aleut's trail. Hiking in the snow was hard work. A little pain was nothing compared to the honor he would earn if he brought in a live prisoner.

He licked his mustache so many times that his tongue was aching at the root. He trailed for twenty minutes before he finally saw a form in the mist. The Aleut was pointing at something. Moon-gon stood deathly still watching the vague shape of the Aleut with his gun trained and ready to fire. Moon-gon adjusted his aim carefully.

Slowly he edged forward. The Aleut was too still. As he watched the Aleut, the surrounding fog thickened. All he could see was a fuzzy dark shape.

As he moved closer, he felt hot blood rushing to his face. He now saw that he was stalking a rusty World War Two anti-aircraft gun that was pointed at the sky over the harbor. The Aleut's tracks led right past the old gun and continued on, a trick to confuse pursuers. Moon-gon had lost a couple of minutes, but that's all. He stepped past the anti-aircraft gun and plodded on.

Soon the tracks led him past another rusty anti-aircraft gun. He wasn't fooled this time. He approached boldly and didn't bother to raise his weapon. He trudged on, but the fog gave him a weird sensation. The air was dead still, and it was so quiet. He listened to his footsteps as his boots squeaked in the snow. The trail he was following only showed fifteen or twenty feet ahead of him before mist obscured visibility.

He pushed on, passing a snow-covered pile of gas drums, ruins and revetments of old structures rising like white patterns in the powder. Occasionally he heard his comrades' voices carrying through the fog. This emboldened him. It was twenty against two.

He drudged on for ten more minutes when he saw another silhouette in the fog. The Aleut. Seizing his moment of opportunity, Moon-gon rushed forward and halted within twenty yards.

The Aleut turned around suddenly, looking completely surprised. He was wounded and carried only a spear. He was shot in the left shoulder, blood soaked through his jacket. Moon-gon lifted his rifle. The moment was alive and he found himself floating in clouds of possibilities. Fortune was spilling on him. He smiled despite his numb lips.

"Drop the spear," he said in English, "or I'll help you by shooting your arm off."

The Aleut hesitated.

Moon-gon swung the AK towards the Aleut's shoulder and was about to pull the trigger, when--

Something slammed down fierce over his head and batted the rifle from his hands into the snow. He started to turn, but a hand came around his neck and dragged him downwards. Suddenly he was on his back--and a rifle butt smashed hard in his face, breaking his jaw. As the world began to spin, he heard the American say to the Aleut, "Thank God you're alive. Take my gun and get out of here. When you're safe, tend to your wound. You've got to stop that bleeding."

Moon-gon thought he saw the Aleut handing his spear to the American. And Moon-gon passed out. . . .

***

Abby tied the reins of her horse around a rock and continued on foot. She remembered what her dad had taught her and checked the switch on the rifle. Aim and squeeze--that's all she had to remember.

Hold the rifle snug and tight. No, be quiet and stay out of sight. She didn't want to shoot if she didn't have to. There were too many of them.

She hiked down out of the pass following the horse tracks. Before long, fatigue slowed her knees to a hesitant pace. Instinctively she sensed that her legs could carry her faster in the other direction. Occasionally she stopped and listened. Once she heard Frank's faraway voice but then nothing. Now she stood where she was for several minutes, listening. She heard footsteps not far off.

Abby froze.

The footsteps were slow and methodical. She couldn't tell exactly how close they were but guessed over thirty yards. She remembered that her gun was ready to fire, and she lifted the weapon. The footsteps were getting closer. She could hear them getting louder, but still couldn't see anyone. Squeak . . . thud . . . squeak . . . thud . . .

She wanted to crouch down but didn't dare move for fear of being heard. The footsteps were getting closer.

She must shoot them before they got her. She aimed her weapon at where the footsteps were coming from. She had the advantage, she was ready, and she waited. And the footsteps got louder. Squeak . . . thud . . .

She hoped the unseen person was Frank or Brian. Her heart drummed harder than the muscle ever had in her life; once it occurred to her that they might hear the thumping. That was silly with all the noise their boots were making.

The footsteps stopped. Abby's insides turned to slush. Her chest expanded and contracted to fast breaths. Had they seen her? It was so quiet now they might hear her breathing. They couldn't have been more than twenty yards away. She held her breath and listened. She couldn't hear them breathing, so she let out her breath and drew in another. She tried to breath slowly, but couldn't. The barrel of her rifle wouldn't hold still . . .

If it weren't so cold, she might have been in a giant steam bath with steam so dense she couldn't see people she could easily talk to. Then she heard a recognizable sound and saw a spark. It happened again, only this time she could make out a tiny flame in the vapor. Somebody was lighting a cigarette. They hadn't seen her. She trained her rifle on the person, but didn't dare pull the trigger because if she did, everyone would know where she was.

Did Brian smoke? She didn't think so, but suddenly she couldn't remember.

The flame vanished, and the footsteps started up again. She stood rigidly, ready to pull the trigger and suffer whatever fate befell her. They couldn't be more than a step or two from visibility. Any moment they'd step into view, and she'd see a look of surprise on their face--and she'd pull the trigger. And then it would be all over for her.

Squeak . . . thud . . . squeak . . . thud . . .

***

Jung Dae-sung followed the tracks through the fog until he came to an area where there had been a scuffle in the blood-stained snow. He stopped and his big round eyes moved slowly back and forth like wet olives. His big mouth curled slightly into a grin. He was tense with fear, but realized it was just a matter of finishing off the wounded. Mok Don had explained that these people were ignorant farmers, and could be easily handled.

After following the tracks for a while longer, he heard an unmistakable groaning sound. He followed the trail of blood. There seemed to be two sets of tracks, but then both tracks were wiped out by something heavy that was being dragged through the snow. The groaning was getting louder, but in the fog he couldn't see anything. One set of tracks broke away, and he followed the dragging thing toward the groaning sound.

He hiked for a long ways and came upon Moon-gon, lying in the snow, his face a bloody mess, his mouth covered with duct tape. He was struggling, but couldn't seem to get up. It appeared he was hurt badly, and there was a wild look in his eyes.

"You idiot," Jung Dae-sung said. "Shut up and be quiet."

Jung Dae-sung set down his rifle and got down on his knees to remove the duct tape from Moon-gon's mouth. Moon-gon's head jerked back and forth. Moon-gon was acting crazy, moaning even louder.

"Shut up or I'll leave you gagged."

Suddenly Moon-gon rolled over with startling quickness.

The American was beneath him, and he sprang up. A knife flashed and rent a gaping wound in Jung Dae-sung's shoulder. Jung Dae-sung attempted diving on the American, but instead he took a stunning blow to the side of his neck which left him disoriented. He buckled onto his side. The American leapt upon him and put a blade to his throat.

***

Abby stood with her gun pointed and ready to fire. An obscure shape emerged from the fog. Her finger touched the trigger. A few more steps and . . .

A scream shrieked in the tense stillness.

The scream was quite a ways off, but Abby gasped and reflexively crouched a few inches. The vague shape made a sudden movement. Abby drew in a deep breath of air. She shifted the rifle slightly. But the shape disappeared. She heard footsteps pounding off into the distance.

***

Lim Ju-jang's head turned back and forth, his jaw rigid, his chest panting beneath his thick brown insulated body suit.

He couldn't see anything and had no idea where he was. The others had strayed from him.

He kept replaying the death-shriek of his comrade Jung Dae-sung. He knew the voice all too well. Every quick breath he took was laborious and strained.

Lim Ju-jang heard something and spun around. Nothing there. Somebody stalking him. He slunk down the gently sloping hill-- movement at the corner of his eye. He turned. Nothing. Nobody. Apparition gone.

More screams in the fog.

Jung Dae-sung was still alive. What were they doing to him? Another scream--

All the tension in Lim Ju-jang's body welled up in a surge of anger.

He closed in, lifting his legs in the snow, lunging forward, over and over. He would avenge Jung Dae-sung. Hatred and wrath fueled his strength. He ran, lifting his legs and lunging forward.

Other voices began yelling out in the fog. "Where are you?"

"Stop," Jung Dae-sung shrieked.

Lim Ju-jang froze. Then moved. Cautious, careful, calculating, panting.

He closed in, his jaw stiff.

He wanted to continue running, but he didn't know where the Americans were. He felt the tension in his body would impair his reactions. He guessed he was within forty meters and slowed down to a cautious pace.

He froze in his tracks. Couldn't remember if he put a fresh clip in his gun. Double checked--clip ready.

English to his left.

Lim Ju-jang spun. A figure loomed in the mist. Figure turned on him. Lim Ju-jang's gun erupted in a burst of sheer power.

The American was blown off his feet and riddled. "I got him, I got him, he's down."

His wrath controlled his faculties. He fired bursts of vengeance, his machine gun arcing as he swept the roaring weapon back and forth. He emptied the magazine, and his trigger onslaught halted.

"American down," he yelled. "Down hard."

Lim Ju-jang heard a few distant cheers of victory.

He tromped over to the body. The snow in the area was sprayed with blood. He had wasted him with numerous hits. "Confirmed," he yelled out. "Confirmed."

But when he got closer—

No. Couldn't be.

He'd shot one of their own. Shaking--fiercely.

"He's alive," Lim Ju-jang yelled. "American alive."

He turned away from the body. On his third step, something slipped out of the fog and took him clean off his feet. He landed on his side--horrified--with a spear imbedded in his upper chest cavity.

His gun. Where was his gun?

"I'm down," he screamed.

He rolled but the pain made him howl.

The American walked out of the fog. Calm and unhurried.

He said, "You prey on the innocent and the helpless. You deserve what you get." He lifted his AK at Lim Ju-jang's head.

Lim Ju-jang shook his head.

The American hesitated. He lowered his AK.

With one hand, he wrenched at the spear in Lim Ju-jang's shoulder. Lim Ju-jang wailed in pain. More twisting unleashed agony. The spear dug in. Finally, the man dislodged it with brute strength, and Lim Ju-jang shrieked.

The American turned away.

Lim Ju-jang still had the 9mm in the shoulder holster. He reached for the weapon with his good arm. The American spun around and stabbed the spear into Lim Ju-jang's thigh.

Lim Ju-jang yelled from his gut.

A boot slammed into his ear. He twisted on the ground.

When he opened his eyes, the American was gone.

***

Frank strapped on his snowshoes and began moving up a snow dune taking long, easy strides. He snowshoed for some time until he heard the voices of two men. Their tone was cautious, but it revealed men who didn't understand how calm water and cold air carried sound. Frank waited and discerned their direction of progress. He began snowshoeing in their direction laying tracks directly in their path. He hiked for some ten minutes to a small hatchway in the ground, which he found easily because he marked it years ago with a tall, thin metal stake so nobody fell in. The hole was small, and snow had accumulated until it completely covered the opening. Frank pulled up the stake. He lunged over the low spot where the hole was, his snowshoes allowing a long stride. He hiked over the next ridge and entered the tunnel.

Little warehouses of food and ammunition, clothing, old bulletproof vests, medical and other supplies were buried all over the harbor area and well camouflaged. The vault was dark, and after removing his snowshoes, Frank hurried down the tunnel.

As he anticipated, the men picked up his trail and he soon heard their voices. Several minutes passed when a body stepped through the snow-covered hatchway and plunged twelve feet down into the vault, landing just inches from Frank. The body buckled on the floor. The man groaned. Frank leapt onto him, delivering a fierce blow to the bifurcation of the carotid artery that immediately left the man unconscious. Frank grabbed his lariat and gained his feet. He held the rope out and waited.

He heard excited Korean chatter up above. He waited perhaps ten seconds, when suddenly an unsuspecting face looked down into the hole. The man's eyes took a moment to adjust to the light.

Frank swung the loop up, pulled the rope tight around his neck, and tugged. The man slid in through the hole and fell twelve feet onto his head. Frank didn't have to neutralize him.

CHAPTER THIRTY-SIX

Chull-su moved very cautiously when he sent out the patrol. Murdoch was dangerous and these greenhorns didn't appreciate what they were up against.

Hang Doo-hee and Bae were walking ahead of him; a sailor with black-rimmed glasses named Won-song brought up the rear. They moved slowly and tightly. Time passed like nagging torment. Since the last attack, Chull-su heard screams and pleas in the distance.

The search was confusing. They followed a set of horse tracks, which led them in a maddening circle. They came upon tracks all over the place now. Most were from his own men. But Chull-su had no way of knowing which ones were which, and each time the tension level rose. With each new set, he sent Hang Doo-hee or Bae to scout it out. They'd follow for twenty or thirty meters and then return. From there they'd all move on until they came across more tracks. And the process was repeated.

They spotted a bridge with tracks over it. Hang Doo-hee felt this was a likely ambush site. He was a former soldier with combat experience. He approached the bridge like a cat stalking a bird. He wore no hat and kept his bald head slightly sideways. His eyes were narrow, curved slits. He searched under the bridge, but found nothing.

They followed the cries, but the cries stopped, and all they found was a body. They worked their way down to the beach. They passed some rusty oil and gas drums and other debris peeking out of the snow. They moved along the beach for a while.

And then the American yelled to them, a voice on the fog: "Too many have died, already. Leave the island now."

And the voice seemed to come in off the water. Chull-su was startled. Was he on the pier? or at one of the points which Chull-su had glimpsed earlier? Or down the beach in one direction or the other? He couldn't be sure.

The whole coast was engulfed in a soupy fog.

"Magook," he yelled. "You're getting desperate, you're getting scared, your luck is running out. Twenty men are hunting you. You cannot possibly get away. Give up."

Silence followed.

***

After tethering his horse, Frank took an old frag grenade from the saddle bag and went to the submarine base. The buildings were now buried ruins, so the midget submarine was the only relic in sight. The "Type A" was a two-man sub, 24 meters long, and 2 meters in width. The conning tower rose roughly 2 meters from the hull.

The beach dune was slowly claiming the old sub, banking up against and burying most of her starboard side. With snow piled on top of that, only her port side was completely exposed. A bomb blast had long ago ripped a large hole just below the conning tower which now provided access; you simply stepped in through the rent in the side.

The old submarine railway was buried, but a ramp-like grade sloped down to the sub between snow-covered dunes. Korean tracks scribbled a busy sketch in the snow around the sub and ramp. He walked up onto the dune behind the tower and ducked down, burying himself in snow. Since the snow in the area was already stirred up, he didn't expect the additional disturbance to attract any attention. And he waited.

He didn't like waiting for the action to come to him. It was axiomatic in the art of war that the side to stay behind its fortified line was always defeated. But guerrilla warfare had its own demands, and waiting was often one of them. Circumstances governed action. Neutralizing the enemy was the only issue; preferred method of warfare was irrelevant.

He heard voices. Two Koreans came down the ramp. Frank saw them through a small peek-hole in the snow just above his rifle.

He rose in the snow and swung his rifle over the conning tower. Hostile greeting awaited as the second man opened up on roaring automatic, swinging his rifle hysterically; flesh-seeking ammo ricocheted and scattered on the conning tower. Frank answered in kind: the blazing muzzle of his AK executed a small arc, the reports coming together as stark thunder. A rainstorm of ordinance made contact with the enemy, punching him backwards like he'd been hit with a jackhammer, socking and thumping him down, leaving him sprawled and terminated in the snow.

The second man dropped to his knees and blasted away on full automatic, swinging his rifle from left to right. Frank squeezed off another burst, two slugs catching his forehead, a crimson mist settling on the snow behind him. Before moving on, Frank executed a tactical reload, slamming in a new magazine against a half-spent one.

***

Hang Doo-hee was on point as they moved down the beach. His ears ached from the cold, but he didn't want to dull his senses by wearing a stocking cap. He wore the military coat that he stole when he deserted the Korean army. He deserted after learning he was about to be arrested and court marshaled for assaulting a superior officer. In the Korean Army, he'd received numerous medals, and finally joined special forces, where he was trained by elite American advisors.

He walked in front of Chull-su, his sick leader. The man deserved to die.

Hang Doo-hee concentrated on listening and watching. He was hunting a living, armed enemy. The high couldn't be matched. More than once he saw himself back in the demilitarized zone, conducting patrols, hunting communist infiltrators.

He held his AK firmly, and due to the fog, moved the selector switch to automatic. When they came to the pier, they searched between and around the four floating pontoon cubes that rested nearby. Someone had been there and gone.

Chull-su snapped his fingers. Hang Doo-hee looked over at him, and Chull-su motioned for him to check the pier. Hang Doo-hee didn't like it. Waves had washed over the big dock and left ice. No tracks were visible on the ice. He had no idea what was out there, who was out there.

The American was in his own territory and was killing Chull-su's men. Hang Doo-hee scowled and slowly started moving down the pier. He moved slowly and carefully, one step at a time.

He focused on survival. He was possibly entering a hot zone, and he felt the tension. The mental drain was tiring. In the DMZ, there were hot zones; he'd nearly died in one. He lived then, he'd live now. The American was formidable, but Hang Doo-hee would kill him.

He moved slowly. After he'd gone a hundred yards, he could go no further. The pier had been ravaged by storms. The pilings leaned at angles as though they'd all been pulled over by some unworldly force. Hang Doo-hee didn't know how much farther the pier went due to the fog, but given the tilt and the ice, he turned back. The fog was so thick on the harbor that he couldn't even see the *Pinisha*, though he could hear the generators, and the ship wasn't far off.

Back at the beach, he shook his head at Chull-su , who pointed up the shoreline.

Hang Doo-hee led the patrol up the beach. At one point he saw footprints in the rocky sand. The American had run at the water's edge and wavelets had washed most of the prints away. If he turned inland, his prints would become visible. They never turned inland. He was on the American's trail.

***

Abby heard the voices echoing through the frosty, damp vapors. Hearing Frank's voice, knowing he was alive gave her purpose, renewed determination to find him, but she wasn't sure which direction his voice came from. She kept replaying his ghostly tone and his ominous warning to the Koreans. She knew there were a lot of Koreans and suspected they were spread out all over the place. She didn't know which way to go.

She heard one man plead in Korean, his voice betraying fear and misery: "Someone help me."

There was no reply. It was eerily silent for a while then the same voice moaned out again. "My leg . . . I'm bleeding . . . help me . . ."

Perhaps this last plea brought help. Abby heard no more of the wounded man's pleading after that.

Fortunately, she was still breathing after nearly coming face-to-face with one of those killers. But she wasn't doing anything to help Frank. Her chances of even finding him were small. The area stretched far in all directions, and she couldn't see more than a few feet.

Better she hiked back up into the hills where she would be safer. Down here, there was nothing she could do but stumble around in the fog. Hiking back up the hill, she found her legs carrying her lightly. She'd gone perhaps fifty yards when she heard a voice--and it was uphill from her.

"See anything?" the voice said in Korean.

Another voice answered, "I've found tracks leading down toward the water. Let's see where they go."

Abby missed a breath. The very tracks she was following uphill, the Koreans were now following downhill, right toward her. She turned and quickly started downhill. After only a few steps, she slipped and fell flat on her face. After wiping the snow from her face, she looked around for her gun. In the snow there were two sets of horse tracks, her own tracks, and the disturbance where she'd fallen. But her gun was lost under the snow.

Frantically she dug in the snow, but she couldn't find her rifle. She reached down into the powder and felt around with her arms. Nothing. Then it occurred to her. The gun had slid like a ski. But how far might it have gone? She made a guess of five or six feet and started digging there. She didn't find it, and the men couldn't be far away.

She heard something. She stiffened, listened intently. The men were closer than she thought. There was no more time to look for her gun. She rose and started down the hill, hiking as fast as she could. She fell a second time, but got up and hurried on into the thickening vapors.

She followed the horse tracks for lack of a better direction to go. Then she decided that if she turned in another direction, there was a fifty-fifty chance her pursuers would continue to follow the horse tracks and she'd lose them. So she broke away and headed down toward the water, hiking through the fuzziness of the island's smoky stretches. The muscles in her legs burned. She slowed down to a more manageable stride since she might have to keep going for a long time. She'd gone quite a ways when she saw a big Korean emerge from the ghostly vapor.

And he was looking straight at her.

CHAPTER THIRTY-SEVEN

After checking out the pier, Hang Doo-hee returned to the beach, where Chull-su and the others awaited him. His senses were heightened enough that if he made contact, his reactions would prove deadly. He assumed point, and the sweep continued. As he progressed down the beach, the terrain steepened. Soon he was moving along rocky cliffs over the water. And it started snowing.

When Chull-su called Mok Don on the walkie-talkie, Hang Doo-hee stood lookout and listened. While they were waiting, Hang Doo-hee reached under his jacket and felt the dog tags on his necklace that rested against his chest. There were four dog tags, and he rubbed them together for good luck. One of the tags was his. The other three tags he took off North Korean infiltrators years ago after killing them in the DMZ.

Mok Don came on the walkie-talkie. *"What's going on out there?"*

"We're trying to flush him out," Chull-su said. "We killed one and wounded the other. Murdoch is still alive."

"He better be. I want him now."

This mission stank. Hang Doo-hee didn't like it when the enemy's life was considered more valuable than his own. Not only that, he was guarding against an attack while Chull-su spoke too loudly. It angered Hang Doo-hee to think the American could probably hear the conversation, too. Chull-su was compromising their position. Easily a fatal mistake.

"We have more casualties," Chull-su said.

"*How many?*"

"Several."

"*With twenty men you can't get him?*"

"Of course we can."

"*Murdoch is an assassin.*"

"What? Why didn't you tell me?" Chull-su said.

An assassin. Hang Doo-hee's adrenaline picked up. He thought he was tracking a fisherman. Now suddenly he's hunting an assassin.

"*Don't question me,*" Mok Don said. "*I tell you what you need to know.*" There was a pause . . . "*I don't care who he is; he can't kill all of you. Bring him in alive.*"

"What about the wounded? Somebody will have to--"

"*Do your job.*"

"We'll get him." Chull-su stuffed the walkie-talkie into his pocket.

Hang Doo-hee turned on Chull-su. "What makes you think you'll get Murdoch? He's already taken out several of your men."

Chull-su was looking angry. "What do you suggest?"

"He may be dangerous, but I can kill him. I'll lead the way. You follow me. Very slowly. And keep quiet."

"I'll cover from behind," Chull-su said. "Bae, you stay next to me. Won-song, you follow."

Wearing a black knit facemask, Bae's head began shifting back and forth.

"Some fisherman." Won-song said, "We're not hunting him, he's hunting us."

Chull-su pointed at him. "Shut up."

"He's killing us, one by one."

"Enough."

"You heard Mok Don. We have no idea who we're dealing with."

"I told you to shut your mouth. You don't respect Mok Don? You don't respect DowKai authority?"

Chull-su lifted his AK-47 and fired a burst into Won-song's face at point-blank range. Brains and gore exploded out the back of his skull. The right side of his face was blown off before he hit the ground.

Hang Doo-hee was shocked. His muscles tensed, ready to swing his rifle at Chull-su if he tried to take him out too.

Chull-su glared over at him and gestured for him to get moving.

Hang Doo-hee nodded, but didn't like having this lunatic behind him. He moved slowly through the fog along the top of the cliff. Occasionally they heard some distant yelling of men, but mostly it was quiet. After a while they started seeing footprints all over. Hang Doo-hee slowed down even more.

"It must be him," Chull-su said. "There are footprints and horse tracks. We're getting close."

"Freeze," Hang Doo-hee said, holding up his hand to warn the others.

"What's going on?" Chull-su said.

Hang Doo-hee looked back at him. "See anything unusual?"

"Get to the point."

"If you want to live, keep your eyes open. See those trip wires?" Hang Doo-hee pointed.

Chull-su took a few steps forward. He gestured to Bae. "Keep back, everybody."

Hang Doo-hee shook his head. "He strung the wires around that white stake, which he thought would blend in with the snow. Thought we wouldn't see it in the fog; and if we did, and stepped over them, one of us would fumble and set off a charge. Wait here."

Hang Doo-hee followed the wires for thirty meters, where he found them attached to another white stake and two hand grenades. It was sloppy work: The snow was tampered with all over, and he spotted a poorly concealed land mine. There were probably several more in the area from the looks of the snow. Carefully he made his way back.

"Looks like Murdoch set up a mine field over there. The mines are rusty, probably left on the island in World War Two. And the wires are attached to corroded hand grenades. I'm not sure if any of that stuff is still capable of detonating, but I don't want to find out the hard way.

There's enough space over by the cliff to go around. The snow hasn't been disturbed over there. Bae, you go first."

Bae nodded and started over toward the edge of the cliff. He looked back, his eyes wide open, peering through the holes in his knit facemask.

Hang Doo-hee said, "Stay away from that stake. The grenades might still work."

Bae nodded again. "No problem. There's plenty of room." He hiked past the stake, very carefully moving along the edge.

"Good," Hang Doo-hee said--but suddenly the edge of the cliff gave way, and Bae screamed. In the blink of an eye, he disappeared down the edge of the cliff. The scream lasted maybe a couple seconds. Hang Doo-hee heard a soft thud and some tumbling rocks; after that, silence. Hang Doo-hee approached the edge and looked down. Bae was buried under a slide of snow and boulders.

Hang Doo-hee returned to Chull-su. "He's dead."

Chull-su cursed.

"It was a snow cornice," Hang Doo-hee said. "The edge was unstable there. The American knew it."

"You knew," Chull-su said.

"I suspected a trap."

Chull-su said, "You try and sacrifice me and I'll put a bullet in your back." He paused and looked around. "Let's head back down to the beach. The whole area's probably booby-trapped." He cursed.

"Keep your voice down," Hang Doo-hee said. "We're in the middle of a kill zone."

Chull-su peered into the fog and suddenly lifted his AK-47. "You hear that?"

"You didn't hear anything," Hang Doo-hee said. "If he was that close, I'd kill him."

Chull-su motioned to proceed.

"Slowly," Hang Doo-hee said, "very slowly." As they started back down, he walked backwards against a rear assault.

Back at the beach, wavelets foamed up on the sand. The noise irritated him because it was more difficult to listen for noise. On the other hand, the water hid the sounds they were making walking along the shore. The fog thickened. The snow continued to fall. They didn't worry about cover. They'd practically have to bump into Murdoch to be seen.

All of a sudden Hang Doo-hee heard something up ahead of them. The moment was shattered as automatic fire blared out from behind him.

He hit the dirt.

"Die!" Chull-su yelled as he blasted his AK-47 blindly into the fog. "Die, you decadent pig!"

Then the shooting stopped. Hang Doo-hee heard his comrades shouting in Korean. "Get down," he yelled at Chull-su. Hang Doo-hee rolled over and saw Chull-su dive to the ground.

A moment later several bursts of return fire clattered out. Then there was more yelling.

"Who's there?" Chull-su said.

"It's Hyun. You nearly killed us! You hit one of our own."

Hang Doo-hee and Chull-su found his brother and a new guy who was quiet and jumpy. Hyun was staring at the body. "He's dead."

"He shot first," Chull-su said.

Hyun nodded. "We saw the American a few minutes ago. We were following his tracks in the sand when this fool panicked."

Hang Doo-hee listened to all this with mounting disgust. "You want him, you'll have him. I'm going after him alone."

                                    ***

After Hang Doo-hee left, Chull-su split them into groups of two. "You head up the hill," he told the others. "Hyun and I will sweep the beach behind Hang Doo-hee."

They were turning to go when Chull-su heard a strange whipping sound. He immediately dropped to his knees. The others followed his example. An earsplitting gunshot rang out. A rumbling was getting closer.

A scream.

A horse charged out of the fog, running. The rider sprayed the beach with his AK on automatic.

There was just enough time for Chull-su to dive out of the way. He rolled twice. When he looked up, he saw a body dragging on a rope. For just a second, he made eye contact with Hang Doo-hee. He saw a look of sheer terror--a grotesque curse twisting on a doomed face as Hang Doo-hee slid off into the fog. Chull-su heard another scream. He lay there in shock for several moments, listening to shots out in the fog.

He was drawing in strained breaths, but the air was too cold and he started coughing. After several minutes of that, he motioned for the other two men to fall in behind him. They followed the American's trail for about five minutes before they found Hang Doo-hee's body in the sand, the rope still around his neck. He'd been shot.

Chull-su heard something down the beach. He turned and saw something moving in the fog--an old gas drum rolling down the embankment.

"Take cover," he yelled.

Automatic fire clattered out--drawing a line across the rolling barrel. A tracer hit.

Whump!

The sky ignited.

A firestorm burst forth. Everyone was knocked down by a stunning concussion. Chull-su landed hard. Fire rained around him. He turned over and the beach was burning in flaming streaks and patches. He saw the quiet new guy thrashing in the sand, his clothes on fire. The man got up, ran for the water, and dove in. Only then did the man scream. He thrashed wildly and came out of the water as rapidly as he'd gone in. How badly he was burned Chull-su didn't know, but his face looked alright and he went for his weapon.

"Let's get out of here," Chull-su said. He got up and led a charge down the beach in the opposite direction.

Suddenly a barrage of gunfire erupted, spraying the area and cutting them off. All three hit the ground. Sand spit up all around them. Nobody moved except to ball up. Chull-su reached for the walkie-talkie to tell Mok Don they were pinned down, but he thought again. A burst of gunfire was followed by several more. Hyun and the quiet one returned fire now. Chull-su emptied another thirty-round clip into the fog. The quiet one screamed again.

Then piercing silence . . .

Silence short-lived. The quiet one cried out in pain. A bullet had pierced his hip. He moaned and made hoarse curses. Chull-su crawled over to the man, who now managed to contain himself. Every breath came like a grievance.

"As soon as we capture him, we'll get you back to the ship. We have to keep moving. I'm taking your gun."

"You can't leave me here without my gun."

Chull-su jerked the rifle from his hands and crawled back to the others. He motioned for them to follow and he got up. "Stay low," he told them.

"Don't leave me," the quiet one said. "I'll freeze." This from a man who was just on fire. "Please, I need help. Oh, please, he'll kill me. I'm part of the group. At least leave my gun. At least do that. Have mercy, please. Please!"

Chull-su led the men about thirty feet down the beach and then dropped to his belly. He motioned for the others to get down. Hyun crawled up next to him.
"What are we doing?"

"Listen to him moaning in pain. In this pea-soup fog, I can just barely make him out from here. The American will come to finish him off. Then we'll hit him."

"It might work," Hyun said, the material of his surgical mask stretching from his smile.

Chull-su waited. The wounded man's pleas grew morbid. Chull-su watched the fog beyond him and falling snow illuminated by the flames. He waited for a shadow to emerge from the fog. Never came. Ten minutes passed.

The others said nothing. They waited another five minutes, but still the American didn't show. "Let's stick together," Chull-su said.

He was in the middle as they patrolled down the beach. They'd just found two bodies by the old Japanese submarine when someone called to them in Korean.

"It's Soo-man. Don't shoot."

Three DowKai men and a woman emerged from the fog, led by the muscular security director. "Look what we found," Soo-man said. "Abby the archaeologist." He slapped her bottom.

Abby was brought to Chull-su. He slapped her hard across the face. "You try something, I'll hurt you bad."

"You're disgusting," she said

Again he slapped her, this time even harder. He almost knocked her down. "I don't like you." He slapped her again.

Soo-man said, "Keep her pretty."

Ignoring him, Chull-su kicked her in the gut. She let out a loud shriek.

"You hear that?" Chull-su yelled into the fog. "We have the woman. Give up or she dies."

No answer . . .

Slowly, Chull-su turned his head toward Abby. While he waited, his stare began to crumble with his growing smile. "Give up," he yelled.

No answer . . .

Chull-su looked at the others and grinned. Soo-man grinned. Chull-su dropped his rifle and lunged at the woman. She screamed when he grabbed her jacket, tearing it. He tackled her. Again she screamed and fought back, but Soo-man dropped his gun and pinned down her arms.

"Let her go," the American said, his voice near in the fog.

Soo-man grabbed his gun and swung it around while staying on his knees.

Chull-su was startled by the sudden proximity of the threat. He rolled off Abby with his nerves bristling and dragged her up onto her feet. He grabbed her by her brown hair and yanked her head back. Pointed the AK-47 at her skull. "I'll kill her."

The American emerged slowly from the fog, anger burning in his green eyes, his gun aimed at Chull-su. "Let her go," he said. "Now."

Chull-su let go of her hair and reached around her neck, pulled her tight and began choking her. "I'll kill her. Give up." The woman was gagging, tugging at his arm.

The American stepped closer in the fog with his gun aimed at Chull-su's face. "Let her go. I'll tell you where the treasure is."

Chull-su loosened his hold on her throat. She gasped for air.

The American raised his gun slightly. "I'll shoot you straight in the eyes. Let her go, or I'll blow your head off at the count of three. After she leaves, I'll go with you. One--"

Chull-su let the woman loose. She picked up her jacket and staggered over to the American. He leaned over and whispered into her ear without taking his eyes off Chull-su.

"No, Frank."

"Do it!"

The woman glared back at Chull-su , then walked off into the fog.

"Now we're giving her time to clear out of the area," the American said.

Over the next hour, there were some distant pleas from the wounded, but nobody helped them. The gun was pointed at Chull-su's head. But power was about to change hands.

CHAPTER THIRTY-EIGHT

Frank walked out in front of the swarthy thugs and every step seemed to have consequence. His cheeks were heavy and he could feel the sag in his face. He felt dark and cold as if his soul had died, like the

batteries were ripped out. The Koreans talked loudly and angrily. The
snow was blowing down harder now in the gusty wind.

There would be no eulogy, no epitaph, no last words. The
Koreans owned him now, and he was all they needed or wanted. At
least Frank had something left to bargain with. If he told them where
the gold was, he could save the lives of the others. He would do
everything he could to save Luke, Abby and Ingrid.

Two of the Koreans walked behind him with their rifles trained
at his back. They directed him into a large, motorized skiff. They rode
over the waves with cold wind blowing in off the mournful sea.

With eyes closed and chin on chest, Frank thought about Luke,
Abby, and Ingrid. Trapped in the dark of the bunker, huddled around
the fire.

The engine cut, and Frank opened his eyes as the skiff coasted
the final stretch to the boarding ladder on the ship's leeward side.
Chull-su led the way, and Frank followed him up the ladder.

Four men climbed onto the stern after them, and Frank heard the
skiff motor shoreward. Two brawny Koreans approached the group
and excused the land party. They seized Frank by the arms and ushered
him down the catwalk and into the accommodation. An elevator let
them off on the second deck, where they locked Frank in a luxurious
stateroom. He heard Korean chatter out in the hall, the two brawny
men on guard duty.

The cabin was fully carpeted in forest green. Furnishings
included a large bed, Persian-silk upholstered divan, antique table,
Dutch captain's desk, Russian lacquer seaman's closet, and mini-
refrigerator. He opened a door and found a sparkling full bath. What a
way to die. When a man created his own hell, no earthly comfort could
ever give him peace. Even unto death.

The round porthole opened to seaward. Gray water and gray
sky converged into distant gray clouds.

He sat down on the bed. The door swung open and a swarthy
Korean man walked in followed by the two guards. The man had gray
hair and cold, obsidian eyes that shifted stealthily before freezing on

Frank. "So you think you can fight Mok Don and get away with it," he said.

Frank returned his glare. Mok Don's eyes were like beholding black ice.

The man dominated silence. He waited as though expecting some grand gesticulation from Frank, perhaps a bow or some motion of deference. Frank waited. Finally Mok Don grew impatient and spoke.

"Where's the gold?"

"And if I tell you?"

"I'll let your son live," Mok Don said quietly. "I'll let the women live. And maybe you too."

"North of here in a cave."

Mok Don's eyes narrowed to cracks of shiny blackness with crow's feet. He began eagerly unfolding a map, walked over to Frank, and laid it out on the bed.

"Show me."

"There." Frank pointed to Musashi Inlet.

Mok Don took a deep breath and spoke softly: "And the cave?"

"You'll find it."

"You better hope I do, or I'll kill your son," Mok Don said, as though murdering children was in the normal course of business. He folded the map and walked out of the cabin, closing the door behind him.

Ten minutes later, Frank heard them heave anchor followed by the grumble of marine diesels. He was being led to the sepulcher; but worse, his life had been a complete and evil failure. He had prematurely ended Brian and Karen's lives through the choices he had made. He felt low. He had many successes in life, yet in the most important things, his history was marked by failure on the road to doom. He remembered the day he first entered the treasure cave with Luke. He recalled the volcanic rumblings and his hellish visions of the molten depths. How appropriate, he thought. Even the grimmest destiny couldn't be any worse than how he already felt.

Soon the *Pinisha* again dropped anchor. Frank didn't get up and look out the port hole. He couldn't stand to look at Kiska, his home, where Luke, Abby, and Ingrid waited for him in a bunker. Only they didn't know he'd never return. Luke needed a father. Frank wasn't much of that, but Luke needed him. He couldn't let his kid down. The boy's faith in Frank was both heartening and humbling. Today the thought of it felt like an indictment.

The *Pinisha* lay at anchor for twenty-four hours. From the decks alow wandered the sounds of shouted commands, of hydraulics and cranes, of the lifting and lowering of treasure. Each sound sucked life and blood from Frank; each sound confirmed his existence and his fate; each sound robbed his son a father. And he could do nothing. Hours rolled by like waves in sets as he waited. When he lay on the bed, he felt like a dirty rag. He thought of Melody, his dear sweet wife who'd given her life to him. She too was dead, and Frank blamed himself for that. He took a blanket and lay on the floor.

He thought of Virgil: of Aeneus ready to abandon hope and he saw himself; except there was no Divine reassurance for Frank Murdoch, only black condemnation. If the Koreans didn't hurry up and kill him, he might die of his own shame. And then came sleep, and with sleep came nightmares, horrible nightmares welling up from deep within his subconscious mind wherein was stored all the horror and disgrace of his past, all the guilt that had ruined his life and ran him through a perpetual living hell.

He dreamt of a man in a field, lined up in the sights of his sniper's rifle. Frank squeezed off a shot and the man buckled and dropped. Then the man's family walked into the field wearing black. They cried and mourned. The wife looked at Frank and screamed, "You murderer! Why did you have to kill him? He was all we had. You destroyed our family!" And Frank saw the face of his own wife.

He awoke shaking, sweating. Anger burned in him. How long he'd slept he didn't know, but light shined brightly through the port hole. He felt like a tormented, caged animal, sapped of life and spirit.

Soon the big marine diesels rumbled. The *Pinisha* sailed, her single screw shoving her seaward. The soft rumblings of the ship's engines gave Frank at least a glimmer of hope. At last they were leaving Kiska. Luke, Abby, and Ingrid would be safe.

Frank looked out the porthole and watched Kiska Island grow small on the gray horizon. As the island got farther away, he knew his own death was getting closer.

The hours seemed endless, tugging by one after another as the *Pinisha* steamed south. Frank had no more visitors, except the steward who grew increasingly rude. Frank ate none of the meals he brought. For two nights, Frank waited, sinister thoughts polluting his mind and dimming his spirit. At times he lay on the floor, unable to sleep, tossing, rolling. He endured his miserable time in oppressive darkness thinking of how he failed his family, about how he regretted his life. But anger grew in him, anger at the vicious predators who killed the innocent, anger at terrorists who exploded bombs in crowded cities; and toward the vicious greed of scum like Mok Don.

He studied his cabin, inch by inch, bolt by bolt. He tried to think of a way to escape, but no plan with a reasonable chance of success formulated in his mind. The boat was full of armed men, and land, hundreds of miles away.

Morning's light filtered in the porthole again. Frank lay huddled on the floor, his body aching, his soul painful. Then came sleep.

He awoke shaking, sweating.

A knock on the door jarred his senses. A pause. The door opened. The steward walked in with a platter of food. He carried the platter to the table, set it down, and picked up the untouched one he had brought hours earlier. He shook his head on the way out.

Frank closed his eyes, falling away, falling back into numb sleep . . . A knock on the door . . . Another knock. Had his last hour arrived?

CHAPTER THIRTY-NINE
Kiska Island

Chull-su searched the houses of the Americans, but found no sign of the women or the boy. Tired and in no particular hurry, he slept in Murdoch's bed. He spent two nights there resting, recovering from the hunt. Finally, it was clear that Chull-su needed to get moving.

Unfortunately, his whiskey and cigarettes had run out, and his flesh demanded attention. Despite a spinning misery, he got up and searched the place, but found no liquor. As he became more desperate, he tore the place apart looking for hidden alcohol, but again came up empty-handed.

He set out on foot, hiking down the beach. The fresh snow made for hard treading when he strayed from the shoreline. Before long, the pains clawed at his gut and he found himself unable to go far without stopping. To make matters worse, a chill moved over him as his under-sweating cooled. To his relief, he arrived at the smaller houses down the beach and took to searching them. In the first home, he found pelt-clothes in the closet and no alcohol. In the second, he found a case of American whiskey that they'd overlooked when they gave the American woman the humiliation she deserved. Chull-su grabbed a fifth and sucked on it. A little infusing therapy. Several more bottles went into his pack. He left promptly, well aware that the Aleut might still be alive on the island.

Soon his headache went away as did the pain in his gut. Now he was ready to hunt again. He decided against following the path they took on the night of the first storm when they saw the ambush party. He didn't want to go near the bodies of the men who had been killed there if he didn't have to.

He doubled back towards the main house and cut inland through a pass between the mountains. The snow made for miserable travel and soon he was reconsidering the coastal route. But recollections of those faces of the dead urged him on. He followed a creek, but kept plenty clear. He wasn't going to fall in and freeze.

As he stayed with this route he was surprised to find himself moving through a herd of thousands of sheep spread out over the snow. The snow was trampled down which made for easy passing.

Beyond the mountains, the snow stretched on endlessly. He spent three hours trudging through some of the bleakest and most hopeless and despairing whiteness he'd ever seen. Every few seconds he checked his backside and searched the horizon.

Finally, humping over a hill, he saw in the distance, a large cove that reached in from the sea. Near the shore of the cove, he saw a rusty old shipwreck rising out of the water.

He now took a rest in hopes of regaining his strength before proceeding. The wind chilled his bones and made his head ache. Chull-su sat down on the bluff by a rusty anti-ship canon and stared at an icy shipwreck, another war ruin. No doubt some Japanese died in that shipwreck. Chull-su would shed no tears on this hill. Bombing that ship was the only good thing the Americans ever did.

He had to get rid of his shakes before he moved on. Whiskey would calm him.

He lifted the bottle to his lips and took a mouthful. He screwed the lid back on and put the bottle into his pack with the others. Finally, after smoking a cigarette butt down to the filter, it was time to get a better look at that cove.

Starting up, he flicked the cigarette butt into the snow and drew a deep breath, but his lungs couldn't take the shot of cold air. He coughed and hacked, squeezing his burning chest. When the attack passed, he sat there thinking for a long time. His independent thoughts began to multiply. New thoughts born of the elemental environment. He was open to independent thinking now that his unquestioned obedience to DowKai philosophy had been tested.

As he started to stand, he began coughing again. The coughing increased in its intensity. Soon he was hacking up blood, spitting, the coughing becoming uncontrollable. Out came the whiskey. He tore open a packet of pills and washed them down with a guzzle. Looking at the nearly empty bottle, he saw blood swirling around from his backwash. He took another swig and packed the bottle. He hiked on.

After twenty minutes, he arrived at the cove-side beach and examined the Japanese shipwreck not far off. He could see a decrepit name plate reading: *Borneo Maru*. He walked on and left the strange ship behind. This island was a death pit. Storms. Shipwrecks. Frostbite. Savages. Traps. Accident. Murder. Everybody who came to this island died. Chull-su would live. Already he'd defied every peril.

How despicable the Americans were. How their western decadence led them to moral decay. How the western disease was spreading. The whole world was being polluted by the ugly Americans and their global influence. Thanks America. Die America.

Where were the women and boy hiding?

CHAPTER FORTY

Pinisha

Frank stood up and faced the door. Something cold and grim told him that dying was the easy way out. He was betraying Luke by leaving him vulnerable and alone.

The door opened.

The little Korean from the museum walked in. Gaudy clothes, slicked-back hair, goatee, fat lips. Frank sat up to get a better look at the killer of Colonel Kim.

A dull blankness loomed behind the redness of bloodshot eyes. He said, "You killed many DowKai men on the island. Mok Don is angry." When Frank didn't answer, the man continued: "Mok Don will make an example of you in front of the crew."

"What do you mean?"

"You, Mr. Murdoch, must come with me." The man laughed, and Frank saw his broken, bloody teeth. "You have a meeting on deck. Sooner you're dead the better."

Frank's head dropped. "Let's get it over with."

"A long time ago, Mok Don killed a man and let his son live. Later, the son tried to kill Mok Don. Mr. Don learned his lesson." Hyun grinned. "My brother Chull-su will clean up the mess and make sure that doesn't happen again."

Frank slowly put on his coat as fear squeezed his guts. Regrets flashed across his mind: His son!

He walked between the two guards. The little man followed behind. They walked out into the hall and started aft. Frank spun around, and seizing the AK off the man behind him, slammed the butt into his face. The man collapsed like he'd been rapped with a baseball bat at the World Series. Spinning the other way, Frank cold-cocked the man in front of him before he could get off a shot. Then Frank broke through a cabin door as he knew the little man had enough time to respond.

There were two Koreans in the cabin and both reached for their weapons. Frank buffeted them both in the face with his swinging rifle butt. Leaving them unconscious, he peeked out into the hall. The little man was gone. One of the guards was coming around. Frank rushed out into the hall and hit him in the back of the head with his rifle. As the man went limp, Frank hurried down the companionway.

He took the elevator to the lower deck. As the elevator doors opened at the boat deck, he gripped his rifle tightly, but saw no one. He walked down the companionway and out the open door to the catwalk outside, broad on the starboard quarter. Holdback hooks kept the door open. They were still in the gray zone. Cold wind blew across the decks. The wavy ocean reeled past. Slowly, he edged for'ard, nervously glancing aft. At any moment a crewman might surprise him from behind. The catwalk ran all the way astern and offered him no cover from behind. He edged for'ard, keeping out of sight of the crew gathering on the main deck alow. Drawing closer, he spied over the rail and down at them. He saw some twenty men along the weather deck's starboard rail.

Rapidly, his eyes scanned across the crew. Mok Don was not there. Frank backed away from the rail, completely out of sight of the men alow. He hurried back inside, his heart pounding, his adrenaline racing, a knot wrenching at his stomach. Within moments every man on the ship would be hunting him. There was no time to lose. Where was Mok Don?

Frank hurried back to the elevator. The wheelhouse was his only chance. He stabbed the button and waited. Around the corner he heard the cook banging pots in the galley. Suddenly, a voice began ranting Korean over the ship-wide intercom system.

That was it.

Every man on board knew of his escape.

His grip tightened on the assault rifle. He stood waiting for the elevator with the tension of stretching hemp rope. Sweat ran down his forehead.

Ding. The elevator doors opened to the shocked, wide eyes of Mok Don and Hyun. Both held AKs across their chests.

CHAPTER FORTY-ONE
Kiska Island

Chull-su trudged over one snowy dune after another as his hunt continued. The food and bottles in his backpack caused the shoulder straps to dig into his shoulders and chafe the skin, but he kept moving. He went on feeling little relief. His breathing was hoarse, his lungs on fire. His legs felt like cement and burned every time he lifted them. Sweat soaked through his black insulated jumpsuit, which made the material stick to his legs. The cold was starting to penetrate him. Coming down the back side of a dune, his legs gave way and he collapsed forward, arms at his sides, his face carving a groove in the snow as he slid several feet. He cursed several times while he got up on his feet and started huffing over the next dune.

At last he came to the bay. He hiked though endless, monotonous, miserable dunes as he strove to circle the body of water.

As he neared the half way mark, the hiking went from miserable to insufferable. The snow gave way beneath his feet and exhausted him.

Forlornly, he kept on. He now doubted the Aleut was following, though the thought still added an edge to his adrenaline. He smoked a cigarette butt and washed down a packet of pills.

Half an hour later he was nearly around the bay, but was still grunting in those wretched hills of snow. Finally, realizing he'd pushed himself too hard without stopping for food and drink, he felt nausea. Then came the flood as he vomited into the snow. He dropped to his knees. Soon there was nothing left, but he continued retching and dry heaving. His headache was unbearable, but it was ghastly cold and he needed to move on.

After some tough hiking, the wavy blanket of snow angled down and gave way to black-sand beaches at Kiska Harbor. Chull-su passed several water tanks in the hills above the harbor. He spotted numerous tunnels in the area and searched them. Along the shore, walking was easier and he picked up the pace by the old submarines. He passed the piers and an icy boat ramp.

The hiking went on past one lake after another. His pace slowed as strength seemed to drain from his legs and his back. He crossed a couple streams safely.

He continued on along the coast, determined to stalk his prey to the death. Only his hatred sustained him as the hiking grew more and more difficult and the slopes, steeper. At times the terrain was rugged and had to be circumvented. Continuing along cliffs over thrashing waves, he passed several enormous, inky-black, lava pillars rising from the whitewater below.

He came to a rugged area which couldn't be scaled, so he started inland, climbing mountainous, backbreaking, snow-cursed hills rising high above the sea. The climbing was debilitating and he spit and hacked ceaselessly.

Toward the top of the hills, he was disheartened by the bleak, dismal, snow-invaded whiteness. Then, panting with infirmity, he crested on the hilltop. There it was. A cabin. The hunt was nearly over.

CHAPTER FORTY-TWO
Pinisha

When the elevator doors opened, Mok Don and Hyun both reacted after a moment's shock. As they lifted their guns, Frank was already in motion, swinging his gun upward as he lunged into the elevator. Hyun took the full brunt of the blow in the head and buckled like he'd been whacked with a sledgehammer; the rising follow through rapped Mok Don across the cheek, slamming him into the wall as his face snapped sideways.

Hyun was instantly knocked unconscious. Mok Don fumbled to regain a hold on his weapon even as he hit the floor. Shifting his grip, Frank swung his rifle like an ax; the muzzle crashed across Mok Don's wrists. He yelled in pain. Frank heard feet slapping down the companionway as the elevator door closed behind him. He shifted his grip, centering the muzzle between Mok Don's horror-stricken eyes. With his free hand he stabbed the elevator button.

"Reach for that weapon and you die." With Mok Don at his mercy--a wave of wrath swept over Frank. His finger began to shake slightly on the hair trigger. But just as rapidly, a wave of reason swept over him.

He thought of Luke, Abby, and Ingrid. The elevator rose.

Mok Don stared at Frank contemptuously, yet warily, unsure what to do. Blood ran freely from the gash on his cheek.

"You're a dead man." He spat blood on the floor. "Give up now and I'll have mercy on you. You haven't a chance. You're trapped on this boat with thirty armed men hunting you down. It's only a matter of minutes."

Frank drew a circle on Mok Don's chest with the bargaining end of his AK-47. "Odds are they'll kill me, but you'll go first."

Mok Don glared at Frank, a trace of fear showing on his face.

Frank picked up both their rifles and took Hyun's pistol.

The elevator door opened. "Let's go," Frank said.

Mok Don struggled to get up. Frank grabbed him by the collar and threw him out of the elevator against the bulkhead. "Hurry up."

Mok Don picked up the pace, walking haggardly down the hall into the wheelhouse.

Frank dug the barrel into his back. "Tell him to drop the gun."

Mok Don relayed the message in Korean. The shipmaster bent down and set his pistol on the floor.

"Slide it over here."

The shipmaster did so, then stood back up and took a deep breath, nervously watching Frank.

Frank laid the extra guns on the floor by the wall. "Order the crew to prepare the life boats. Tell him that. You're gonna do some rowing."

"You can't do that," Mok Don said.

"If you want to stay here and die, that's fine."

Mok Don translated the order. The shipmaster went to the control consul, pushed a button, and barked Korean into the ship-wide intercom system.

Frank pushed the muzzle into Mok Don's lower back and walked him to the starboard-aft window by the wing deck. He looked out at the life boat on the quarter-deck. Two crewmen rushed out on deck to the davit and began lowering the boat. "Good," Frank said. "I want every man in those boats. They're casting off in five minutes."

Mok Don spoke to the shipmaster in Korean. The shipmaster said something back. Mok Don looked up at Frank. "Shipmaster Chung will have to stop the ship to cast off the life boats. He can't do it in five minutes."

"Wrong," Frank said. "The ship will not slow down."

Anger flashed across Mok Don's face. "He must stop the ship. He must."

"Don't touch the controls. You tell him that either the crew casts off now or he dies." Frank jabbed Mok Don with the muzzle.

Mok Don squalled at Shipmaster Chung. Frank understood nothing, but the shipmaster got into action fast, giving another order over the intercom, eyeing Frank nervously as he did so.

"Good," Frank said. "Apparently you want to live. Tell the shipmaster to get down on deck with the others. I want every man off the ship in five minutes. And tell him to take that filth in the elevator with him. Nobody stays and lives. I'm getting impatient."

Fury rushed up Mok Don's face. "You can't do this."

Frank looked at his watch. "Go ahead. Take your time."

Mok Don began frantically shouting at Shipmaster Chung. The shipmaster yelled another order over the intercom and hastened out of the wheelhouse.

Mok Don looked at Frank; desperation gleamed in his eye. "Don't do this. I'll give your gold back."

"The time to negotiate is over."

Frank returned Mok Don's stare for a long silence.

Mok Don's chest heaved to fast breaths. Blood was running down his cheek and soaking his collar. His eyes darted around in desperation, suddenly freezing on Frank.

"What--what about me?"

"Well, now, that depends on how fast your friends are. Why don't you move over to that intercom and give them a little pep talk."

Mok Don hurried to the consul and barked orders into the mike. Then he moved to the window and looked alow. Frank looked too. Already two life rafts were in the water falling behind the ship, and Frank watched a third splash down. Crewmen were abandoning ship without hesitation.

"Lucky for you, they're listening," Frank said. "You'd better hope they all listened."

"Of course they did. Do you think they fear the ocean more than they fear me?"

Frank didn't answer.

"They need food and water," Mok Don said.

"If your men were smart they grabbed some. Now I want all the men off the island. Call off Chull-su."

"I can't."

"Call him on his SatPhone."

"He has nothing. But Shipmaster Chung can take us back. Then I'll stop him."

"That won't be necessary."

Couple of minutes crawled by . . . Sweat was running down Mok Don's face and turning red as clear drops passed over the bleeding gash. . . . Moment to moment existence flew past, lofty in the heightened awareness of Frank's quickened perception. The life boats were shrinking in the distance.

Staring back at Frank and up the black muzzle of the AK, Mok Don was now soaked with sweat, blood still running down the side of his face.

"Go." Frank jabbed Mok Don with the gun, prodding him toward the elevator. Hyun was gone, the rug bloodstained where he fell. Mok Don was silent as they descended to the boat deck. The elevator doors opened, and they walked out into the empty companionway. Frank said, "Move out that open door." They walked down the passage and stepped outside. Cold wind blew at their hair and clothing. The savage sea fell quickly past.

"Hurry up," Frank said. He pushed Mok Don who was leading the way aft. The covered catwalk led to the stern by the after house and covered swimming pool. Frank eyed the *Hector*, which was towing behind on a hawser line belayed to a bollard. Evidently Mok Don had considered the crab boat part of his plunder.

"Take your shoes off," Frank said. "It's hard to swim with them on."

"Don't do this. I'll make you rich."

"Now."

Mok Don kicked his shoes off. He wouldn't look at Frank.

"That's better," Frank said. "You'll swim faster that way. And I recommend you swim real fast. You got a ways to go to catch up with the rest of them. Life boats aren't too far off. Yeah, I'd swim real fast. Bleeding in the water's a bad thing. But you should be alright if you swim real fast."

Simmering with anger, Mok Don glowered at Frank.

"I don't know what you're waiting for," Frank said. "Every second is putting space between you and those life rafts. That's cold water."

Mok Don's eyes went past Frank. For a moment they scanned the superstructure, looking for something. Then he looked back at Frank. "You're a dead man, Murdoch."

Frank dropped his rifle on the deck. His palm leapt forth bare and hard, connecting with Mok Don's nose. Mok Don's heels came off the ground and he landed on his back with an ill-mannered groan. When he looked up, blood was pouring from his nose, down over his mouth.

"That's from a friend of mine in Korea who claims you're scum," Frank said.

Mok Don struggled to get up. Frank pounded him in the eye, again flattening him. "You have any more grievances you'd like to voice?"

On his next try, Mok Don won his feet. He climbed up on the rail and jumped. He dropped twenty feet and splashed into the water. After a couple of seconds, his head broke the surface and he started swimming toward the life boats. Frank stood there and watched him fall away with the wake. Soon he was far past the *Hector*. Frank turned and went forward.

***

Mok Don swam for some twenty minutes before he got within hailing distance of the life rafts. The men yelled to him and waved. He waved back. They began rowing in his direction. He swam toward them. The water was choppy and the distant life rafts were occasionally whelmed from sight. He swam on, occasionally spotting them, hearing their cheers. Soon he was close enough to one of the boats to glimpse the expressions on their faces.

Something was wrong!

The men were waving and shouting frantically. They were pointing beyond Mok Don. He stopped swimming and listened, treading water with his ears clear of the water to listen.

"Shark!" the men were yelling. "Shark!"

Mok Don gasped for breath and hit his stride sprinting and splashing. Terror alone more than tripled his swimming speed.

Then his kick was intercepted. His leg was stuck as if suddenly in a clamp. Saws ripped into his thighs, and he began spinning violently. He let loose a shrill shriek as he was dragged underwater. His breath was gone and yet his body spun so violently nothing mattered. There was no pain, only shock--horror.

It all happened so fast. Next thing he knew he was above water again, flailing by the lifeboats, which he could almost touch. He gasped in absolute horror. The *thing* would be back! He was almost safe now. But he had taken a proper thrashing and his leg was useless-- in fact he couldn't feel it at all. There was no pain and he thrashed toward the boats.

The men shouted back and rowed alongside of him. He was pulled up over the side of the boat and in.

Immediately the men were gasping and groaning. "His leg! The shark took his leg!"

"*No!*" Mok Don yelled. He turned over and looked down. Blood was spurting from his thigh. His leg had been taken from above the knee. "*No!*"

CHAPTER FORTY-THREE

Gray water slipped by at eighteen knots. The wind blew cool and fresh. Walking fore, Frank stepped through the doorway to the inboard companionway.

He climbed a stairwell to the accommodation deck, where he checked several cabins, finding them empty. He climbed to the boat deck, which was also abandoned and silent. On the bridge deck, he expected to find the best accommodations and probably the shipmaster's quarters which were usually positioned near the wheelhouse.

The first two staterooms were empty but for personal effects. The third stateroom contained dozens of the finest relics from the Kiska treasure, carefully arranged across the room's floor. Frank's eyes fixed on the gold suit of armor. Next to the armor helmet lay the gold crown Frank showed Abby on the eve of their arrival at Kiska. Clipped to the gold girdle, was Luke's prize gold sword. Frank thought of Chull-su being left behind on the island.

He scowled and began kicking the relics aside, working his way towards the suit of armor. The noise was terrible. He seized the gold sword and bashed the gold crown, which folded around the blade and hit the wall. Fragments of splintering curved jade shot in every direction. Frank's next hack bent the breastplate. He turned and walked out carrying the gold sword next to his rifle. He climbed up another deck and walked into the wheelhouse with his AK-47 leading the way.

He stood there momentarily, looking over the control center of the *Pinisha*. He walked to the control consul and looked at her position on the electronic chart. She was over the Aleutian Trench, east of Kamchatka. He glanced at the CRT display of the satellite receiver, noting her position, then entered several numbers into the digital readout on the autopilot to indicate the new heading in degrees.

He was going home. He hoped it wasn't too late for Luke, Abby, and Ingrid.

The wretched treasure. The treasure caused it all. All the tragedy.

Today he'd shown mercy. He let murderers go free. Wasn't that a crime in itself? He gave them a fair chance at sea. If they survived, their future victims would have Frank to blame.

Carrying Luke's sword, he clamored down three decks and went astern. The *Hector* was a beautiful sight, and he was eager to board her. He sheathed the sword by sticking it through his pants, slung the rifle over his shoulder, and climbed over the taffrail. Then, hanging from the tow rope, he climbed hand over hand above the *Pinisha*'s wake and back to the *Hector*.

Once aboard his rolling crab boat, he hastened to his office in the house. Hands numb, he set the rifle on his desk and sat down. He leaned back in the chair.

Emotionally, he felt as numb as if Novocain were running through his veins rather than blood. He thought only of stopping the man who was hunting down Luke, Abby, and Ingrid, hunting them like animals. He fell into a trance and found himself staring at the small bottle that lay upon the edge of his desk. He focused his eyes and stared at it for several minutes, stared with traces of hostility well-known to the unforgiven. Slowly, he leaned forward and reached out for the little bottle. He picked it up and looked at it more closely. Inside was his seed, his symbol of faith. He set it down gently and looked at it for a few minutes.

His eyes closed leaving tight wrinkles. He leaned over on his desk.

Rising, he took the spiral staircase down to the engine room and walked to the aft engine room supply locker. Finding the key atop the beam, he opened the locker and removed a box from the bottom shelf. He slipped the box into a knapsack, which he put on.

Back onboard the *Pinisha*, he opened the door to the after deckhouse and went inside. He found a flashlight hanging on the wall. The deckhouse was used for stores: gears, fittings, etc. Frank inspected the floor for a round hatch. He opened the hatch and climbed down the ladder to the steering gear space below. The hatch closed behind him, and blackness enveloped.

He turned on the flashlight. The steering gear space berthed oily hydraulic machinery. Probing the darkness with his flashlight, he spotted two round deck hatches and an access hatchway. The access hatchway led to hold #5. As he recalled from boarding ships years ago, one round hatch opened to a tunnel escape leading to the after peak, a recess below; the second hatch opened to the rudder trunk which housed the upper rudder stock used to turn the rudder.

He opened the hatch to the tunnel escape and started down the ladder. Slowly, he made the vertical descent into the bowels of darkness. The booming noise of the shaft below stunned his senses and swamped him with a strange feeling of isolated vulnerability. The ladder ended in the after peak. Looking around he noticed a round hatch that lay on the floor.

Frank opened the hatch and climbed down into the lowest bowels of the *Pinisha*. This deep recess housed the noisy propeller shaft tunnel. He climbed down amidst the harsh-sounding clamor, his feet stepping into a quarter inch of water. He splashed through the damp, dark passageway, his roving shaft of light cutting through blackness, stabbing at imprisoned night. He was walking forward, but stopped short of the big watertight door through the crosswise bulkhead.

He removed his knapsack and took out the square package-- about the size of three dictionaries--plastic explosives. Holding the flashlight under his arm, he removed the wrapping and molded the block of explosives to the bulwark above the bilge water against a horizontal girder. He attached a detonator unit to the top of the block and ran a wire from his wire coiler to a timer which he also placed on the explosives. He set the timer for forty minutes, took his flashlight, and stood up.

Frank quickly scanned the blackened obscurity with his probing needle of light.

The big metal door through the forward bulkhead led into the main propeller shaft tunnel. Opening the door and passing into the next section, he kept moving, splashing through bilge water as he went.

Suddenly, despite the booming engine and shaft noise, he heard metal clank to aft. Switching off his light, he froze in total darkness and waited several seconds, tension tight in his gut. He took the AK-47 in his hands. He waited. No more sounds. Perhaps the ship's rocking had caused something to fall over. He stood as still as a statue. Perhaps it was nothing.

Flashing on his light, he followed the narrow column of dancing white illumination, looking nervously backwards several times. He arrived at another metal door and spun the dogs. Opening the door, a flood of bright light blinded his unadjusted eyes. Squinting, he edged his way inside the lower engine room. Calculating boundaries, he recalled the forward bulkhead separated the lower engine room from the wing fuel tank. The only way out was up or back. He slid the flashlight tightly into his pocket. He set a second charge by the forward bulkhead, synchronizing the timer to coincide with the first.

The metal grate staircase led up to the 'tween engine room, and Frank hurried past pipes, generators, valves, engines, and boilers; as he did so, creaks, hisses, whirrs, hums, and murmurings streaming out of ventilators changed pitches and volumes against his position. The heat from the engines was stifling. Another clank.

He walked fore on metal walkway gratings over machinery and passed through the forward bulkhead into the soundproof engine control room and closed the door behind him. Shivers ran up and down his spine. He turned to the window and watched his trail for several minutes.

CHAPTER FORTY-FOUR

Leaving the control center, Frank returned to the deafening blare of the engine room. Carefully, warily, he ducked and searched through pipes, ventilators, pumps and knobs, looking for a cranny with a good angle on all the approaches. While he foraged around, he kept an eye on the stairway. Finding what he was looking for, he slipped in a nook by a vent shaft. He couldn't crouch down with the sword sheathed through his pants, so he withdrew the blade and set the weapon aside. Then he waited . . . Unbearably hot . . . Sweating . . . The flashlight digging into his gut.

Several minutes passed. Then Frank saw the nose of an assault rifle poke into view. Someone stopped a foot before Frank's nook. Frank remained still. Slowly, the gun's barrel began moving forward into view. Frank saw a hand. Scabbing rope burns ringed around the wrist. A feverish, hugely muscular Korean moved into view as slowly as a crawling lion. Frank recognized him as one of the men who attacked him at the monastery. The man's eyes orbed wide as he looked into the nook and straight at Frank.

Frank shook his head negatively, his rifle trained between the man's eyes. He yelled to be heard over the mains: "Move fast and you die."

Intensity gripped the man's face. He showed no fear, but seemed to realize that he was one false move from the end. Slowly the man laid down his weapon.

Frank reached over for the sword with one hand and grasped the handle. He stood up, sheathed the long blade under his belt, and eased out of the nook.

The man watched him closely.

Frank ducked beneath a vent as he stepped out on the grated walkway. When his arm brushed against a searing hot pipe, he flinched reflexively and jerked away from the hot surface. The big man seized the moment, his hands exploding outward, batting the gun out of Frank's hands and pushing him backwards. Frank landed on his back and slid on the grating.

The man dove at Frank, who grabbed the sword, pulling the blade upward. The man crashed down onto the upturning sword. He wailed in shock and pain as the blade came out of his back.

The man's eyes swarmed with primordial rage as he grabbed Frank's neck and throttled, cutting off breathing. Frank was choking, and the man squeezed harder. Murder raged in his eyes until they turned up unnaturally in the sockets and started twitching violently. Frank tried to wrestle him off but was in too awkward a position. The grip around his neck became murderous, and he thought his lungs would explode. Those eyes over him were windows of suffering. Then the man's grip faltered as he began heaving in violent spasms.

Frank gasped for air. The man atop him made horrible wailing sounds that gave way to a pitiful cry. Frank tried pushing him off, but the sword had them attached. Using all his strength, Frank rolled to port. The man hit the grating and yelled desperately. As Frank stood up, his belt pulled the sword out of the man's guts, causing him to let out a hideous gasp. Frank kneeled down to the man and ripped his shirt open. Blood gushed from the wound.

"Shouldn't have done that," Frank said, catching his breath, his lungs still burning.

The Korean was trying to speak, "It'ae--"

Frank couldn't hear or understand what he was saying. "What?"

"It'aewon--"

Frank knelt down. "What are you saying?"

The man grabbed his collar and pulled him close. He was gagging but he rasped his dying words into Frank's ear in English.

"Are you sure?" Frank asked.

The man was gasping deeply and harshly. Frank tried to stop the bleeding with the man's shirt, but within a few minutes the man's eyes rolled back again, froze, and he was dead.

Frank picked up his AK-47 and walked back into the engine control room, closing the door behind him against the clamoring mains. He walked to the center of the sound-proof room and stared at the watertight door through the crosswise bulkhead.

Thunder blasted through the glass, sending the exploding window shattering to the deck; simultaneously, something batted Frank's legs out from under him, sending him twisting, crashing down upon the steel decking. The deafening marine diesel engines now wailed into the control room. At the same moment he was dazed and shocked. Adrenaline was clawing in him. He was shot beneath the knee.

Frank crawled for cover, dragging his leg. Another burst of gunfire batted the decking just beyond him. Bullets ricocheted inches from him. He balled up and rolled. A snapping catapult of wretchedness told him that his leg was broken.

Rising up on his elbows, he pushed the control room door open a crack. He just barely peaked up over the metal doorway sill, which reached twelve inches above the deck level. He ducked.

The big man lay where he fell. There was someone else in the engine room.

Frank reached around and pulled a piece of glass out of his back and threw it on the glass-sprayed floor, pulled a bloody shard from his elbow.

Where was the shooter? The answer came in a question: How did Frank get shot in the lower leg? Behind the waist-high bulkhead, his legs should have been shielded—unless the sniper was elevated. The grated stair landing. He must be on the stair landing aloft. Frank looked up over the doorway sill and this time looked high. He couldn't believe his eyes. Looking under and beyond a big round horizontal vent shaft, he saw movement by a vertical pipe. Frank was in the man's blind spot.

He raised the AK-47 into position, aimed, and squeezed off a single shot. The report slapped back with a loud boom. Over the clamorous marine diesel engines, he heard the sound from aloft of a body crashing down on the stair grating. He heard the man ranting hysterically in Korean.

After that, Frank heard only the big marine engines. He waited several minutes. His entire leg was numb, but with the slightest pressure on it--strokes of pain smote him. He was fairly immobilized. The explosives would soon detonate. He glanced at his watch. Stared in disbelief.

Only nineteen minutes remained till the *Pinisha* would explode.

He had to get out of there. Again he looked up over the raised sill of the doorway. Gunfire rang out, battering the bulkhead next to his face. The man was still alive and had a new angle on him. Frank was pinned down, could hardly contain his adrenaline. There was no going back the way he came and certainly no going up with the sniper waiting for him. Time was going too fast.

Using guesswork and calculation, Frank lifted the AK over the sill and fired a burst in the direction of the sniper. In the moment afterwards, he scrambled across the floor, crawling wildly across the shattered, splintered glass. He scrambled through the deadly window of vision where he was shot. The pain in his leg hurt like stabbing knives, but he reached cover beyond the sniper's view. Blood soaked his pant leg and seeped from cuts in his hands. He pulled several pieces of glass from his knee.

A watertight door secured with dog latches opened fore. With his shot leg dangling, Frank muscled the dogs and moved awkwardly into the darkness of 'tween hold #4, latching the door tightly behind him. With a tap on the deck, a shaft of pain speared up his bad leg all the way to the back of his head. Frank stiffened against the shock. When the torment passed, he noticed that his elbow felt wet and he withdrew glass. He quickly pulled jagged fragments out of his knee and the palms of his hands. He could feel the warm blood soaking his clothes, causing them to stick to his skin.

He withdrew the flashlight from his pocket and turned the light on, flashing the beam around the expansive, dark compartment. The hold was empty.

He hopped a few times, but excruciating hurt brought him to his bloody, slippery hands and knees. Dragging his leg, he crawled along the edge of the hold. His every movement was tempered by the need to minimize pressure on his broken leg. Despite his best efforts, the leg was constantly jarred, jammed, twisted and jolted, spawning shutters of pain. His progress was slow, but he grappled on.

At the forward bulkhead, he struggled up onto his good leg and stepped through another doorway into 'tween hold #3. The compartment was laden with unmarked crates of some unknown commodity.

He crawled through the darkness as fast as he could, knowing the timer on the explosives was ticking and every second could be the difference between life and death; but with awkward movements, the whip of pain would snap him out of the numbness. His pace erratic . . . The toil endless . . . Minutes ticking away. . . .

As he progressed through the dark, vibrating compartment, he wondered how he could get off the ship. He had a broken leg; time was running out; he was moving at a slug's pace; and he had no idea the condition of the sniper in the engine room. He kept looking back to make sure nobody was following him through the holds. His ears were ringing and he kept thinking he heard noises, all the way expecting to take a bullet in the back. He wanted to pick up the pace, but couldn't go any faster.

He passed through a doorway in the forward bulkhead into 'tween hold #2. He flashed his light around. Wooden crates were stacked neatly atop one another and no crates impeded his passage along the perimeter. Frank persisted doggedly.

His leg was jolted hard climbing into 'tween hold #1. He grit his teeth and shined the flashlight into the ghostly darkness.

A spilling mound of gold treasure glittered against the light beam.

"Treasure for the devil," he said.

He crawled around the gold mound. Blood flowed steadily from his hands and knees. He struggled to think clearly. If he had his holds right, were he to continue fore, he'd hit a dead end as the compartment for'ard of 'tween hold #1 would be the deep tank used for ballast and trimming.

Getting up on one leg, he started up the ladder, took a step . . . another . . .   At the deck above, a round hatch opened to upper 'tween hold #1. He spun the dog latch and heaved it upward, the hatch slamming down on the steel deck overhead.

Passing through, he endured on. Should have shot it out with the man back in the engine room. There wasn't enough time for this.

Frank got up wearily and hobbled for'ard to the next bulkhead, the assault rifle doubling as a cane. He moved through the doorway into the bosun's store. He won the ladder and proceeded stubbornly up into the foc'sle, blood from his hands lubricating the rungs. Climbing took too long. He gained the foc'sle 'tween deck. Light shined in through a porthole, and Frank threw off the flashlight, crawled to the foc'sle door.

He pushed open the door and climbed up on one leg, using the AK as something between a crutch and a cane. The sunlight was nearly blinding, so he squinted. Shielding his aching eyes, he searched the superstructure for snipers.

He glanced at his watch. In seven minutes the *Pinisha* would explode in an apocalyptic flash.

Carrying the rifle, Frank began hopping furiously down the main deck. Pain clawed through his leg. He kept thinking about Luke.

He was on a race against death and barely cared if the sniper was watching. He wouldn't give up. Couldn't give up. But his pace was sticky, his good leg stiffening from glass cuts through the muscles. Haggardly, slowly, failingly, using the rail for support, he hopped one-legged, one step at a time, along the port rail. He kept going. Struggling. By the time he was half way across the main deck, he was crawling, his glass-cut hands and knees slippery on the metal decking and leaving a trail of blood. He wrestled his way down the length of the main deck. He felt groggy. Dizzy.

Finally, laying hand upon the main superstructure, he climbed through the doorway on bleeding hands and knees. He climbed a stairwell to the accommodation deck like an animal. He adjusted the AK-47, which was now strapped around his neck and under his arm. Top of the stairs, he glanced at his watch.

Five minutes.

He pulled and grappled and finally managed to stand up on his good leg. He began hopping, using the rail for support, but again the grinding bones drove him onto his hands and knees. Onward he crawled, dragging his leg. Finally he arrived astern.

Four minutes until the ship exploded into a fireball and dragged the *Hector* into the deep.

CHAPTER FORTY-FIVE

Suffering for every inch, Frank staggered across the *Pinisha*'s stern. He travailed over the taffrail and realized he felt numb to pain now. Only adrenaline and a vision of his son kept him going. He began another ship-to-ship, hand-over-hand rope crossing. His arms were dead-man's arms, stiff and numb, his grip weak and unsteady. His hands were soaked with hot and slippery blood.

The ships were traveling at eighteen knots and the *Pinisha*'s churned up white water slipped rapidly beneath him as he put one hand in front of the other. He could feel the extreme tension in the three-inch rope. Half way across, the *Hector* sank into a wave trough, dipping Frank's feet in cold seawater. A seism of pain burst through him, striking at his core. He held on, but his arms felt rubbery. His grip faltered. A churning froth of seawater raced beneath him and under the *Hector,* beckoning him unto the soft caress of easy surrender.

His hands stung where rope fibers cut into his open wounds. One shaky hand at a time, he tussled for the crab boat.

As the rope pulled tight again, it made squeaking, stretching sounds. He grappled on, his arms and shoulders growing toilworn, the ocean's spray slapping him across the face, leaving salt in his mouth and wounds.

Frank reached the *Hector* and strained every nerve climbing up on the bow.

If the explosion detonated with the *Hector*'s hawser belayed to the *Pinisha*, he'd be plunging into the nadir of the ocean. The depths of the Kuril Trench would be a mausoleum for the *Pinisha* and an abysmal suboceanic catacomb for the gold…and him.

He pulled the sword free and glanced at his watch. Thirty seconds.

Grabbing the rail, Frank pulled himself up onto his good leg. Suddenly, a burst of gunfire ricocheted off an anchor winch.

Looking back over his shoulder, Frank saw a hunched figure on the *Pinisha*'s wheelhouse wing deck.

Frank dropped the sword. With only seconds till detonation, he swung the AK around and aimed it at the rope. He squeezed the trigger to no report. "Damn it!"

Only seconds till detonation.

He dropped the gun, swept up the sword, and lifted it high over his head. With a full swing stabilized on his good leg, he sank the blade in the three-inch rope. The crackle of automatic gunfire played at his nerves, but he was still standing. Into his second swing, he put all of his might. The blade severed the shaft. Rope exploded in a fraying whip out over the water. The *Hector* lunged against the water's resistance and sudden halting of pull, sending Frank tumbling overboard and the sword splashing into the ocean.

In mid air, Frank's hands clamped onto the rail, his body swung down, slammed into the hull, flailed. Hanging over the ocean, he felt the electricity of adrenaline and a zap of pain through his leg and hip. Estimating no time till detonation, he exerted with everything left in him and climbed back onto the bow. He crawled haggardly across the foc'sle. Pulling himself erect, planting his hands on the railings on either side of the stairwell, he lifted his feet and slid down.

A titanic blast sent a shock wave exploding outward from its source, striking the *Hector* with devastating force, blowing out every fore window. Sliding down the metal rails to the weather deck, Frank was thrown, twisted in the air, and landed on the steel deck, hitting his head.

He regained consciousness with the painful realization that Luke and the others might already be dead. Then again, maybe there was still time. He slowly rose up onto his hands and knees. His world spun. Pain mocked his flesh. He grit his teeth and crawled for the rail.

***

Kiska Island

Ingrid opened the door to the emergency bunker and looked out across the meadow. Her eyes scanned the horizon carefully, spotting no sign of Frank or Brian. She felt Luke brush up against her.

"Is he coming?" Luke said.

"He will be," Ingrid said. "But not yet." She felt the moisture in her eyes as she thought of what Abby had told her about the Koreans taking Frank hostage. If she ever got off this island, she was never coming back. She turned and took Luke's hand. "Come on. Let's go back inside."

***

On the *Hector,* using all his resources, Frank stood up and staggered to the rail. His boat was drifting. The *Pinisha* gone.

Fresh air blew over him and he breathed deeply. Fresh salt air on a gray ocean.

He made his way to the wheelhouse and started the engines. He set a course and activated the autopilot.

CHAPTER FORTY-SIX

Groggy. Mok Don was so groggy. But the pain was so intense he couldn't sleep. He had been awake for several minutes, staring at his leg, unable to believe it was no longer there. He wanted to kill Murdoch, but felt powerless and hopeless. What would become of Mok Don now? The world as he'd known it was over with. Everything was different now. Nothing would ever be the same. He would see Murdoch dead if it took him the rest of his life.

The three lifeboats were tied together, drifting in the waves. Mok Don looked around. Finally, his mind was clearing. The aftermath of the attack had been *agony* and *shock* and *chaos*--like a hallucination of some horrible monstrosity. He remembered being pulled into the boat--panic and hysteria among the men. He remembered only one man who had taken charge, one man who had remained calm, one man who acted to save his life. The rest had been totally incapable of decision. He remembered being sewed up. He had never known such suffering then or now—physical or mental.

Now all the men were mute, staring at him as though nauseated. Shocked—that's what they were, more than twenty seamen shocked by an abominable spectacle: Mok Don, their immortal leader, missing a leg.

Mok Don must have been in shock himself. He was lightheaded and thought he might pass out.

He glared at the man directly in front of him. "What did you do to me?" he demanded.

"I fixed your leg if that's what you're asking."

"You're a cook, a steward—*a scullion worker!*"

The cook's head dropped humbly, then lifted. "I brought the first aid kit, so I thought I should be the one to sew you up. There was no time for anything else."

Sitting next to the steward, Shipmaster Chung nodded. "He's the only one who knew how to sew."

The steward nodded. "Occasionally I've trussed this or that in the galley. Stitching you up was more difficult, the way you were thrashing and cursing. But I got it closed and stitched up tight. My only concern was saving your life. The bleeding nearly stopped after you passed out. The first aid kit had lots of codeine. That's what I gave you for the pain. You may be feeling tired from the pills and blood loss."

"Will I live?"

"I found an antibiotic in the first aid kit. Hopefully that should stop any infection. I'm no doctor, but I had to do something. I couldn't let you bleed to death."

The cook lifted a plastic water jug to Mok Don's lips and poured. Only then did Mok Don realize how thirsty he was, and he drank greedily. When he was satisfied, he nodded, and the cook put down the water jug. Mok Don's head was spinning. Dizzy. Groggy.

"What about food?" he asked.

The cook shook his head shamefully. "Lost overboard during the panic of abandoning ship. I expect we'll be rescued soon."

Suddenly, the water thrashed not far off. Mok Don recoiled in horror. "What was that?"

"Ever since the attack," Shipmaster Chung said, "the sharks have been following us, swarming around the boats."

Coldly with a threatening tone, Mok Don said, "So we have no food to go around, and those monsters are looking upon us for a meal?"

The men were petrified by the prospect of Mok Don's wrath. Mok Don glared at Shipmaster Chung and then at the cook.

"Is there anything more you can do for my leg?" he asked the cook.

"Not unless you need more sewing."

"You ought to be thrown to the sharks for losing the rations," Mok Don said. "But since you saved my life and might be called on to do so again, I'll let you live." Mok Don glared down at his leg as pain shuttered through him. "Give me more pills!" he demanded.

The cook obeyed, and Mok Don washed the pills down with more water.

"How much water do we have?" Mok Don demanded.

"Five gallons," said the cook.

Mok Don made rough calculations. With twelve men, they'd be lucky to survive a week. It could take several weeks to be rescued. There were too many thirsty mouths.

He looked across a miserable lot of stony faces until his eyes found Hyun. As his eyes bored wrathfully into Hyun, Mok Don watched his face mask suck in and out more and more rapidly.

"Someone will pay for this tragedy," Mok Don said. "The Kim brothers—Chull-su and Hyun—have plunged into the cesspool of shame and dishonor. Chull-su let the Americans escape; Hyun has also demonstrated gross insubordination. Now let every eye see how Mok Don deals with incompetence; let every ear hear and remember. It's only fitting that Hyun should feed the sharks because it was his blood that whet their appetite."

Hyun's eyes expanded to rounded orbs. His face mask stretched as his mouth opened wide and he made a terrified gasping sound. His head began shaking rapidly. "No, Mok Don, no, no. *Please. Not that.*"

Mok Don nodded at the sailors next to him and said, "In with him. We'll waste no water on the disgraced."

Two sailors grabbed his arms at the shoulders and lunged the runt into the water. He splashed into the ocean and began thrashing against his sinking body.

"*Help me. Please. You don't under--*"

A fourteen-foot form raced at him--cutting the surface with a menacing fin. Hyun began screaming, but the fish took him in crushing jaws—took him underneath into a slicing, thrashing whitewater. Suddenly, sharks converged on the prey from all over. Under several feet of water, they shot at Hyun like torpedoes. Contact was made with terrifying ferocity as the beasts sank their teeth and spun violently—several sharks at a time ripping meat off their prey.

Water churned white and red. Fins raced around in a soulless frenzy--thrashing wildly. Savage. Feasting. Splashing. Tearing. Bumping into lifeboats. Deranged, bloodthirsty chaos.

CHAPTER FORTY-SEVEN
Kiska Island

Chull-su was thrilled. Surely the women and the boy were hiding in the cabin. He'd visit them and get off the island. Deal the cards and get out--that's all he wanted now. His own survival was at stake.

His feet sank in the snowy powder as he struggled down the side of the massive hill. Near the bottom, the blanket of swallowing whiteness began its blinding reaches. He made the hike to the cabin quicker with an oncoming second wind. Knowing they'd be caught by surprise, he kicked in the door and jumped inside, rifle swinging, ready to send blood flying.

Nobody. Empty.

Chull-su cursed. Depression snapped loose in his head. His second wind vanished. He nearly collapsed in the doorway of exhaustion. He lifted one leg after another toward the bed. He collapsed.

***

Moving slowly around the *Hector*, Frank got a crowbar from the tool room and tore up several planks from the iron-bark deck. Back down in the tool room, the big engines booming into his numbness, he made a wooden splint which he duct-taped to his leg. He cut two planks to crutch size, cut out handles which he chiseled round for solid grip, and screwed plate-size square boards on for feet.

For a test run, he crutched up and down the stairs to the wheelhouse. The plate-size wooden feet were cumbersome on board, but otherwise, no problem.

***

Chull-su didn't know how long he was out. He must have fainted, blacked out or something. He was on the bunk. More rest would restore him. He bunked down for the night. Next morning he was too sick to go on and snow was sifting down again. His legs were too sore to walk. He spent the day feverish and shaky, finally regaining his strength the second night. Morning came again and now he was ready. He resumed his hunt for the women and the boy.

***

Frank anchored the *Hector* in 25 fathoms with a sand bottom, a mile South of Witchcraft Point. He rowed ashore. The plate-size boards attached to the feet of the crutches gave a snow-shoe effect, sinking in the snow, but not into the tundra beneath. He started the three-mile hike to the bunker. Frank crutched along the beach of the west shore. Fortunately, the sand was packed hard, but his shoulder muscles burned from the exertion. When the beach played out, he headed inland, and he hadn't gone more than half a mile when he heard an anguished groan. On instinct, Frank dropped to the ground and stayed still. After a minute, he got up on his knees for a better look but saw nothing. He left his crutches behind and began to crawl in the direction from which he'd heard the noise, dragging his broken leg, wincing from pain, the smell of rancid sweat filling his nostrils. The collapsed tunnel slowly came into view. Frank heard another moan, so he crawled up to the edge. The first thing he saw was the fur pelt of a caribou. It was Clay Krukov's coat.

"Are you alright?" Frank said.

"I feel like hell, but I'll survive if you get me out of here."

"Where are the others?"

"I was looking for them when this happened."

It took an hour to rig up a rope and haul Clay out. It was not easy because Clay's shoulder was still in pain and he was weak from the loss of blood.

Sitting next to his old friend, Frank said, "You go to the ranch and look for them there. Get yourself patched up. I'll go back to the bunker. I'll meet you back at the house tomorrow."

***

For hours, Chull-su continued the hunt despite his sickness. The wind started blowing again, and by the horizon, he guessed another killer storm was moving in. He knew he wouldn't survive another storm if he didn't find shelter.

He was moving inland along the base of the volcano through a valley that appeared to lead all the way across the island. Thirst and dehydration were inflicting their ravages upon him. He came to a lake only partially frozen over. Approaching the water's edge very carefully so he didn't slide in, he reached down, filled his cupped hands and greedily drank a mouthful. Swallowing, he tasted the salt in the water. Spitting and cursing, he continued on, suffering worse than before.

He hiked for another stretch and came to several arms of lava that reached out across the tundra. He wearily plodded through each of the meadows between the arms. He was surprised to find wild horses resting in the protective meadows.

Nearly exhausted to the point of collapse, he breathed in raucous gasps. His whole upper-chest cavity burned and ached. Sweat was freezing, sending chills deeply through him. Now even Chull-su would fall victim to the forbidding elements. Barely ambulatory, he was hobbling back into the second meadow, near the biggest herd of horses he'd seen yet, when he saw what appeared to be a bunker built into the lava. Relief swept over him.

Taking the long way around, he came up alongside the bunker so he couldn't be seen. He moved the selector switch on his AK to automatic. He heard voices inside the bunker. Female voices.

Perfect. Chull-su snaked up by the door latch, hesitated, jerked the door open. A woman stood just inside. Chull-su sprang up behind her and got his arm around her neck as she turned. She tried to scream but was instantly gagging. He put the AK to her head, yelled at the woman and the boy by the fire: "Move and I'll kill her."

The woman by the fire screamed. The boy jumped back and fell down.

Chull-su threw Abby to the ground and moved for the pistol on a ledge. He recovered it and shoved the pistol into the waist of his pants. He saw the AK laying on the white duffel bag.

"Get to the fire," he said.

Abby and the boy did as they were told.

Chull-su looked the place over. "More guns. Where are they?"

"Over there," Abby said, pointing at the AK-47. "That's the only one."

Chull-su glared at her. "Don't lie to me. That would be a mistake." As he waited for Abby to change her story, an itch spread inside his chest and throat. "You thought you could hide from me in your little hole." Chull-su coughed. "Water. Get me water now."

Abby got up and started for the door, picking up a water container from the floor.

Chull-su grabbed her by the arm and squeezed hard. "If you don't come back, your friends will die for it, and then I'll find you."

She nodded and went out. Chull-su coughed several times. He saw a cup by the golden-haired woman. "What's that?"

Ingrid looked at the cup, then at Chull-su. "Tea."

"Give it to me."

She brought the cup to him, and he tasted it. The tea was cold, but he didn't care. He gulped the cool liquid and tossed the mug aside. "Good," he said. "You do what I tell you and we'll get along."

Chull-su coughed as he took off his pack and laid it on the ground. The boy was watching, so Chull-su grinned at him. The boy turned away. Chull-su stripped off his gloves and looked at his bony fingers. They were almost yellow. He rubbed his moist hands together. He moved to the fire and held his hands over the flames to warm them. "Why isn't she back yet?"

"It takes a while," Ingrid said.

"How long?"

"She'll be back soon."

Chull-su opened the bunker door, and the meadow was spread out before him. He hated this place and wanted to get back to the city.

He sat back down and leaned against the wall with his AK pointed at the boy. His eye lids were heavy. He was feeling good because when Mok Don learned that the mission was a success, he would richly reward Chull-su.

When Abby returned, Chull-su said, "Next time hurry up. I'm hungry, get me food."

Chull-su took the jug and drank the ice-cold water. He drank slowly but kept drinking. When the jug was half empty, he put it down. He watched Abby, who was rummaging through a storage tin.

"Faster," Chull-su said.

Abby stirred soup. She brought him a bowl.

With a gun in his lap, Chull-su ate quickly. As he spooned the food down his throat, he felt his strength returning. A warm meal was just what he needed. He finished his bowl and then a second, never taking his eyes off his prisoners. After his last spoonful, he threw the bowl on the ground. He grabbed his AK and got up onto his feet.

He pulled out his bottle and tipped it . . . empty. He threw it on ground, withdrew a new bottle from his pack and unscrewed the lid. He washed down a packet of pills.

He glanced at the boy, whose scared eyes were following him. Chull-su stared at him for a while, knowing the boy would be dead shortly. Chull-su heard a dog bark in the distance. He pointed his gun at Luke's head.

"Leave him alone," Ingrid said.

Chull-su walked to Ingrid and kicked her onto her back. "Shut up."

The boy moved quickly and a rock slammed into Chull-su's face. Pain shot through his right eye. He stumbled backwards, but kept hold of his gun and pointed it at the boy.

"You'll die for that. Outside. I don't want this bunker messed up." Chull-su walked over and kicked the boy in the face. The boy hit the ground, and Chull-su kicked him again and again.

Ingrid screamed. "Stop it. Stop."

"Leave him alone," Abby shouted.

Now Chull-su turned on the women. "You want some too?" He feinted an attack on them, drawing back his rifle to strike. When they shrank back in fear, he laughed at them.

The boy was wheezing and gasping for air. Chull-su attacked him again with a barrage of kicks, which the boy broke by curling up tighter. Blood dripped from the boy's nose and at the corner of his mouth. Chull-su heard something outside the bunker. He left the boy alone while he went over to the viewing slash and looked out. Nothing there. He spotted a black lava rock in the snow that had fallen from the lava wall over the bunker. He turned on the boy, who was sitting up now.

Ingrid was checking the boy over, trying to make him feel better with her attention. Chull-su advanced on her and slapped her.

"Get away from him. Let him suffer alone, like a man. He's gonna die alone."

"You're psychotic," Abby yelled at him.

Chull-su leered at her. "And I thought we were getting along so nicely. I thought we could get through this next storm the easy way.

The boy looked up with tears in his eyes.

"Get up," Chull-su said. "We're going outside."

The boy got up and walked outside.

"No," Ingrid screamed. "Leave him alone." She started after the boy, but Chull-su shoved her to the ground and kicked her head. The woman broke out in tears.

"Stay there," Chull-su commanded. Carrying his AK, he went after the boy. One step out the door, he stopped and carefully scanned the meadow. He approached the boy. It was cold outside and he wanted to get this over with quickly.

"Boy, I'll give you a chance to live. Run. If you can get away, you can go free."

Chull-su pointed the AK skyward. Squeezed the trigger. Thunderclap invaded the meadow as gunfire erupted. Spooked horses rose, panicked, and fled for open country. The earth rumbled under hundreds of pounding hooves and flying snow. The boy shrank back. Chull-su smiled at him. Chull-su would give him six or seven steps, then hew him down.

"Go," Chull-su shouted. "Run."

The boy started running. Chull-su grinned and pointed his weapon.

***

From five feet above the bunker, Frank Murdoch stood on a volcanic ledge. He dove from the ledge, flew with his limbs outstretched, and came down hard on Chull-su's shoulders. Chull-su buckled, all of Frank's weight behind the impact. Chull-su's body broke Frank's fall, and Frank rolled away on impact.

***

Against all pain, Chull-su got up and faced the wounded American. He shot a flat-palm at Frank with a yell. Frank grabbed his extended arm by the wrist--and with crushing force from the outside-- he flat handed the back of Chull-su's elbow joint. The elbow snapped in the socket--bursting out of joint. Bones crunched. Tendons and cartilage ripped. Chull-su's left arm was dangling in the wrong direction in the socket.

He screamed in agony.

He fell to the ground, twisting in pain and shock. But he strained to ignore the pain. He sat up first, then got up onto his feet. Frank once again leaned on his crutches, obviously in pain, too. Chull-su looked at his gun, which was in the snow between them. His firing arm was still good. Chull-su moved for the weapon. He leaned over, got the fingers of his right hand around it--

A crutch slammed into his chin. His head snapped back and he heard something crack. And when he opened his eyes he could barely move. The snow had numbed his face. Cold wind blew over him, making him shake.

Murdoch was still standing there, except now he was holding Chull-su's AK-47. Chull-su suddenly remembered the pistol. Frank was turned away, looking toward the distant horses.

Chull-su made his move. He rose up onto his knees. With his right hand, he went for the pistol tucked in the waist of his pants.

Frank turned and fired. A slug ripped through Chull-su's chest. Some connection sparked in his brain and he lifted the pistol. A burst erupted from Frank's gun. Lead tore through Chull-su's chest. His head snapped back. He hit the ground. Cold darkness.

CHAPTER FORTY-EIGHT
March 9th, 1996

Mok Don crutched across his office and stared out the window at the haze and cityscape of Seoul. There were dark pouches under his black eyes. New wrinkles reached across his forehead and a patch of gray hair fell over his forehead. Like always, people told him he looked well, but lately it was hollow flattery from the lips of grovelers who were quietly revolted by his handicap. Mok Don knew his appearance reflected his severe depression over losing his leg and the treasure. His daily existence was now bitter disgrace: Crutching into the building, taking the elevator, passing people, his secretary . . . pure humiliation. Losing the treasure he could recover from, but losing a leg . . .

Mok Don's head hung forward, and the creases in his forehead deepened.

Today Mok Don would steer the ill-fated course of events in a new direction. He felt fresh hate approaching the hour of expression and vindication. Mok Don breathed deep, ominous breaths, eyes closed. Slowly he moved his head from left to right with his hands on his stressed temples. He would not suffer alone. He would take his revenge on Frank Murdoch. And the revenge would be as sweet and cruel as he could fathom.

Mok Don crutched over to his desk and looked at the solid gold burial urn resting on the edge. He brought this priceless treasure from his collection at home as a symbol of the occasion. It was magnificent. A totally rare artifact. Since he first unearthed this wonder decades ago, he shared it with no one. Only he and the long-dead monarchs of the Three Kingdoms Era had ever laid eyes upon it.

Water-drop, flower, and spangle designs covered the urn in intricate detail. Four animal-head eyelets protruded from the pot's shoulder. Holes drilled through the heads allowed threading and hanging of the urn. Burial urns such as this came into usage during the Three Kingdoms Period. As Buddhism became the state religion of the Shilla Dynasty between the 7th and 10th centuries, cremation was widely practiced. It was the only ancient, pure-gold burial urn on earth with this exact design.

As Mok Don admired the priceless relic, he thought of the ocean: the biggest burial urn on earth. He thought of Frank Murdoch . . . It was time to commit Murdoch to the immense abysmal deep-blue soul. It was time to commit him to the deep. Mok Don would throw Frank Murdoch to the sharks and beasts of the ocean, just as Murdoch did to Mok Don. Only for Murdoch it would be final—his miserable live burial at sea. Then he would know the suffering of Mok Don.

Mok Don crutched around his desk and sat down. He picked up the phone receiver and dialed a number. He got an answer. He said, "What are you doing? . . . Uh-huh . . . Everything is set to go? . . . Get that plane ready by tomorrow . . . I don't care if you have to go to the airport personally and motivate those loafers. Make it ready. Get the men outfitted, they drop everything, get their passports ready, double check every detail. The time has come: We're returning to the Aleutians . . . What? . . . We need to arm twenty-five men with AK-47 rifles and night vision equipment . . . I changed my mind. I want fifty. Get on it--"

The secretary broke in on the intercom. "Mr. Don—"

"I told you I'm busy. Don't bother me." Mok Don hissed. "Get that plane ready," he ordered, returning to his phone conversation. "I won't tolerate any delays. I'll hold you personally responsible."

Mok Don hung up and pushed his chair back. He struggled to push himself into a standing position. He looked down at the temporary wooden leg and stared at it. It was all like a horrible nightmare. He wasn't even a man. He was a freak with a wooden leg. Even poor people would think themselves superior to him now. Write him off as a cripple. Perhaps doing business with him would even become taboo.

This wasn't America, after all. In America there was no shame in having a handicap. Americans often looked at successful cripples as inspirational. Koreans, on the other hand, were shocked by handicaps. In P'yongyang, North Korea, people with handicaps weren't even allowed on the streets. In South Korea, they drew stares. Nobody would take him seriously in the business world now, he would have to command respect with fear.

Again the secretary came over the intercom. "Mok Don."

Now Mok Don was being humiliated by a—*woman*. She hadn't even called him Mr. Don. Even his own secretary was talking down to him. Lines tightened on his face. It was time to start making some examples. He stretched his hands and clenched his fists. He picked up his cane and contemplated the pain he could inflict with it.

"*Mok Don*." Again the secretary on the intercom.

"Get in here," he demanded, tightening the grip on his cane till he felt pain in the joints of his fingers. "We're gonna have a little training session."

"Mok Don! The President is on the telephone. He says he must speak to you immediately. It's an emergency. He *must* speak with you."

Mok Don's gaze froze on his desktop during a void of silence. He didn't move until he said, "After this telephone call, you come in here so we can redefine your job description." Mok Don pushed the button to the speaker phone. "President Paek, my dear friend. How are you?"

"No dear friend of yours could be in good standing, Mok Don, and I'm certainly not one of them."

Shock and dread hit Mok Don. He found himself unable to speak.

"In fact," the President said, "you're a disgrace to this country. Our relationship has been one of sufferance for a very long time. Reckoning always comes, nobody escapes it. Not even the great Mok Don. Your day of reckoning has finally come."

"President Paek," Mok Don said coolly, "you are a stinking politician on a temporary pass. I was here long before you, and I'll continue long after you're removed from the Blue House."

"I don't think so, Mok Don. As we speak, the police are in the lobby of your building. They are waiting for my go-ahead to take you into custody. You see, we got a tip recently, a dying confession made by your late security director. Apparently he was a disgruntled employee. His last words gave the location of a special warehouse in Seoul. My police raided the warehouse this morning and found highly incriminating records about your business operations. We also found an enormous amount of hidden cash that we haven't even been able to count. The figure will be staggering. I can guarantee that you're behind on your laundry. Oh, yes, your security director also said if you keelhaul a man, you better kill him."

"What? . . . You're lying, President Paek. No such warehouse exists."

"It's in It'aewon. I wanted to call you personally because I've awaited your downfall for years. You began your quest dealing in human misery and that is how you shall end it. You'll deserve everything you get. I wanted to tell you personally." The President paused. "There will be no pity for you in court. You can expect life in prison. In three minutes, my police will enter your office and take you into custody. Good-bye, Mok Don. You're finished." The line went dead.

Mok Don was gulping for air. Other than his panting chest he could barely move. He stared at the door to his office with his mouth open and his fingers shaking. Suddenly, he glanced at the clock on his desk.

Three minutes.

Soo-man gave up the It'aewon warehouse, gave up . . . Mok Don was trapped. The President was prepared to bury him. If they knew about the It'aewon warehouse, the President was telling the truth: Mok Don *was* finished.

And he had less than three minutes.

Mok Don had been too great for too long. He sat on too high a throne and wielded too much power. The detestable, peasant-loving President demanded his bitter, jealous revenge. Mok Don would never allow himself to go to trial.

Never to prison!

His proud days of victory spanned decades. For thirty years he let nothing stand in the way of his remorseless conquest. He ran his businesses like a glorious conqueror. For thirty years he preyed on the weak and exploited the vulnerable. To survive adrift at sea, he even resorted to cannibalizing his dead salarymen after thirst and starvation licked them.

Mok Don didn't resort to cannibalism only to spend the rest of his life in jail.

He was a glorious international symbol of success. He couldn't give it up now. Mok Don couldn't allow his glory to crumble and be remembered as a disgraced, imprisoned cripple. He would do what he did for his entire life. He would take the easy way. He would rob President Paek of the victory and satisfaction he sought by victimizing Mok Don. He would take his own life. And he would do it with the .45 caliber handgun he was given by the greatest Korean President of all.

Mok Don spun around to the red-oak credenza. He lifted the lid to the black mother-of-pearl inlaid lacquer box. *And he stared in shock . . .*

slowly realizing what had happened. *The gun was gone.* He'd taken the
pistol to be cleaned after bashing Chull-ho's squalid teeth.

Mok Don had no means of killing himself!

A knock shook the door.

Mok Don froze, realizing he had only seconds till he would be
humiliated and later paraded before the country in disgrace. Even the old
women and street beggars would laugh at him.

No! Mok Don would dive through the glass and fall to his death.
Or was the glass too thick? If it didn't break, and Mok Don was knocked
out—he'd become the President's greatest propaganda windfall . . .
Korea's symbol of disgrace.

Another knock on the door.

Mok Don jumped up onto his feet, but his wooden leg gave way
and he collapsed to the floor. With one leg he'd never make it through the
glass.

The doors to his office burst open.

Mok Don climbed up on his hands and his knee and lunged for the
envelope knife on his desk. Police poured into his office. He plunged the
knife into his heart. Machine-like he yanked the blade out and plunged it
in again and again. He wrenched the point around. The pain was hell and
he screamed. He plunged the knife into his belly and twisted the blade all
around.

"I win," he shrieked. "I win, you rotten scum." Then he hit the
floor.

CHAPTER FORTY-NINE
Three months later

Frank anchored the *Hector* in Musashi Inlet.

For a moment his eyes fixed on the mass of fallen cliff,
thousands of tons of igneous rock. The boulder would have eclipsed an
apartment building. It had always been there, he knew, but it now sat

in a different angle than before the tsunami. He felt his heart rate pick up as he considered the awesome force that had moved it.

He rowed the skiff ashore and crawled up onto the lava. He lifted the aluminum skiff with its bow line, pulling it up over the edge of the lava and dragging it across the flat-rock shelf toward the massive boulder. He pulled it around the obstacle and stood there for a moment.

A slope of blasted rockfall used to be piled along the base of cliff here, yet the tsunami had stripped it all away. Not a single pebble remained on the ground. The lava had been licked clean of the thousands of tons of broken lava rock, and only the watery cave remained now, yawning wide like the reaper's mouth calling out to the doomed.

Frank cringed at the thought of going inside another cave. Caves and the heavy toll they charged had become a living nightmare—his personal hell, the articles of which were written in blood.

Warm and damp air that stank of sulfur wrapped around him in the entrance chamber. The eerie sounds of a wind tunnel howled the melancholy chant of monks. Frank sat down on a warm rock. He removed the caving helmet from his backpack and turned on the helmet lamp. The beam illuminated sulfur steam rising from vents in the floor and snow melt dripping from cracks in the ceiling. Volcanic geothermal heat streamed up vents created by water percolating in the bowels of the earth. He pulled the skiff into the river that led into the depths of the island.

Frank breathed heavily and tried to force the memories of tragedy out of his mind even though they played in his head like a movie. He thought of Melody, and his eyes watered up. Her tones sang through his thoughts like the beautiful cries of a loon. Powerful feelings of love and regret and devastation saddened him and distracted him. The bird song faded away and he heard the thunder of gunshot, a report that had echoed though his mind for years, the bad report that deprived him of the woman he loved. He had heard that gunshot a thousand times since her death, but now it rang louder than ever.

The soft howl of the wind tunnel played its funeral song as if a spirit knew it was time for Frank to join his wife. Frank shoved the aluminum skiff away from the riverbank and rowed through the darkness.

He glided into a massive cavern that was coffin dark, and lit a flare. Red light filled the cavern. His helmet lamp illuminated blood-red cave walls and stalactites that hung from the ceiling like long, wild Viking hair. The stalactites looked wet as if they dripped crimson fluids. The gentle current pulled his boat into a large cavern where the water slowed as the river widened from ten feet to a hundred feet across. The cave wall frowned at him where a gaping stone mouth opened to another run of the deep volcanic throat. Above the crooked mouth, dark eye-like pits watched Frank, and he wanted to turn around and leave. Hot wind moaned through the openings of gloom and foreboding.

Visions of Frank's past raced through his mind like a film on fast forward, and his record condemned him. He wiped puddles of sweat out of his eyes. The water under the boat was actually simmering now. The heat grew so intense that he pulled the hood over his head. It was like Dante's river crossing for the unforgiven. Frank thought of Mok Don. The man got better than he deserved, but Frank also lacked angel's wings. His deeds and his life's work would never save him.

Frank couldn't understand why Mok Don hadn't fought the charges in court. Many had survived similar battles. Not only that, Mok Don had survived three tortuous weeks at sea while others died around him.

Strange thoughts raced through Frank's mind. He thought of a Phoenix rising from the ashes. He remembered a house he had blown up in Columbia after the cartels had tortured four American military advisors and burned them alive on video. After the explosion, Frank watched a man climb out of the rubble and walk away with no serious injuries. All the others had perished while this one walked away, and

Frank, thinking he had just seen some kind of miracle of destiny, let him go. Sometimes things didn't go the way they should.

The cave was a subterranean dungeon with weird formations. Sacrificial tables along the shore waited for victims. Time-sculpted hands on the ceiling waited, ready to drop their spikes. As he swung his flare around, a forest of treelike shadows stretched and tilted. Frank felt like they hid evil spirits eager to torment the latest arrival at the gates of the underworld.

Frank rowed his boat through the open mouth and into the deeper throat of the cave where the windy breath howled and stirred the steaming water into a state of undulating turmoil. The cave narrowed, and as he came around the corner. His helmet lamp illuminated a dark, man-shaped outline, but it was only a rock formation. Behind it, Frank saw a boiling mud pit. This was a hellish place. He remembered the little bottle with the seed. No, there was nothing to fear anymore.

Sweat soaked through Frank's clothes as hot wind pushed the boat backwards. Steam burned his throat, so he breathed through his nose.

He rowed as he followed the rock beach around another corner into a huge cavern. Frank crawled onto a lava table and walked into the darkness toward a side cavern. There in the deep he saw it—a huge mound the size of a car covered with tarps. With a buck knife, he cut away the canvas that had been attached to stakes driven into the rock floor. He pulled away the tarps. Most of them crumbled as he did so.

"The Kobukson," he whispered. It rested on black sand that covered the rock floor. He kneeled down, beholding the thousand-pound golden turtle ship replica. He wondered what Mok Don would have done to get his hands on this.

Frank ran his finger along the golden bulwark and touched a spike that protruded from a plate of gold. He moved around to the front. He tapped his finger on the turtle head and gunwales.

Steam and sulfur fumes swirled around the cavern. How ironic, Frank thought. The bowsprits of the real ships had carried smoke generators that emitted sulfur fumes to confuse the enemies.

Frank stepped back and looked at the whole ship: the humped turtle-shell with spiked gold plates; the eight oars reaching out on each side; the square sails intricately knitted with thin gold wire. A treasure worth millions.

He walked around the ship admiring the amazing craftsmanship of the artifact.

He'd bring Abby back tomorrow to take photos. She would be so pleased.

Frank turned his attention to the cave and looked it over closely. He considered the black sand on the floor. The tsunami had swept perpendicular to the cave entrance before impacting the coast. The turtle ship had been shielded and protected from the awesome, destructive forces that stripped away the rocks at the mouth of the cave.

So this was the kobukson, the most amazing artifact he'd ever seen. He'd call Dane Leisbeth back tomorrow and follow through with his plans for a world tour to raise money for North Korean widows and to eventually return the relic to South Korea, where it belonged. He could live with that, but more importantly, he could live with himself. He had made so many mistakes in his life, but he'd done the best he could at the time. Frank never claimed to be an angel anyway. He looked around the gloomiest cavern he'd ever seen and wasn't worried anymore—about anything.

END

About the Author:

Thriller writer Roger Weston has worked on various vessels at sea, from a commercial fishing boat in the Puget Sound and a salmon processing ship in the Gulf of Alaska to a yacht off the coast of Hawaii. He has traveled in Russia during the Cold War, foiled a well-planned gang mugging in a Moroccan medina, and escaped a gun wielding taxi cab driver in Madrid, Spain.

Also by Roger Weston:

The Assassin's Wife
Fatal Return: A Thriller
The Recruiter: A Chuck Brandt Thriller (Brandt Series Book 1)
The Handler: A Chuck Brandt Thriller (Brandt Series Book 2)

Coming Soon:

A Chuck Brandt Thriller (Brandt Series Book 3)

Visit the author's blog: http://rogerweston.blogspot.com/
Contact Roger Weston at RogerWeston7@gmail.com